Where Animals Talk
West African Folk Lore Tales

By
Robert Hamill Nassau

PUBLISHED BY: 2024 by BTB Publishing

ISBN : 978-1-63652-365-1

WHERE ANIMALS TALK

WEST AFRICAN FOLK LORE
TALES

ROBERT HAMILL NASSAU

CONTENTS

BENGA TRIBE

PREFACE

The typical native African Ekano or legend is marked by repetition. The same incidents occur to a succession of individuals; monotony being prevented by a variation in the conduct of those individuals, as they reveal their weakness or stupidity, artifice or treachery.

Narrators, while preserving the original plot and characters of a Tale, vary it, and make it graphic by introducing objects known and familiar to their audience. These inconsistencies do not interfere with belief or offend the taste of a people with whom even the impossible is not a bar to faith; rather, the inconsistency sharpens their enjoyment of the story.

Surprise must not be felt at the impossibility of some of the situations; *e.g.*, the swallowing by an animal of his wife, baggage and household furniture, as a means of hiding them. The absurdity of such situations is one of the distinctive attractions to the minds of the excited listeners.

Variations of the same Tale, as told in different Tribes, were inevitable among a people whose language was not written until within the last hundred years; the Tales having been transmitted verbally, from generation to generation, for, probably, thousands of years. As to their antiquity, I believe these Tales to be of very ancient origin. No argument must be taken against them because of the internal evidence of allusion to modern things, or implements, or customs of known modern date; *e.g.*, "cannon," "tables," "steamships," etc., etc. Narrators constantly embellish by novel additions; *e.g.*, where, in the original story, a character used a spear, the narrator may substitute a pistol.

Almost all these Tales locate themselves in supposed pre-historic times, when Beasts and Human Beings are asserted to have lived together with social relations in the same community. An unintended concession to the claims of some Evolutionists!

The most distinctive feature of these Tales is that, while the actors are Beasts, they are speaking and living as Human Beings, acting as a beast in human environment; and, instantly, in the same sentence, acting as a human being in a beast's environment. This must constantly be borne in mind, or the action of the story will become not only unreasonable but utterly inexplicable.

The characters in the stories relieve themselves from difficult or dangerous situations by invoking the aid of a powerful personal fetish-charm known as "Ngalo"; a fetish almost as valuable as Aladdin's Lamp of the Arabian Nights. And yet, with inconsistency, notwithstanding this aid, the actors are often suffering from many small evils of daily human life. These inconsistencies are another feature of the Ekano that the listeners enjoy as the spice of the story.

From internal evidences, I think that the local sources of these Tales were Arabian, or at least under Arabic, and perhaps even Egyptian, influences. (Observe the prefix, Ra, a contraction of Rera equals father, a title of honor, as "Lord," or "Sir," or "Master," in names of dignitaries; *e.g.* Ra-Marânge, Ra-Mbora-kinda, Ra-Meses.)

This is consistent with the fact that there is Arabic blood in the Bantu Negro. The invariable direction to which the southwest coast tribes point, as the source of their ancestors, is northeast. Such an ethnologist as Sir H. H. Johnston traces the Bantu stream southward on the east coast to the Cape of Good Hope, and then turns it northward on the west coast to the equator and as far as the fourth degree of north latitude, the very region from which I gathered these stories.

Only a few men, and still fewer women, in any community, are noted as skilled narrators. They are the literati.

The public never weary of hearing the same Tales repeated; like our own civilized audiences at a play running for a hundred or more nights. They are made attractive by the dramatic use of gesture, tones, and startling exclamations.

The occasions selected for the renditions are nights, after the day's works are done, especially if there be visitors to be entertained. The places chosen are the open village street, or, in forest camps where almost all the population of a village go for a week's work on their cutting of new plantations; or for hunting; or for fishing in ponds. The time for these camps is in one of the two dry seasons: where the booths erected are not for protection against rain, but for a little privacy, for the warding off of insects, birds and small animals, and for the drying of meats. At such times, most of the adults go off during the day for fishing; or, if for hunting, only the men; the children being guarded at their plays in the camp by the older women, who are kept occupied with cooking, and with the drying of meats. At night, all gather around the camp-fire; and the Tales are told with, at intervals, accompaniment of drum; and parts of the plot are illustrated by an appropriate song, or by a short dance, the platform being only the earth, and the scenery the forest shadows and the moon or stars.

The Bantu Language has very many dialects, having the same grammatical construction, but differing in their vocabulary. The name of the same animal therefore differs in the three typical

Tribes mentioned in these Tales; *e.g.*, Leopard, in Mpongwe, equals Njĕgâ; in Benga, equals Njâ; and in Fang, equals Nzĕ.

PRONUNCIATION

In all the dialects of the Bantu language, consonants are pronounced, as in English; except that g is always hard.

The vowels are pronounced as in the following English equivalent:—

a	as in father	e.g., Kabala
â	as in awe	e.g., Njâ.
e	as in they	e.g., Ekaga.
ĕ	as in met	e.g., Njĕgâ.
i	as in machine	e.g., Njina.
o	as in note	e.g., Kombe.
u	as in rule	e.g., Kuba.

A before y is pronounced ai as a diphthong, *e.g.*, Asaya. Close every syllable with a vowel, *e.g.*, Ko-ngo. Where two or more consonants begin a syllable, a slight vowel sound may be presupposed, *e.g.*, Ngweya, as if iNgweya.

Ng has the nasal sound of ng in "finger," as if fing-nger, (not as in "singer,") *e.g.*, Mpo-ngwe.

Robert Hamill Nassau

PART FIRST
MPONGWE

Robert Hamill Nassau

FOREWORD

The following sixteen Tales were narrated to me, many years ago, by two members of the Mpongwe tribe (one now dead) at the town of Libreville, Gaboon river, equatorial West Africa. Both of them were well-educated persons, a man and a woman. They chose legends that were current in their own tribe. They spoke in Mpongwe; and, in my English rendition, I have retained some of their native idioms. As far as I am aware none of these legends have ever been printed in English, excepting Tale 5, a version of which appeared in a British magazine from a writer in Kamerun, after I had heard it at Gaboon. Also, excepting Tale 14. It appeared, in another form, more than fifty years ago, in Rev. Dr. J. L. Wilson's "Western Africa." But my narrator was not aware of that, when he told it to me.

DO NOT TRUST YOUR FRIEND

Place
Country of the Animals
Persons

Njĕgâ (Leopard)	Ngowa (Hog)
Ntori (Wild Rat)	Nkambi (Antelope)
Ra-Marânge (Medicine Man)	Leopard's Wife; and others
Nyare (Ox)	

NOTE

A story of the treachery of the Leopard as matched by the duplicity of the Rat.

In public mourning for the dead, it is the custom for the nearest relative or dearest friend to claim the privilege of sitting closest to the corpse, and nursing the head on his or her lap.

At a time long ago, the Animals were living in the Forest together. Most of them were at peace with each other. But Leopard was discovered to be a bad person. All the other animals refused to be friendly with him. Also, Wild Rat, a small animal, was found out to be a deceiver.

One day, Rat went to visit Leopard, who politely gave him a chair, and Rat sat down. "Mbolo!" "Ai, Mbolo!" each saluted to the other. Leopard said to his visitor, "What's the news?" Rat replied, "Njĕgâ! news is bad. In all the villages I passed through, in coming today, your name is only ill-spoken of, people saying, 'Njĕgâ is bad! Njĕgâ is bad!' "

Leopard replies, "Yes, you do not lie. People say truly that Njĕgâ is bad. But, look you, Ntori, I, Njĕgâ, am an evil one: but my badness comes from other animals. Because, when I go out to visit, there is no one who salutes me. When anyone sees me, he flees with fear. But, for what does he fear me? I have not vexed him. So, I pursue the one that fears me. I want to ask him, 'Why do you fear me?' But, when I pursue it, it goes on fleeing more rapidly. So, I become angry, wrath rises in my heart, and if I overtake it, I kill it on the spot. One reason why I am bad is that. If the animals would speak to me properly, and did not flee from me, then, Ntori, I would not kill them. See! you, Ntori, have I seized you?" Rat replied, "No." Then Leopard said, "Then, Ntori, come near to this table, that we may talk well."

Rat, because of his subtlety and caution, when he took the chair given him on his arrival, had placed it near the door.

Leopard repeated, "Come near to the table." Rat excused himself, "Never mind; I am comfortable here; and I came here today to tell you that it is not well for a person to be without friends; and, I, Ntori, say to you, let us be friends." Leopard said, "Very good!"

But now, even after this compact of friendship, Rat told false-hoods about Leopard; who, not knowing this, often had conversations with him, and would confide to him all the thoughts of his heart. For example, Leopard would tell to Rat, "Tomorrow I am going to hunt Ngowa, and next day I will go to hunt Nkambi," or whatever the animal was. And Rat, at night, would go to Hog or to Antelope or the other animal, and say, "Give me pay, and I will tell you a secret." They would lay down to him his price. And then he would tell them, "Be careful tomorrow. I heard that Njĕgâ was coming to kill you." The same night, Rat would secretly return to his own house, and lie down as if he had not been out.

Then, next day, when Leopard would go out hunting, the Animals were prepared and full of caution, to watch his coming. There was none of them that he could find; they were all hidden. Leopard thus often went to the forest, and came back empty-handed. There was no meat for him to eat, and he had to eat only leaves of the trees. He said to himself, "I will not sit down and look for explanation to come to me. I will myself find out the reason of this. For, I, Njĕgâ, I should eat flesh and drink blood; and here I have come down to eating the food of goats, grass and leaves."

So, in the morning, Leopard went to the great doctor Ra-Marânge, and said, "I have come to you, I, Njĕgâ. For these five or six months I have been unable to kill an animal. But, cause me to know the reason of this." Ra-Marânge took his looking-glass and his harp, and struck the harp, and looked at the glass. Then he laughed aloud, "Kĕ, kĕ, kĕ—"

Leopard asked, "Ra-Marânge, for what reason do you laugh?" He replied, "I laugh, because this matter is a small affair. You, Njĕgâ, so big and strong, you do not know this little thing!" Leopard acknowledged, "Yes: I have not been able to find it out." Ra-Marânge said, "Tell me the names of your friends." Leopard answered "I have no friends. Nkambi dislikes me, Nyare refuses me, Ngowa the same. Of all animals, none are friendly to me." Ra-Marânge said, "Not so; think exactly; think again." Leopard was silent and thought; and then said, "Yes, truly, I have one friend, Ntori." The Doctor said, "But, look! If you find a friend, it is not well to tell him all the thoughts of your heart. If you tell him two or three, leave the rest. Do not tell him all. But, you, Njĕgâ, you consider that Ntori is your friend, and you show him all the thoughts of your heart. But, do you know the heart of Ntori, how it is inside? Look what he does! If you let him know that you are going next day to kill this and that, then he starts out at night, and goes to inform those animals, ' Now, look! if you wish to be able to kill other animals, first kill Ntori." Leopard was surprised, "Ngâ! (actually) Ntori lies to me?" Ra-Marânge said, "Yes."

So, Leopard returned to his town. And he sent a child to call Rat. Rat came.

Leopard said, "Ntori! these days you have not come to see me. Where have you been?" Rat replies, "I was sick." Leopard says, "I called you today to sit at my table to eat." Rat excused himself, "Thanks! but the sickness is still in my body; I will not be able to eat." And he went away.

Whenever Rat visited or spoke to Leopard, he did not enter the house, but sat on a chair by the door. Leopard daily sent for him; he came; but constantly refrained from entering the house.

Leopard says in his heart, "Ntori does not approach near to me, but sits by the door. How shall I catch him?" Thinking and thinking, he called his wife, and said, "I have found a plan by which to kill Ntori. Tomorrow, I will lie down in the street, and you cover my body with a cloth as corpses are covered. Wear an old ragged cloth, and take ashes and mark your body, as in mourning; and go you out on the road wailing, 'Njĕgâ is dead! Njĕgâ, the friend of Ntori is dead!' And, for Ntori, when he shall come as a friend to the mourning, put his chair by me, and say, 'Sit there near your friend.' When he sits on that chair, I will jump up and kill him there." His wife replies, "Very good!"

Next morning, Leopard, lying down in the street, pretended

that he was dead. His wife dressed herself in worn-out clothes, and smeared her face, and went clear on to Rat's village, wailing "Ah! Njĕgâ is dead! Ntori's friend is dead!" Rat asked her, "But, Njĕgâ died of what disease? Yesterday, I saw him looking well, and today comes word that he is dead!" The wife answered, "Yes: Njĕgâ died without disease; just cut off! I wonder at the matter—I came to call you; for you were his friend. So, as is your duty as a man, go there and help bury the corpse in the jungle." Rat went, he and Leopard's wife together. And, behold, there was Leopard stretched out as a corpse! Rat asked the wife, "What is this matter? Njĕgâ! is he really dead?" She replied, "Yes: I told you so. Here is a chair for you to sit near your friend."

Rat, having his caution, had not sat on the chair, but stood off, as he wailed, "Ah! Njĕgâ is dead! Ah! my friend is dead!"

Rat called out, "Wife of Njĕgâ! Njĕgâ, he was a great person: but did he not tell you any sign by which it might be known, according to custom, that he was really dead?" She replied, "No, he did not tell me." (Rat, when he thus spoke, was deceiving the woman.) Rat went on to speak, "You, Njĕgâ, when you were living and we were friends, you told me in confidence, saying, 'When I, Njĕgâ, shall die, I will lift my arm upward, and you will know that I am really dead.' But, let us cease the wailing and stop crying. I will try the test on Njĕgâ, whether he is dead! Lift your arm!"

Leopard lifted his arm. Rat, in his heart, laughed, "Ah! Njĕgâ is not dead!" But, he proceeded, "Njĕgâ! Njĕgâ! you said, if really dead, you would shake your body. Shake! if it is so!" Leopard shook his whole body. Rat said openly, "Ah! Njĕgâ is dead indeed! He shook his body!" The wife said, "But, as you say he is dead, here is the chair for you, as chief friend, to sit on by him." Rat said, "Yes: wait for me; I will go off a little while, and will come."

Leopard, lying on the ground, and hearing this, knew in his heart, "Ah! Ntori wants to flee from me! I will wait no longer!" Up he jumps to seize Rat, who, being too quick for him, fled away. Leopard pursued him with leaps and jumps so rapidly that he almost caught him. Rat got to his hole in the ground just in time to rush into it. But his tail was sticking out; and Leopard, looking down the hole, seized the tail.

Rat called out, "You have not caught me, as you think! What you are holding is a rootlet of a tree." Leopard let go of the tail. Rat switched it in after him, and jeered at Leopard, "You had hold of my tail! And you have let it go! You will not catch me again!" Leopard, in a rage, said, "You will have to show me the way by which you will emerge from this hole; for, you will never come out of it alive!"

Some narrators carry the story on, with the ending of Tale No. 6, the story of Rat, Leopard, Frog and Crab.

Leopard's pretence of death appears also in Tale No. 3.

TALE 2
LEOPARD'S HUNTING CAMP

Persons

Ntori (A very large forest Rat)   And other Animals

Njĕgâ (Leopard)

NOTE

Besides the words for "hunger" and "famine," the Bantu languages have a third word meaning, "longing for meat." In this story, Leopard's greed is matched by the artifice of Rat:—It was a practice of African natives to hide their ivory tusks in streams of water until a time convenient for selling them.

Polite natives will neither sit uninvited in the presence of their superiors, nor watch them while eating. If need be, to secure privacy, a temporary curtain will be put up, and the host will retire, leaving the guest alone. Rude or uncivilized tribes are offensive in their persistent effort to see a white foreigner's mode of eating.

One of the tricks of native sorcerers is to jump into a fire.

It was a time of ngwamba (meat-hunger) among the Animals in Njambi's Kingdom.

Leopard, being the eldest in his tribe, said to Rat, "Ntori! child! this is a hard time for meat. I think we better go to the forest, and make a olako (camp) for hunting." Rat replied "Good! come on!"

So they began to arrange for the journey. The preparation of food, nets, baskets, and so forth, occupied several days. When all was ready, they started. Having come to a proper place in the forest, they selected a site where they would build up their booths. Leopard was to have his own separate camp with his wives and his children and his people; and Rat his, with his wives and his children, and his people.

So they began to make two camps. Leopard said, "Ntori! child! I have mine here. You go there yonder." So they built their booths for sleeping-places; and rested another day; and then built their arala (drying frames) over their fire-places for smoke-drying the meat that they hoped to obtain. Next day, they prepared their guns, and started out on the hunt. On that very first day, they met game, and, ku! (bang) went their guns, killing an Elephant, and, ku! a wild Ox. Then Leopard said, "Ntori! child! we are successful! Let us begin the work of cutting up!"

After all the carcasses had been cut up, came the time to divide the meat between the two companies. So, Leopard said, "As I am your Uncle, I precede; I will choose first, and will give you the remainder." So Leopard chose, taking out all the best pieces. When Rat saw that most of the meat was going to Leopard's side, he thought it time to begin to get his share. But when Rat laid hold of a nice piece, Leopard would say, "No! child! do not take the best: that belongs to your Uncle"— and Leopard would claim the piece, and hand it over to his women. So it went on in the same way; to every nice piece that Rat chose, Leopard objected that it belonged to him. After Leopard had taken all he wanted, there were left only the bowels and the heads and legs for Rat.

Then they each went to their own camping-place, to spread the meat on their arala, and to cook their dinner. But, all the while that Rat was spreading bones and bowels on his orala, he was vexed; for, there was very little meat on those bones; while Leopard's people's arala were full of meat, and savory portions were simmering on their fires tied in bundles (agⱥwu) of plantain leaves. At the noon meal, Leopard sat down with his family, and Rat with his. But Rat had only poor food; while Leopard and his people were rejoicing with rich meat.

The second day was very much the same as the first. It was Rat who did most of the hunting. With him it was, ku! (bang!), and some beast was down; and, ku! and some other beast was down. Whenever Rat fired, Leopard would shout out, "Ntori! child! what have you got?" And it was Rat who would shout in reply, "Nyare" (ox), or "Njâku" (elephant), or "Nkambi!" (antelope), or whatever the game might be. And it was Leopard who offensively patronized him, saying, "That is a good boy, Tata! (Little Father); bring it here to your Uncle." Then Rat and all the servants would carry the carcass to Leopard. So that day, the cutting and dividing was just like the first day; Leopard claiming and taking the best, and leaving the skeleton and scraggy pieces and the bowels for Rat.

After that second day's hunt, Rat was tired of this way of dividing, in which he got only the worthless pieces. So he decided to get back some of Leopard's meat by artifice, for his own table, even if he had to take it from Leopard's orala itself. He began to devise what he should do. As he was out walking, he came to a brook in which were sunken logs of hard heavy wood. They had lain there a long time, and were black with outside decay. With his machete in hand, he dived; and remaining under the water, he scraped the logs till he had removed the dark outside, and exposed the white inner wood. He kept on at the job scraping and scraping until the logs appeared white like ivory. Then he went back to Leopard's camp, and, with pretence of excitement, exclaimed, "Mwe Njⵣgâ! I think we will be going to be rich. You don't know what I've found! Such a big ivory-tusk hidden in the water! I think we better leave off hunting meat, and go to get this fine ivory." Leopard replied, "Good! come on!"

The next day, they first arranged their fires so that the smoke-drying of their meat might continue during their absence; and then started for the ivory. They all prepared themselves, for diving, by taking off their good clothing, and wearing only a small loin-cloth. Their entire companies went, men, women, and children, leaving not a single person in the camps.

Leopard says, "You, Ntori, go first, as you know where the place is." Rat says, "Good! come on!" And they went on their way.

Arrived at the brook, Rat says, "You all come on, and dive." Leopard asks, "My son! is it still there?" Rat, pointing, answers, "Yes! my ivory is there." Leopard, looking down in the water says, "I see no ivory!" Rat, still pointing, replies, "There! Those white things! Don't you see them?" Leopard says, "I never saw ivory look like logs." Rat answered, "No? But this is a new kind. I assure you they are ivory! I have been down there, and I cleaned the mud off of them." Leopard was satisfied, and said, "Good! come on!" And they all dived. They laid hold of the supposed ivory, and pulled, and pushed, and lifted, and worked. But it was stuck fast, and they could not move it.

While they were thus working, Rat suddenly cried out, "Njⵣgâ! O! I forgot something! I must go quickly back to the olako. I will not be gone long. I shall return soon."

Rat came out of the brook; ran to the camp; took of his own bundles of bones and scraggy pieces, and put them on Leopard's drying-frames, and took the same number of bundles of good meat from Leopard's frames. Then he ran back to the brook, to continue the work at the so-called ivory.

Soon after that, Rat says, "Mwe Njĕgâ! it is time to return to the olako; we have worked long; I am hungry." Leopard says, "Good! come on!" So they returned to the camp to eat.

Rat says, "Njĕgâ! as I am so hungry, I will not wait with you, but will go to my own olako at once. And I will put up a curtain between us, as it is a shame for one to eat in the presence of his elder."

So Rat put up a curtain; and opened a bundle of nice meat; and he and his people began to eat.

When Leopard took down one of his bundles, and opened it to share with his women, he was amazed, and said, "See! only bones and mean pieces! Ah! what is this matter!" And he called out to the other camp, "Ntori! Tata!" Rat responds, "Eh! Mwe Njĕgâ?" Leopard inquires, "What kind of meat are you eating?" Rat answers, "My own, from my own bundles. But what kind have you, Mwe Njĕgâ?" Leopard says, "My women prepared meat that was nice; but now I have only bones. I am surprised at that."

The next, the fourth day, Rat said to Leopard, "I think we better change from the hard work on the ivory. Let us go hunting today; and tomorrow we will resume the ivory." Leopard assented "Good! come on!" And they started out to hunt. They were successful again as on the previous days. At the time of the division of the meat, Rat showed no displeasure at Leopard's taking the best pieces; as he had now his own artifice to get them back. And the meats of the day were placed on their owners' respective drying-frames. By this day's doings, many of Leopard's baskets were full, ready to be taken to town, while most of Rat's were still empty.

On the fifth day, they went to the brook again, to their fruitless work of pulling at the so-called ivory. The same things happened as before; Rat remembers that he has forgotten something; has to go in haste to the camp; rapidly changes the bundles on his and Leopard's frames; returns to the brook; they all come back to the camp to eat; and there were repeated Leopard's surprise, and his questions to Rat about the kinds of meat they were eating. Thus they continued; on alternate days hunting, and working at the ivory that was stuck immovably fast in the mud; and Rat stealing; and Leopard complaining.

Finally, Leopard became tired of his losses; and, one day, without letting anyone know what he intended doing, he said, "I will take a little walk." Rat says, "You go alone? May I accompany you?" Leopard said, "No! I go alone; I won't be long away; and I do not go far."

So Leopard went to the wizard Ra-Marânge, whom as soon as he saw him, exclaimed, "What are you come for? Are you in trouble?" Leopard told him the matter of the losses of the meat. Then Ra-Marânge jumped into his fire, and emerged powerful and wise. And he said, "I will make for you something that will find out for you who it is that takes your meat."

So Ra-Marânge made a little image of a man, and conferred on it wisdom and power, and gave it to Leopard, who took it to his camp, and hid it in his hut.

The next day they all resumed the work at the brook, with the ivory. There was the same diving, the same fruitless pulling, Rat's same need of going back to the camp, and his same attempts at stealing. While he was doing this, he sees something like a little man standing near him. Rat puts out his hand to take from Leopard's bundles as usual, and the image catches him by the wrist of that hand. Rat indignantly says, "You! this little fool! leave me! What do you catch me for?" But the image was silent; nor did it let go its hold. So Rat struck at it with his other hand. And the image caught that hand with its other hand. Then Rat was angry and kicked with one foot at a leg of the image. And that foot was retained by that leg of the image. Rat kicked with his remaining foot; it also was retained by the image's other leg. He was thus held in the power of the image.

Rat, in desperation, said, "Let me go!" The image spoke, and simply said, "No!" Rat felt he was in a bad situation; but he put on a bold face. He knew that, by his long delay, the others must have given up the work at the brook, and would by now be returning to the camp; and, in a little while, he would be discovered. To forestall that discovery, he shouted out, "Mwe Nĕjgâ, come quickly! I've found the person who changes your bundles!" Leopard, on the path, heard his voice, and replied, "My child, is that so? Hold him fast!" Rat still daringly said, "Come quickly! He wants to get away from my grasp!" Leopard replied, "Hold fast! I am coming!" They all came hastily, both of Rat's people, and of Leopard's people; and there they saw Rat held fast by the hands and legs of the image. Leopard asked, "Where is he?" Rat, daring to the last, said, "This little man here that I am holding." Leopard said, "Now that I am here, let go of him, for I will take charge of him." Rat struggled, but in vain. Leopard several times repeated his direction to Rat, "Let go of him!" But Rat was utterly unable to withdraw his limbs from the power of the image. And he gave up the effort, in shame. Then Leopard had to help release Rat; the conferred power of the image being subservient to him. He did not strike Rat, he being his relative. But rebuked him, "Ah! Ntori! now I know it was you who made all the trouble about my meat!" And he took back all his fine bundles, and returned Rat his poor bundles. Rat went to his own camp ashamed, but still angry at the unjust division of the meat.

As Leopard's baskets were now full, he announced that they should prepare to break camp, and return to town. Rat's women murmured, "Ah! all going away, and our baskets almost empty!" Rat comforted them, "Yes; it is so; but, we will find a way to fill them!"

So, the next day, while the others were gone to get leaves and vines with which to tie up their baskets, Rat took his empty ones to the brook and filled them with stones, and tied them up with leaves, as if they contained meat.

On the following day, as they were about to start on their journey, Rat said to Leopard, "As you are the elder, go you first, and I will follow." Leopard said, "Good! come on!" And they went on the path, Rat keeping close behind Leopard's people. (Baskets being carried tied on the back with a strap over the forehead, the bearer leans heavily forward, and cannot see what is happening behind.) Rat had prepared a hook with a handle. From time to time, as they came to narrow places in the path where thorny branches met, he would strike the hook into some basket before him, and in pretence, would say, "Wait! a thorn on this branch has caught your basket! Let me unfasten it." While the carrier would stand still for Rat to release the branch, the latter seized the chance to take pieces of meat from the basket, and substitute stones from his own baskets. The way was long; and, at every obstructed place, Rat kept on at his pretence of helping to free some basket of Leopard's from the thorns that caught it, and changed pieces of good meat for his stones.

Before they reached Leopard's town, darkness began to fall, and both companies were very tired, especially that of Leopard;

for, their baskets seemed to have grown heavier. Rat said, "Njĕgâ! All this hard day's walk! Hide our baskets, yours in one place, and mine in another, and let us go on to town and sleep; and we will send back our women for the baskets in the morning." Leopard assented, "Good! come on!" So they left their baskets, and all went to town.

The next morning, Rat sent his people very, very early. Leopard sent his later, at the usual time of morning business. When his people were going they met Rat's people coming back with their loads, and exclaimed, "You are loaded already!"

When Leopard's people brought their baskets to the town, and opened them, they were amazed to find that they had little else than stones and bones. Leopard was very angry; and, going to Rat, he began to scold, "You have taken away my meat!" "No I have my own. Look! these baskets, you know them, they are mine! Perhaps some one stole your meat in the night and put the stones in place. But, as you are in such a trouble, I will share with you of mine." So he called to his women, "Give Njĕgâ a few pieces of meat." Leopard took the meat, and Rat and his people went away to their own town.

But Leopard was not satisfied. He was sure that Rat had played him a trick. He had forgiven Rat his stealing at the camp; but, for this last trick, he meditated revenge.

TESTS OF DEATH—1ST VERSION

Persons
Njǔgâ (Leopard)   Ntori (Wild-Rat)

NOTE

It is the proper and most friendly mode, that relatives and friends should hasten to visit their sick, on the very first information, without waiting to be invited or summoned.

Leopard told his head-wife, "Ntori has taken our meat and deceived me in all these ways; I will kill him and eat him."

So he pretended to be sick.

The next day, news was sent to Rat that his Uncle Leopard was sick of a fever.

The following day, word was again sent that he was very sick indeed, and that he wanted a parting word with Rat. Rat sent back a message, "I hear; and I will come tomorrow."

Rat suspected some evil, and did not believe that Leopard was sick. So he went to the forest, and collected all kinds of insects that sting, and tied them into five little bundles.

Next day, word came to him, "Njǔgâ is dead." Rat went quickly, taking the five little bundles with him.

When he reached Leopard's town, he joined the crowd of

mourners in the street, and lifted up his voice in wailing. Leopard's head-wife went to him, and said, "Come into the house, and mourn with me, at your Uncle's bed-side." Rat went with her; but he did not take the seat that was offered him, as a near relative, at the supposed dead man's head. He first explained, "After a person is reported dead, it is proper to make five tests to prove whether he is really dead, before we bury him."

So he stood by the bed, at a point safe from Leopard's hands, and opened a bundle, and lifting the shroud, quickly laid the bundle on Leopard's naked body. The insects, infuriated by their imprisonment, flew out and attacked Leopard's body, as it was the object nearest to them, and they were confined under the shroud. Leopard endured, and did not move.

Rat opened a second bundle, and thrust it also on another part of Leopard's body. Leopard could scarcely refrain from wincing.

Rat opened a third, and laid it in the same way on another part. Leopard's face began to twitch with the torture. Rat opening a fourth, used it in the same way; and Leopard in pain began to twist his body; but, when Rat opened the fifth bundle, Leopard could endure the stings no longer. He started up from the bed, holding a dagger he had hidden under the bed-clothing.

But Rat was too agile for him, and ran out before Leopard could fully rise from his supposed death-bed, and escaped to his own place. The mourners fled from the furious insects, and Leopard was left in agony under the poison of their stings.

TALE 3
TESTS OF DEATH—SECOND VERSION

Persons

Njǒgâ (Leopard) Ekaga (Tortoise)

Ibâbâ (Jackal) With Ndongo (Pepper)

With Ngomba (Porcupine) Hako (Ants)

Nkambi (Antelope) And Nyoi (Bees)

Njâgu (Elephant) And Others

Ihǒli (Gazelle)

NOTE

All of a neighborhood go to a mourning for a dead person. Failure to go would have been regarded, formerly, as a sign of a sense of guilt as the cause of the death. Formerly, at funerals, there was great destruction. Some of a man's wives and slaves were buried with him, with a large quantity of his goods; and his fruit trees adjacent to the houses were ruthlessly cut down. All, as signs of grief; as much as to say, "If the beloved dead cannot longer enjoy these things, no one else shall."

The ancestor of the leopards never forgave the ancestor of the gazelles, but nursed his wrath at the trick which the latter had played on him with the insects. Unable to catch gazelles, because of their adroitness, the leopard wrecks his anger on all other beasts by killing them at any opportunity.

These two beasts, Leopard and Jackal, were living together in the same town. Leopard said to Jackal, "My friend! I do not eat all sorts of food; I eat only animals." So, one day, Leopard went to search for some beast in the forest. He wandered many hours, but could not find any for his food.

On another day, Leopard said to Jackal, "My friend! let us arrange some plan, by which we can kill some animal. For, I've wandered into the forest again and again, and have found nothing." Leopard made these remarks to his friend in the dark of the evening. So they sat that night and planned and, after their conversation, they went to lie down in their houses. And they slept their sleep.

Then soon, the daylight broke. And Leopard, carrying out their plan, said to Jackal, "Take up your bedding, and put it out in the open air of the street." Jackal did so. Leopard laid down on that mattress, in accordance with their plan, and stretched out like a corpse lying still, as if he could not move a muscle. He said to Jackal, "Call Ngomba, and let him come to me." So Jackal shouted, "Come! Ngomba, come! That Beast that kills animals is dead! Come!"

So Porcupine came to the mourning, weeping, and wailing, as if he was really sorry for the death of his enemy. He approached near the supposed corpse. And he jeered at it. "This was the person who wasted us people; and this is his body!" Leopard heard this derision. Suddenly he leaped up. And Porcupine went down under his paw, dead. Then Leopard said to his friend Jackal, "Well! cut it up! and let us eat it." And they finished eating it.

On another day, Leopard, again in the street, stretched himself on the bedding. At his direction, Jackal called for Antelope. Antelope came; and Leopard killed him, as he had done to Porcupine.

On another day, Ox was called. And Leopard did to Ox the same as he had done to the others.

On another day, Elephant was called in the same way; and he died in the same way.

In the same way, Leopard killed some of almost all the other beasts one after another, until there were left only two.

Then Jackal said, "Njⵊgâ! my friend! there are left, of all the beasts, only two, Ihⵊli and Ekaga. But, what can you do with Ihⵊli? for, he has many artifices. What, also, can you do against Ekaga? for, he too, has many devices." Leopard replied, "I will do as I usually have done; so, tomorrow, I will lie down again, as if I were a corpse."

That day darkened into night.

And another daylight broke.

And Leopard went out of the house to lie down on the bedding in the street. Each limb was extended out as if dead; and his mouth open, with lower jaw fallen, like that of a dead person.

Then Jackal called, "Ihⵊli! come here! That person who wastes the lives of the beasts is dead! He's dead!"

Gazelle said to himself, "I hear! So! Njⵊgâ is dead? I go to the mourning!" Gazelle lived in a town distant about three miles. He started on the journey, taking with him his spear and bag; but, he said to himself, "Before I go to the mourning, I will stop on the way at the town of Ekaga."

He came to the town of Tortoise, and he said to him, "Chum! have you heard the news? That person who kills Beasts and Mankind is dead!" But Tortoise answered, "No! go back to your town! that person is not dead. Go back!" Gazelle said, "No! For, before I go back to my town, I will first go to Njặgâ's to see." So Tortoise said, "If you are determined to go there, I will tell you something." Gazelle exclaimed, "Yes! Uncle, speak!"

Then Tortoise directed him, "Take ndongo." Gazelle took some. Tortoise said, "Take also Hako, and take also Nyoi. Tie them all up in a bundle of plantain leaves." (He told Gazelle to do all these things, as a warning.) And Tortoise added, "You will find Njặgâ with limbs stretched out like a corpse. Take a machete with you in your hands. When you arrive there, begin to cut down the plantain-stalks. And you must cry out 'Who killed my Uncle? who killed my uncle?' If he does not move, then you sit down and watch him."

So Gazelle went, journeyed and came to that town of mourning. He asked Jackal, "Ibâbâ! This person, how did he die?" Jackal replied, "Yesterday afternoon this person was seized with a fever; and today, he is a corpse." Gazelle looked at Leopard from a distance, his eyes fixed on him, even while he was slashing down the plantains, as he was told to do. But, Leopard made no sign, though he heard the noise of the plantain-stalk falling to the ground. Presently, Jackal said to Gazelle, "Go near to your Uncle's bed, and look at the corpse."

Leopard began in his heart to arrange for a spring, being ready to fight, and thinking, "What time Ihặli shall be near me, I will kill him."

Gazelle approached, but carefully stood off a rod distant from the body of Leopard. Then Gazelle drew the bundle of Ants out of his bag, and said to himself, "Is this person, really dead? I will test him!" But, Gazelle stood warily ready to flee at the slightest sign. He quickly opened the bundle of insects; and he joined the three, the Ants, the Bees, and the Pepper, all in one hand; and, standing with care, he threw them at Leopard.

The bundle of leaves, as it struck Leopard, flew open. Being released, the Bees rejoiced, saying, "So! I sting Nj⊠gâ!" Pepper also was glad, saying, "So! I will make him perspire!" Ants also spitefully exclaimed, "I've bitten you!"

The pain of all these made Leopard jump up in wrath; and he leaped toward Gazelle. But he dashed away into the forest, shouting as he disappeared, "I'm not an Ih⊠li of the open prairie, but of the forest wilderness!"

So, he fled and came to the town of Tortoise. There he told Tortoise, "You are justified! Nj⊠gâ indeed is not dead! He was only pretending, in order to kill."

And Tortoise, remarked, "I am the doyen of Beasts. Being the eldest, if I tell any one a thing, he should not contradict me."

Robert Hamill Nassau

TASKS DONE FOR A WIFE

Place
In Njambi's Kingdom

Persons

A Rich Merchant and his Daughter	Nguvu (Hippopotamus)
Njâgu (Elephant)	Ekaga (Tortoise)
Njᴇgâ (Leopard)	Mbodi (An Enormous Goat)
Njina (Gorilla)	Servants, and Townspeople

NOTE

The artifices of Tortoise compete with the strength of Leopard. The story of the Giant Goat is a separate Tale in No. 32, of Part Second.

In the time when Mankind and all other Animals lived together, to all the Beasts the news came that there was a Merchant in a far country, who had a daughter, for whom he was seeking a marriage. And he had said, "I do not want money to be the dowry that shall be paid by a suitor for my daughter. But, whosoever shall do some difficult works, which I shall assign him, to him I will give her."

All the Beasts were competing for the prize.

First, Elephant went on that errand. The merchant said to him, "Do such-and-such tasks, and you shall have my daughter. More than that, I will give you wealth also." Elephant went at the tasks, tried, and failed; and came back saying he could not succeed.

Next, Gorilla stood up; he went. And the merchant told him, in the same way as to Elephant, that he was to do certain tasks. Gorilla tried, and failed, and came back disgusted.

Then, Hippopotamus advanced, and said he would attempt to win the woman. His companions encouraged him with hopes of success, because of his size and strength. He went, tried, and failed.

Thus, almost all beasts attempted, one after another; they tried to do the tasks, and failed.

At last there were left as contestants, only Leopard and Tortoise. Neither was disheartened by the failure of the others; each asserted that he would succeed in marrying that rich daughter. Tortoise said, "I'm going now!" But Leopard said, "No! I first!" Tortoise yielded, "Well, go; you are the elder. I will not compete with you. Go you, first!" Leopard went, and made his application. The merchant said to him, "Good! that you have come. But, the others came, and failed. Try you." Leopard said, "Very well." He tried, and failed, and went back angry.

Tortoise then went. He saluted the merchant, and told him he had come to take his daughter. The merchant said, "Do so; but try to do the tasks first."

Tortoise tried all the tasks, and did them all. The first was that of a calabash dipper that was cracked. The merchant said to him, "You take this cracked calabash and bring it to me full of water all the way from the spring to this town." Tortoise looking and examining, objected, "This calabash! cracked! how can it carry water?" The merchant replied, "You yourself must find out. If you succeed, you marry my daughter."

Tortoise took the calabash to the spring. Putting it into the water, he lifted it. But the water all ran out before he had gone a few steps. Again he did this, five times; and the water was always running out. Sitting, he meditated, "What is this? How can it be done?" Thinking again, he said, "I'll do it! I know the art how!" He went to the forest, took gum of the Okume (mahogany tree) lighted a fire, melted the gum, smeared it over the crack, and made it water-tight; then, dipping the calabash into the spring, it did not leak. He took it full to the father-in-law, and called out, "Father-in-law! this is the calabash of water." The merchant asked, "But what did you do to it?" He answered "I mended it with gum." The father said, "Good for you! The others did not think of that easy simple solution. You have sense!"

Tortoise then said, "I have finished this one task; today has passed. Tomorrow I will begin on the other four."

The next morning, he came to receive his direction from the merchant, who said, "Ekaga! you see that tall tree far away? At the top are fruits. If you want my daughter, pluck the fruits from the top, and you shall marry her."

Tortoise went and stood watching and looking and examining the tree. Its trunk was all covered with soap, and impossible to be climbed. He returned to the merchant, and asked, "That fruit you wish, may it be obtained in any way, even if one does not climb the tree?" He was answered, "Yes, in any way, except cutting down the tree. Only so that I get the fruit, I am satisfied."

Tortoise had already tried from morning to afternoon to climb that tree, but could not. So, after he had asked the merchant his question, he went back to the tree; and from evening, all night and until morning, he dug about the roots till they were all free. And the tree fell, without his having "cut" the trunk at all. So he took the fruit to the Merchant, and told him that he had not "cut down" the tree, but that he had it "dug up." The merchant said,

"You have done well. People who came before you failed to think of that. Good for you!"

On the third day, the merchant said to the spectators, "I will not name the other three tasks. You, my assistants, may name them." So they thought of one task after another. But one and another said, "No, that is not hard; let us search for a harder." Finally, they found three hard tasks. Tortoise was ready for and accomplished them all.

Then the merchant announced, "Now, you may marry my daughter; and tomorrow you shall make your journey." They made a great feast; an ox was killed; and they had songs and music all night, clear on till morning.

But, while all this was going on, Leopard, who was left at his town, was saying to himself, "This Ekaga! He has stayed five days! Had he failed, he would not have stayed so long! So! he has been able to do the tasks! Is that a good thing?" (On the day that Tortoise started on the journey to seek the merchant's daughter, Leopard had been heard to say, "If Ekaga succeeds in getting that wife, I will take her from him by force.")

When Tortoise was ready to start on his return journey with his wife, the father-in-law gave him very many things, slaves and goats and a variety of goods, and said, "Go, you and your wife and these things. I send people to escort you part of the way. They are not to go clear on to your town, but are to turn back on the way."

Tortoise and company journeyed. When the escort were about to turn back, Tortoise said, "Day is past. Make an olako (camp) here. We sleep here; and, in the morning, you shall go back." That night he thought, "Njɛ̂gâ said he would rob me of my wife. Perhaps he may come to meet me on the way!" So, he swallowed all of the things, to hide them,—wife, servants, and all.

While Tortoise was thus on the way, Leopard had planned not to wait his return to town, but had set out to meet him. So, in the morning, the two, journeying in opposite directions, met. Tortoise gave Leopard a respectful "Mbolo!" and Leopard returned the salutation. Leopard asked, "What news? That woman, have you married her?" Tortoise answered, "That woman! Not at all!" Leopard looking at Tortoise's style and manner as of one proud of success, said, "Surely you have married; for you look happy, and show signs of success." But Tortoise swore he had not married.

Leopard only said, "Good." Then Tortoise asked, "But, where are you going?" Leopard answered, "I am going out walking and hunting. But you, where are you going?" Tortoise replied, "I did not succeed in marrying the woman; so I am going back to town. I tried, but I failed."

"But," said Leopard, "what then makes your belly so big?" Tortoise replied, "On the way I found an abundance of mushrooms, and I ate heartily of them. If you do not believe it, I can show you them by vomiting them up." Leopard said, "Never mind to vomit. Go on your journey."

And Leopard went on his way. But, soon he thought, "Ah! Ekaga has lied to me!" So he ran around back, and came forward to meet Tortoise again.

Tortoise looked and saw Leopard coming, and observed that his face was full of wrath. He feared, but said to himself, "If I flee, Njŏgâ will catch me. I will go forward and try artifice." As he approached Leopard, the latter was very angry, and said, "You play with me! You say you have not married the woman I wanted. Tell me the truth!" Tortoise again swore an oath, "No! I have not married the woman! I told you I ate mushrooms, and offered to show you; and you refused." So Leopard said, "Well, then, vomit."

Tortoise bent over, and vomited and vomited mushrooms and mushrooms; and then said triumphantly, "So! Njⵧgâ you see!" Leopard looked, and said, "But, Ekaga, your belly is still full,—go on vomiting." Tortoise tried to excuse himself, "I have done vomiting." Leopard persisted, "No! keep on at it." Tortoise went on retching; and a box of goods fell out of his mouth. Leopard still said, "Go on!" and Tortoise vomited in succession a table and other furniture. He was compelled to go on retching; and slaves came out. And at last, up was vomited the woman!

Leopard shouted, "Ah! Ekaga! you lied! You said you had not married! I will take this woman!" And he took her, sarcastically saying, "Ekaga, you have done me a good work! You have brought me all these things, these goods, and slaves, and a wife! Thank you!"

Tortoise thought to himself, "I have no strength for war." So, though anger was in his heart, he showed no displeasure in his face. And they all went on together toward their town. With wrath still in his heart, he went clear on to the town, and then made his complaint to each of the townspeople. But they all were afraid of Leopard, and said nothing, nor dared to give Tortoise even sympathy.

There was in that country among the mountains, an enormous Goat. The other beasts, all except Leopard, were accustomed to go to that Goat, when hungry, and say, "We have no meat to eat." And the Goat allowed them to cut pieces of flesh from his body. He could let any part of the interior of his body be taken except his heart. All the Animals had agreed among themselves not to tell Leopard where they got their meat, lest he, in his greediness, would go and take the heart. So they had told him they got their meat as he did, hunting.

Tortoise, angry because Leopard has taken his wife, said to himself, "I will make a cause of complaint against Njɛgâ that shall bring punishment upon him from our King. I will cause Njɛgâ to kill that Goat." On another day, Tortoise went and got meat from the Goat, and came back to town, and did not hide it from Leopard. Leopard said to him, "Ekaga! where did you get this meat?" Tortoise whispered, "Come to my house, and I will tell you." They went. And Tortoise divided the meat with him, and said, "Do not tell on me: but, we get the meat off at a great Goat. Tomorrow, I go; and you, follow behind me."

So, the next day, they went, Tortoise as if by himself, and Leopard following, off to the great Goat. Arrived there, Leopard wondered at the sight, "O! this great Goat! But, from where do you take its meat?" Tortoise replied, "Wait for me! You will see!" He went, and Leopard followed. Tortoise said to the Goat, "We have meat-hunger: we come to seek meat from you." The Goat's mouth was open as usual; Tortoise entered, and Leopard followed, to get flesh from inside. In the Goat's interior was a house, full of meat; and they entered it. Leopard wondered at its size; and Tortoise told him, "Cut where you please, but not from the heart, lest the Goat die." And they began to take meat. Leopard, with greediness, coveting the forbidden heart, went with knife near to it.

Tortoise exclaimed, "There! there! be careful." But Leopard, though he had enough other flesh, longed for the heart, and was not satisfied. He again approached with the knife near it: and Tortoise warned and protested. These very prohibitions caused Leopard to have his own way, and his greediness overcame him. He cut the heart: and the Goat fell dying.

Tortoise exclaimed, "Eh! Njɛgâ! I told you not to touch the

heart! Because of this matter I will inform on you." And he added, "Since it is so, let us go."

But Leopard said, "Goat's mouth is shut. How shall we get out? Let us hide in this house." And he asked, "Where will you hide?" Tortoise replied, "In the stomach." Leopard said, "Stomach! It is the very thing for me, Njⓧgâ, myself!" So Ekaga consented, "Well! take it! I will hide in the gall-bladder." So they hid, each in his place.

Soon, as they listened, they heard voices shouting, "The Goat is dead! A fearful thing! The Goat is dead!"

That news spread, and all who had been accustomed to get flesh there, came to see what was the matter. They all said that, as the Goat was dead, it was best to cut and divide him. They slit open the belly, and said, "Lay aside this big stomach; it is good; but throw away the bitter gall-sac." They looked for the heart; but there was none! A child, to whom had been handed the gall-bladder to throw it away, was flinging it into some bushes. As he did so, out jumped something from among the bushes; and the child asked, "Who are you?" The thing replied, pretending to be vexed, "I am Ekaga; I come here with the others to get meat, and you, just as I arrived, throw that dirty thing in my face!" The other people pacified him, "Do not get angry. Excuse the child. He did not see you. You shall have your share."

Then Tortoise called out, "Silence! silence! silence!"

They all stood ready to listen, and he said, "Do not cut up the Goat till we first know who killed it. That stomach there! What makes it so big?" Leopard, in the stomach, heard; but he did not believe that Tortoise meant it, and thought to himself, "What a fool is this Ekaga, in pretending to inform on me, by directing attention to the stomach!" Tortoise ordered, "All you, take your spears, and stick that stomach! For the one who killed Goat is in it!" And they all got their spears ready.

Leopard did not speak or move; for, he still thought Tortoise was only joking. Tortoise began with his spear, and the others all thrust in. And Leopard holding the heart, was seen dying! All shouted, "Ah! Njⓧgâ killed our Goat! Ah! he's the one who killed it." Tortoise taunted Leopard, "Asai! (shame for you) you took my wife; and now you are dead!" Leopard died. They divided the Goat, and returned to town. Tortoise took again his wife and all his goods, now that Leopard was dead. And he was satisfied that his artifice had surpassed Leopard's strength.

A TUG-OF-WAR

Persons

Ekaga (Tortoise)   Ngubu (Hippopotamus)
Njâgu (Elephant)

NOTE

African natives are sensitive about questions of equality and senior-ity. A certain term, "Mw☐ra" (chum) may be addressed to other than an equal, only at risk of a quarrel.

A story of the trick by which Tortoise apparently proved himself the equal of both Elephant and Hippopotamus.

Observe the preposterous size of Elephant's trunk! But every-thing, to the native African mind, was enormous in the pre-his-toric times.

Leopard was dead, after the accusation against him by Tortoise for killing the great Goat. The children of Leopard were still young; they had not grown to take their father's power and place. And Tortoise considered himself now a great personage. He said to people, "We three who are left,—I and Njâgu and Ngubu, are of equal power; we eat at the same table, and have the same authori-ty." Every day he made these boasts; and people went to Elephant and Hippopotamus, reporting, "So-and-so says Ekaga." Elephant and Hippopotamus laughed, and disregarded the report, and said, "That's nothing, he's only to be despised."

One day Hippopotamus met Elephant in the forest; salutations were made, "Mbolo!" "Ai, mbolo!" each to the other. Hippopotamus asked Elephant about a new boast that Tortoise had been making, "Have you, or have you not heard?" Elephant answered, "Yes, I have heard. But I look on it with contempt. For, I am Njâgu. I am big. My foot is as big as Ekaga's body. And he says he is equal to me! But, I have not spoken of the matter, and will not speak, unless I hear Ekaga himself make his boast. And then I shall know what I will do." And Hippopotamus also said, "I am doing so too, in silence. I wait to hear Ekaga myself."

Tortoise heard of what Elephant and Hippopotamus had been threatening, and he asked his informant just the exact words that they had used, "They said that they waited to hear you dare to speak to them; and that, in the meanwhile, they despised you."

Tortoise asked, "So! they despise me, do they?" "Yes," was the reply. Then he said, "So! indeed, I will go to them." He told his wife, "Give me my coat to cover my body." He dressed; and started to the forest. He found Elephant lying down; his trunk was eight miles long; his ears as big as a house, and his four feet beyond measure.

Tortoise audaciously called to him, "Mwĕra! I have come! You don't rise to salute me? Mwĕra has come!" Elephant looked, rose up and stared at Tortoise, and indignantly asked, "Ekaga! whom do you call 'Mwĕra'?" Tortoise replied, "You! I call you 'Mwĕra.' Are you not, Njâgu?" Elephant, with great wrath, asked, "Ekaga! I have heard you said certain words. It is true that you said them?"

Tortoise answered, "Njâgu, don't get angry! Wait, let us first have a conversation." Then he said to Elephant, "I did call you, just now, 'Mwⵗra'; but, you, Njâgu, why do you condemn me? You think that, because you are of great expanse of flesh, you can surpass Ekaga, just because I am small? Let us have a test. Tomorrow, sometime in the morning, we will have a lurelure (tug-of-war)." Said Elephant, "Of what use? I can mash you with one foot." Tortoise said, "Be patient. At least try the test." So, Elephant, unwilling, consented. Tortoise added, "But, when we tug, if one overpulls the other, he shall be considered the greater; but, if neither, then we are Mwⵗra."

Then Tortoise went to the forest, and cut a very long vine, and coming back to Elephant, said "This end is yours. I go off into the forest with my end to a certain spot, and tomorrow I return to that spot; and we will have our tug, and neither of us will stop, to eat or sleep until either you pull me over or the vine breaks." Tortoise went far off with his end of the vine to the town of Hippopotamus, and hid the vine's end at the outskirts of the town. He went to Hippopotamus and found him bathing, and going ashore, back and forth, to and from the water. Tortoise shouted to him, "Mwⵗra! I have come! You! Come ashore! I am visiting you!" Hippopotamus came bellowing in great wrath with wide open jaws, ready to fight, and said, "I will fight you today! For, whom do you call 'Mwⵗra'?"

Tortoise replied, "Why! *you!* I do not fear your size. Our hearts are the same. But, don't fight yet! Let us first talk." Hippopotamus grunted, and sat down; and Tortoise said, "I, Ekaga, I say that you and I and Njâgu are equal, we are Mwⵗra. Even though you are great and I small, I don't care. But if you doubt me, let us have a trial. Tomorrow morning let us have a lurelure. He who shall overcome, shall be the superior. But, if neither is found superior, then we are equals." Hippopotamus exclaimed that the plan was absurd; but, finally he consented.

Tortoise then stood up, and went out, and got his end of the vine, and brought it to Hippopotamus, and said, "This end is yours. And I now go. Tomorrow, when you feel the vine shaken, know that I am ready at the other end; and then you begin, and we will not stop to eat or sleep until this test is ended."

Hippopotamus then went to the forest to gather leaves of Medicine with which to strengthen his body. And Elephant, at the other end, was doing the same, making medicine to give himself strength; and at night they were both asleep.

In the morning, Tortoise went to the middle of the vine, where at its half-way, he had made on the ground a mark; and he shook it towards one end, and then towards the other. Elephant caught his end, as he saw it shake, and Hippopotamus did the same at his end. "Orindi went back and forth" (a proverb of a fish of that name that swims in that way), Elephant and Hippopotamus alternately pulling. "Nkᵭndinli was born of his father and mother" (a proverb, meaning distinctions in individualities). Each one, Hippopotamus and Elephant, doing in his own way. Tortoise smiled at his arrangement with each, that, in the tug, if one overcame, it would be proved by his dragging the other; but, if neither overcame, they were not to cease, until the vine broke.

Elephant holding the vine taut, and Hippopotamus also holding it taut, Tortoise was laughing in his heart as he watched the quivering vine.

He went away to seek for food, leaving those two at their tug, in hunger. He went off into the forest and found his usual food, mushrooms. He ate his belly full, and then took his drink; and then went to his town to sleep.

He rose in late afternoon, and said to himself, "I'll go and see about the tug, whether those fools are still pulling." When he went there, the vine was still stretched taut; and he thought, "Asai! shame! let them die with hunger!" He sat there, the vine trembling with tensity, and he in his heart mocking the two tired beasts. The one drew the other toward himself; and then, a slight gain brought the mark back; but neither was overcoming.

At last Tortoise nicked the vine with his knife; the vine parted; and, at their ends, Elephant and Hippopotamus fell violently back onto the ground. Tortoise said to himself, "So! that's done! Now I go to Elephant with one end of the broken vine; tomorrow to Hippopotamus." He went, and came on to Elephant, and found him looking dolefully, and bathing his leg with medicine, and said, "Mwㄢra! How do you feel? Do you consent that we are Mwㄢra?" Elephant admitted, "Ekaga, I did not know you were so strong! When the vine broke, I fell over and hurt my leg. Yes, we are really equal. Really! strength is not because the body is large. I despised you because your body was small. But actually, we are equal in strength!"

So they ate and drank and played as chums; and Tortoise returned to his town.

Early the next morning, with the other end of the broken vine, he went to visit Hippopotamus, who looked sick, and was rubbing his head, and asked, "Ngubu! How do you feel, Mwㄢra?" Hippopotamus answered, "Really! Ekaga! so we are equals! I, Ngubu, so great! And you, Ekaga, so small! We pulled and pulled. I could not surpass you, nor you me. And when the vine broke, I fell and hurt my head. So, indeed strength has no greatness of body." Tortoise and Hippopotamus ate and drank and played; and Tortoise returned to his town.

After that, whenever they three and others met to talk in palaver (council) the three sat together on the highest seats. Were they equal? Yes, they were equal.

AGĔNDA: RAT'S PLAY ON A NAME

Persons

Njɤgâ (Leopard)   Rângi (Frog)

Ntori (Rat)   Igâmbâ (Crab)

NOTE

In native African etiquette, a company of persons is saluted with the use of the verb in the plural; but only the oldest, or the supposed leader, if his name is known, is mentioned by name.

The native custom among polite tribes, is to leave a guest to eat without being watched.

The twitching of a muscle of an arm, or any other part of the body (called okalimambo) is regarded as a sign of coming evil. Compare Macbeth, Act 4, Scene 1.

> "By the pricking of my thumb
> Something wicked this way comes."

The absurd and the unreasonable (*e.g.*, the swallowing of a wife, goats, servants, etc.) are a constant feature of the native legends in their use of the impossible.

All native Africans have more than one name, and often change their names to suit circumstances. But, while all their names have a meaning (just as our English names, "Augustus,"

"Clara," etc.) those meanings are not thought of when denominating an individual; *e.g.*, "Bwalo" which means *canoe.*

Leopards do not like to wet their feet.

Leopard wanted a new wife. So he sought for a young woman of a far country, of whom he heard as a nice girl, a daughter of one of the Kings of that country. He did not go himself, but sent word, and received answer by messenger. Neither the woman nor her father had ever seen Leopard. They knew of him only by reputation.

The King was pleased with the proposed alliance, and assented, saying, "Yes! I am willing. Go! get yourself ready, and come with your marriage company." So Leopard went around and invited many other beasts, "Come! and help me get a new one!" They all replied, "Yes!" And they all started together for the King's town.

When they had gone half-way, one of their number, a big forest Rat said, "Brothers! let us begin here to change our names, so that when we get to the town, we shall not be known by our usual names." But Leopard refused, "No! I won't! I stick by my old name. My name is Njᴀgâ." All the others said the same, and retained their own names.

But Rat insisted for himself, "I will not be called Ntori. I will be called 'Strangers.' My name is Agᴀnda," (the plural of ogᴀnda which means "stranger").

When they approached the town, the inhabitants, with great politeness, ran out to welcome them, shouting, "Agᴀnda! Saleni, Saleni!" (Strangers! Welcome ye! welcome ye!) Rat turned to the company and said, "Hear that! you see they are saluting me as the leader of this company."

Upon their entering the town, they were shown to the

large public Reception-House; and the people said to them, "Now! strangers (Agⓧnda!), march in!" Rat turned again to his companions, and said, "You see! they have again addressed me specially by name, asking me to take possession of this room."

They all went in feeling uncomfortably; but Rat said to them, "Never mind! though this room was evidently prepared specially for me, I am not selfish, and I invite you to share it with me."

After the visitors had all been seated, the people came to give them the formal final salutation, saying "Strangers (Agⓧnda), mbolani! (long life to ye)." Rat promptly whispered to his companions, saying, "This mbolo is to me for you, I alone will respond to it." So, only he replied, "Ai Mbolani! Ai." (Mbolani is the second person plural of the irregular defective verb Mbolo equal to "live long.")

The day passed. In the evening, the people brought in an abundant supply of food, and set it down on the table, saying, "Strangers (Agⓧnda!), eat! Here is your food!" And they went out, closing the door, so that the guests in their eating should not be annoyed by spectators. Then Rat said, "You see! All this food is mine, though I am not able to eat it all." He alone began to eat of it. When he had satisfied his appetite, he said, "Truly this food is my own, but I am sorry for you, and I will give you of it." So he gave out to each, one by one, very small pieces of fish and plantain.

In the morning, the people thoughtfully sent water for the usual morning washing of hands and face. Rat hasted to open the door; and the slaves carrying the vessels of water, said to him, "These are sent to the strangers (Agⓧnda)." So Rat took the water and used it all for himself.

This second day was a repetition of the first. The townspeople continued their hospitality, sending food and drink and tobacco and fruits; and making many kind inquiries of what "the Ag⊠nda" would like to have. Rat, received all these things as for himself; while the rest of the company felt themselves slighted, and were hungry and disgusted.

On the third day, the company said among themselves, "Nj⊠gâ told us that our visit was to last the usual five days; but we cannot stand such treatment as this!" And they began to run away, one by one. Even Leopard himself followed them, provoked at his expected father-in-law's supposed neglect of him. But, before Leopard had gone, Rat went to the bride elect, and said, "I never saw such a party as this! They do not eat, and are not willing to await the Marriage Dance for the Bride on the fifth day."

When they were all secretly gone, leaving Rat alone, he said to the woman, "I will tell them all to go, even my friend Nj⊠gâ whom I brought to escort me. But I will not go without you, even if we have not had the dance; for, I am the one who was to marry you." And the father of the girl said to Rat, "Since they have treated you so, never mind to call them again for the Dance. You just take your wife and go."

So the King gave his daughter farewell presents of boxes of clothing, and two female servants to help her, and a number of goats, and men-servants to carry the baggage.

Rat and wife and attendants set out on their journey. When they were far away from the King's town, Rat exclaimed, "I feel okalimambo (premonition)." (He suspected that Leopard was somewhere near.) So he dismissed the men-servants, and sent them back to the King. And then quickly, in order to hide them, he swallowed the woman and the two maid-servants and all the boxes of clothing, and the goats.

Rat then went on, and on, and on, with his journey, until at a cross-roads, he saw Leopard coming cross-ways toward him; and he called out, "Who are you?" The reply came, "I am Njɛgâ. And who are you?" Rat answered, "Ntori."

Then Leopard called to him, "Come here!" "No!" said Rat, "I am in a hurry, and want to get home—" And he went on without stopping. So Leopard said, "Well, I pass on my way too!" "Good!" said Rat, "Pass on!" And they went on their separate ways.

But Leopard, at a turn in his road, rounded back, and hasted by another path to get in front of Rat. When Leopard again saw Rat a short distance before him, he calls out, "Who are you?" The reply was "Ntori; and who are you?" Leopard answered, "I'm Njɛgâ. Stop on your way, and come here to me!" Rat replied, "No! you asked me once before to stop, and I refused. And I refuse now; I must pass on."

Because of Rat's unwillingness to stop, Leopard began to chase him, and to shout at him, "You have my wife!" Rat answered back, "No! I have no wife of yours!" "You lie! You have the woman with you. What makes your body so big?"

Rat ran as fast as he could, with Leopard close after him. Rat's home is always a hole in the ground; and, as he was hard pressed in his flight, he dashed into the first hole he came to, which happened to be a small opening into a cave. But his tail was not yet drawn in and Leopard was so near that he seized it. Projecting from the mouth of the hole there was also the small root of a tree. Rat called out, "Friend Njɛgâ! what do you think you have caught hold of?" "Your tail!" said Leopard. Said Rat, "That is not my tail! this other thing near you is my tail!" So Leopard let go of the tail, and seized the root. Rat slid quickly to the bottom of the hole, and called out, "O! Njɛgâ! I did not think you were so silly! You had hold of my tail, and you let me go! You just look at your hand; you will see my tail-hairs clinging to it!"

Leopard went away in wrath; and, finding Frog at a near-by brook, he said to him, "Râgi! you just watch. I do not want Ntori to escape from that hole. Watch, while I go to get some fire, with which to burn him out."

Shortly after Leopard had gone, Rat began to creep out. Seeing Frog standing on guard, he said, "Good Râgi! let me pass!" But Frog replied, "No! I have my orders to watch you here." Then said Rat, "If that is so, why don't you come close here, and attend to your duty? You are too far from this hole. If a person is set to watch, he should be near the thing he watches. As far as you are there, I could, if I tried, get out without your catching me. So, it is better for you to have a good look down this hole." While Rat was saying all this, he was near the mouth of the hole; but, as Frog approached, he receded to the bottom, and went to the back end of the cave, where cayenne pepper bushes were growing. Frog came to the edge of the hole, and looking down, saw nothing.

During this while, Rat was plucking pepper-pods and chewing them, retaining them in his mouth. Returning again to the entrance, he saw Frog still watching, and he said, "Râgi! get out of my way, and let me pass. Let me out!" Frog replied, "I will not!" Rat asked, "Do you know me?" Frog replied, "Not very well." Then Rat said, "Come near! Open your eyes wide, and take a good look at me!" As soon as Frog's eyes were wide open, Rat blew the pepper into them. This so startled Frog that he fell back, his eyes blinded by the smarting; and Rat jumped out and ran away. Frog, heedless of his prisoner, was jumping about in pain; and, abandoning his post, crawled to the water of the brook not far away, and tumbled into it to wash his eyes.

Now, by this time, Leopard had returned with his fire. Seeing no one on guard, he called out, "Rângi! Rângi! where are you?" Frog, at the bottom of the brook, was still in agony with his eyes. He knew well that Rat was gone; but, in his vexation, he answered, "Ntori is there! Put in your fire!" So, Leopard put fire into the hole, and made a great smoke, but there was no sign of Rat.

After a long time, Leopard became tired at not finding Rat, and called out, "Rângi! Rângi! Where indeed is Ntori? He has not come out by this fire!" Then Frog answered, "Ntori is not there. I just lied to you in vexation of the pain I got through serving you." So, Leopard was very angry and said to Frog, "You have deceived and fooled me! I will just come and eat you up!" Said Frog, "Good! come on!"

Leopard ran to the brook, but, as Frog was at the bottom, Leopard had first to drink all the water, before he could reach him. Leopard drank and drank. But, as soon as the water was nearly drunk up, Frog jumped out, and hopped away to an adjacent pond. There Leopard followed, and began to drink up that water also. He drank, and drank, and drank, until he became so full and his belly so swollen that his feet no longer touched the ground; and he fell over on his back, before he had entirely emptied the pond. He was in such great pain, in his swollen belly, that he was helpless, and cried out to passersby, "Please, open a little hole in my body, and let out this water!" But each of the passersby said, "No! I am afraid that after I have helped you, then you will eat me."

At last, among those who passed by, came Crab. Leopard pleaded with him, "Igâmbâ! please! open my skin. Let out this water, so that I may live!" At first, Crab replied as the others, "No! I fear that after I help you, you will eat me." But Leopard begged so piteously that Crab consented, and scratched Leopard's skin with one of his claws. And the water spurted out! It came in so fast a current that it began to sweep Crab away. So Leopard cried out, "Igâmbâ! Please! do not let yourself be taken away! Catch hold on some root or branch!" Crab did so, holding on to a projecting root. When the water had subsided, and Crab was safe, Leopard was able to rise; and he said, "Igâmbâ! you have been kind to me; let me take you home, and I will be good to you; I will cook dinner, so we can eat together." Crab agreed, and they went together.

Leopard began to cook a kind of yam called nkwa, making a pot full of it. (When it is thoroughly cooked, it is soft and sticky.) The yam being finally ready to be eaten, Leopard said, "We do not put this food out on plates, but we bring the entire pot, and every one will help himself from it with his hands." Leopard thereupon began to take out handfuls of the nkwa, and to eat it. Crab tried to do the same, putting a claw into the sticky mass. But its heat burned his tender skin, and, in jerking his claw away, it stuck fast in the nkwa, and broke off. As soon as that happened, Leopard snatched up the claw and ate it. Crab protested, "Ah! Njᵉgâ! you are eating my claw!" Said Leopard, "Excuse me! No, I thought it was nkwa." So the dinner went on; Leopard greedily eating, Crab trying in vain to eat, and losing claw after claw, which Leopard in succession promptly ate.

Now, when Leopard had finished eating all the food, Crab's claws were all gone, and he had not been able to eat at all, and was left hungry. So Leopard says to Crab, "Now, as you are so helpless, what must I do for you?" He hoped that Crab, in despair, would tell him to eat him. But Leopard really was not hungry just then; and, when Crab said, "If you will just put me into some shallow water for two months, then all my claws will grow all right again," Leopard replied, "Good!" and he took Crab and placed him in a small stream of water.

The next day, Leopard, being now hungry to eat Crab, came to the water and called out, "Igâmbâ! Igâmbâ! have you your claws grown now?" The reply was, "Why! No! I told you two months yesterday, when you put me in here."

On the third day, Leopard came again to the water, and cried out to Crab, "Have your claws sprouted? Have they grown again?" "No!" said Crab curtly.

Leopard continued thus day by day, vexing Crab with inquiries, as if anxious about his health, but really desirous of an excuse to eat him, yet ashamed to do so by violence, because of Crab's kindness to him when he had the water-colic.

At last, Crab became tired of Leopard's visits. Hopeless to defend himself if Leopard should finally use force, he gave up in despair, and said, "So! I see why you ask me every day. You know that I told you two months. If you are determined to eat me, come on, and end the trouble at once!" With this permission as an excuse, Leopard was glad. He stepped to the edge of the water and took away Crab for his dinner. That was the return for Crab's kindness to him. After this, Leopard went out again to try to find Rat, but he never found him.

"NUTS ARE EATEN BECAUSE OF ANGÂNGWE"; A PROVERB

Places

Kingdom of the Hogs; The Forest; and Towns

Persons

Angângwe, King of Hogs	Nyare (Ox)
A Hunter	Nkambi (Antelope)
Ingowa (Hogs; singular Ngowa)	Njâgu (Elephant)
Njina (Gorilla)	

NOTE

"Inkula si nyo o'kângâ 'Ngângwe."

This is a proverb expressing the obligation we all owe to some superior protecting powers.

The Hogs had cleared a space in the forest, for the building of their town. They were many; men and women and children.

In another place, a Hunter was sitting in his town. Every day, at daybreak, he went out to hunt. When he returned in the afternoons with his prey, he left it a short distance from the town, and entering his house, would say to his women and children, "Go to the outskirts of the town, and bring what animal you find I have left there."

One day, having gone hunting, he killed Elephant. The children went out to cut it up and bring it in.

Another day, he killed Gorilla.

And so, each day, he killed some animal. He never failed of obtaining something.

One day, his children said to him, "You always return with some animal; but you never have brought us Ngowa." He replied, "I saw many Ingowa today, when I was out there. But, I wonder at one thing; that, when they are all together eating, and I approach, they run away. As to Ingowa, they eat nkula nuts and I know where the trees are. Well, then, I ambush them; but, when I go nearer, I see one big Ngowa not eating, but going around and around the herd. Whether it sees me or does not see, sure when I get ready to aim my gun, then they all scatter. The reason that Ingowa escape me, I do not know."

The Hogs, when they had finished eating, and were returning to their own town, as they passed the town of Elephant, heard mourning; and they asked, "Who is dead?" The answer was, "Njâgu is dead! Njâgu is dead!" They inquired, "He died of what disease?" They were told, "Not disease; Hunter killed him." Then another day, when Ox was killed, his people were heard mourning for him. Another day, Antelope was killed; and his people were mourning for him. All these animals were dying because of Hunter killing them.

At first, the Hogs felt pity for all these other Beasts. But, when they saw how they were dying, they began to mock at them, "These are not people! They only die! But, as to us Ingowa, Hunter is not able to kill us. We hear only the report that there is such a person as Hunter, but he is not able to kill us."

When Hogs were thus boasting, their King, Angângwe, laughed at them, saying, "You don't know, you Ingowa! You mock others, that Hunter kills them?" They answered, "Yes, we mock at them; for, we go to the forest as they do, but Hunter does not touch us." Angângwe asked, "When you thus in the forest eat your inkula-nuts, you each one eat them by his own strength and skill?" They answered, "Yes; ourselves we go to the forest on our own feet; we ourselves pick up and eat the inkula. No one feeds us." Angângwe said, "It is not so. Those inkula you eat si nyo o'kângâ wa oma (they are eaten because of a person)." They insisted, "No, it is not so. Inkula have no person in particular to do anything about them." Thus they had this long discussion, the Hogs and their King; and they got tired of it, and lay down to sleep.

In the morning, when daylight came, the King said, "A journey for nuts! But, today, I am sick. I am not able to go to gather nuts with you. I will stay in town." The Hogs said, "Well! we do not mistake the way. It is not necessary for you to go."

When they went, they were jeering about their King, "Angângwe said, 'Inkula si nyo o'kângâ w' oma'; but we will see today without him." They went to the nkula trees, and found great abundance fallen to the ground during the night. The herd of Hogs, when they saw all these inkula, jumped about in joy. They stooped down to pick up the nuts, their eyes busy with the ground. They ate and ate. No one of them thought of Hunter, whether he was out in the forest.

But, that very morning, Hunter had risen, taken his gun and ammunition-box, and had gone to hunt. And, after awhile, he had seen the Hogs in the distance. They were only eating and eating, not looking at anything but nuts.

Hunter said in his heart, "These Hogs, I see them often, but why have I not been able to kill them?" He crept softly nearer and nearer. Creeping awhile then he stood up to spy; and again stooping, and again standing up to spy. He did not see the big Hog which, on other days, he had always observed going around and around the herd. Hunter stooped close to the ground, and crept onward. Then, as he approached closer, the Hogs still went on eating. He bent his knee to the earth, and he aimed his gun! Ingowa still eating! His gun flashed! and ten Hogs died!

The Hogs fled; some of them wounded. Those who were not wounded, stopped before they reached their town, and said, "Let us wait for the wounded." They waited. When the hindmost caught up and joined the others, they showed them their wounds, some in the head, some in the legs. These wounded ones said, "As we came, we saw none others behind us. There are ten of us missing; we think they are dead." So, they all returned toward their Town; and, on their way, began to mourn.

When they had come clear on to the town, Angângwe asked, "What news, from where you come?" They answered, "Angângwe! evil news! But we do not know what is the matter. Only we know that the words you said are not really so, that 'nuts are eaten because of a certain person.' Because, when we went, each one of us gathered by his own skill, and ate by his own strength, and no one trusted to any one else. And when we went, we ate abundantly, and everything was good. Except that, Hunter has killed ten of us. And many others are wounded."

The King inquired, "Well! have you brought nuts for me who was left in Town?" They replied, "No; when Hunter shot us, we feared, and could no longer wait." Then Angângwe said, "I told you that inkula are eaten because of a person, and you said, 'not so.' And you still doubt me."

Another day, the Hogs went for inkula; and the King, remained in town. And, as on the other day, Hunter killed them. So, for five successive days, they went, the King staying in town; and Hunter killing them.

Finally, Angângwe said to himself, "Ingowa have become great fools. They do not consent to admit that nuts are eaten by reason of a certain person. They see how Hunter kills them; and they still doubt my words. But, I pity them. Tomorrow, I will go with them to the nuts. I will explain to them how Hunter kills them."

So, in the morning, the King ordered, "Come all to nuts! But when we go for the nuts, if I say, 'Ngh-o-o!' then every one of you who are eating them must start to town, and not come back, because then I have seen or smelt Hunter; and I grunt to let you know." All the Hogs agreed. They went on clear to the nkula trees, and ate, they stooping with eyes to the ground. But Angângwe, not eating, kept looking here and there. He sniffed wind from south to north, and assured them, "Eat you all! I am here!" He watched and watched; and presently he saw a speck far away. He passed around to sniff the wind. His nose uplifted, he caught the odor of Hunter. He returned to the herd, grunted "Ngh-o-o." And he and they all fled. They arrived safely at town.

Then he asked them, "Who is dead? who is wounded?" They assured, "None." He said, "Good!"

Thus they went nutting, for five consecutive days, they and their King, Angângwe only keeping watch. And none of them died by Hunter.

Then Angângwe said to them, "Today let us have a conversation." And he began, "I told you, inkula si nyo o'kângâ w' oma; you said, 'Not so!' But, when you went by yourselves to eat nuts, did not Hunter kill you? And these five days that we have gone, you and I together, and you obeyed my voice, who has died?"

They then replied, "No one! no one! Indeed, you spoke truly. You are justified. Inkula si nyo o'kângâ wa 'Ngângwe. It is so!"

WHO ARE CROCODILE'S RELATIVES?

Persons
Ngando (Crocodile)   Sinyama (Beasts)
Sinyani (Birds)

NOTE

An Argument in Evolution—When and How does Life begin?

Crocodile was very old. Finally he died. News of his death spread abroad among the Beasts; and his relatives and friends came to the Mourning. After a proper number of days had passed, the matter of the division of the property was mentioned. At once a quarrel was developed, on the question as to who were his nearest relatives.

The tribe of Birds said, "He is ours and we will be the ones to divide the property." Their claim was disputed, others asking, "On what ground do you claim relationship? You wear feathers; you do not wear plates of armor as he." The Birds replied, "True, he did not wear our feathers. But, you are not to judge by what he put on during his life. Judge by what he was in his life's beginning. Look you! In his beginning, he began with us as an egg. We believe in eggs. His mother bore him as an egg. He is our relative, and we are his heirs."

But the Beasts said, "Not so! We are his relatives, and by us shall his property be divided."

Then the Council of Animals demanded of the Beasts on what ground they based their claim for relationship, and what answer they could make to the argument of the birds as to Crocodile's egg-origin.

The Beasts said, "It may be true that the mark of tribe must be found, in a *beginning*, but not in an egg. For, all Beings began as eggs. *Life* is the original beginning. Look you! When life really begins in the egg, then the mark of tribe is shown. When Ngando's life began, he had four legs as we have. We judge by legs. So we claim him as our relative. And we will take his property."

But, the Birds answered, "You Beasts said we were not relatives because we wear feathers, and not ngando-plates. But, you, look you! Judge by your own words. Neither do you wear ngando-plates, you with your hair and fur! Your words are not correct. The *beginning* of his life was not, as you say, when little Ngando sprouted some legs. There was *life* in the egg before that. And his egg was like ours, not like what you call your eggs. You are not his relatives. He is ours."

But the Beasts disputed still. So the quarrel went back and forth. And they never settled it.

WHO IS KING OF BIRDS?

Places
The Country of Birds in Njambi's Kingdom   Njambi's Town
Persons
Ra-Njambi (Lord or Master   Ngwanyâni (Eagle)
of all)   Ugulungu (Schizorhis, Plan-
Njâgâni (Chicken)   tain-Eater)
Ngozo (Parrot)

NOTE

1st—Ability to Speak a greater gift than ability in Walking, Flying, or any other Force.

2nd—Why Chickens live with Mankind.

All the Birds had their dwelling-place in a certain country of Njambi's Kingdom. The pelicans, chickens, eagles, parrots and all other winged kinds all lived together, separated from other animals, in that country under the Great Lord Njambi.

One day, they were discussing together on the question, "Who is King of the Birds?" They all, each one, named himself, *e.g.*, the Chicken said, "I!;" the Parrot, "I!" the Eagle "I!" and so on. Every day they had this same discussion. They were not able to settle it, or to agree to choose any one of their number. So, they said, "Let us go to Ra-Njambi, and refer the question to him." They agreed;

and all went to him so that he might name who was the superior among them. When they all had arrived at Njambi's Town, he asked, "What is the affair on which you have come?" They replied, "We have come together here, not to visit, but for a purpose. We have a discussion and a doubt among ourselves. We wish to know, of all the Birds, who is Head or Chief. Each one says for himself that he is the superior. This one, because he knows how to fly well; that one because he can speak well; and another one, because he is strong. But, of these three things,—flight, speech, and strength, we ask you, which is the greatest?"

Immediately all the Birds began a competition, each one saying, "Choose me; I know how to speak!" Njambi silenced them, and bade them, "Well, then, come here! I know that you all speak. But, show me, each one of you, your manner of speaking."

So Eagle stood up to be examined. Njambi asked him, "How do you speak? What is your manner of talking?" Eagle began to scream, "So-o-we! so-o-we! so-o-we!" Njambi said, "Good! Now call me your wife!" The wife of Eagle came, and Njambi said to her, "You are the wife of Ngwanyâni, how do you talk?" The wife replied, "I say, 'So-o-we! So-o-we! So-o-we!' " Ra-Njambi said to Eagle, "Indeed! you and your wife speak the same kind of language." Eagle answered, "Yes; I and my wife, we speak alike." They were ordered, "Sit you aside."

Then Ra-Njambi directed, "Bring me here Ngozo." And he asked, "Ngozo, how do you talk? What is your way of speaking?" Parrot squawked, "I say, 'Ko-do-ko!' " Ra-Njambi ordered, "Well, call me your wife!" She came; and he asked her, "How do you talk? Talk now!" The wife replied, "I say, 'Ko-do-ko!' " Njambi asked Parrot, "So! your wife says, 'Ko-do-ko?' " Parrot answered "Yes; my wife and I both say, 'Ko-do-ko.' "

Njambi then ordered, "Call me here, Ugulungu." He came, and was asked, "And how do you talk?" He shouted, "I say, 'Mbru-kâ-kâ! mbru-kâ-kâ! mbru!' " Njambi told him, "Call me your wife!" She came, and, when asked, spoke in the same way as her husband. Njambi dismissed them, "Good! you and your wife say the same thing. Good!"

So, all the Birds, in succession, were summoned; and they all, husband and wife, had the same mode of speaking, except one who had not hitherto been called.

Njambi finally said, "Call Njâgâni here!" The Cock stood up, and strutted forward. Njambi asked him, "What is your speech? Show me your mode of talking!" Cock threw up his head, stretched his throat, and crowed, "Kâ-kâ-re-kââ." Njambi said, "Good! summon your wife hither." The wife came; and, of her, Njambi asked, "And, what do you say?" She demurely replied, "My husband told me that I might talk only if I bore children. So, when I lay an egg, I say 'Kwa-ka! Kwa-ka!' " Njambi exclaimed, "So! you don't say, 'Kâ-kâ-re-kââ,' like your husband?" She replied, "No, I do not talk as he."

Then Njambi said to Cock, "For what reason do you not allow your wife to say, 'Kâ-kâ-re-kââ?' " Cock replied, "I am Njâgâni, I respect myself. I jeer at all these other birds. Their wives and themselves speak only in the same way. A visitor, if he comes to their towns, is not able to know, when one of them speaks, which is husband and which is wife, because they both speak alike. But I, Njâgâni, as to my wife, she is unable to speak as I do. I do not allow it. A husband should be at the head; and in his wife it is not becoming for her to be equal with him or to talk as well as he does."

Njambi listened to this long speech; and then inquired, "Have you finished?" Chicken answered, "Yes."

Njambi summoned all the Birds to stand together in one place near him, and he said, "The affair which you brought to me, I settle it thus:—Njâgâni is your Head; because you others all speak, husband and wife, each alike. But, he speaks for himself in his own way, and his wife in her way; to show that a husband has priority and superiority over a wife. Therefore, as he knows how to be Head of his family, it is settled that Njâgâni is Head also of your Tribe."

But, Njambi went on to say, "Though this is true, you, Njâgâni, don't you go back again into the Forest, to your Kingship of the Birds. For the other birds will be jealous of you. You are not strong, you cannot fight them all. Lest they kill you, stay with me in my Town."

Cock went to get his wife and children, and returned and remained there with Ra-Njambi. Therefore, the original bird to dwell among Mankind was the chicken.

When the other Birds scattered and went back to their own forest country without their king, they said, "Let it be so! We will not choose another King. Our King has left us, and has emigrated to another country, and has sat down in Njambi's Town."

So, the Birds have lived in the forest without any King.

There is another story which gives a different explanation of chickens being the first of birds to dwell among Mankind.

The Birds had no fire. They had to eat their food raw, and to shiver on cold days. In flying over the other countries, they saw Mankind using, in the preparation of their food, a thing which birds did not have. They observed that that thing seemed to add much to the comfort of Mankind. So, they chose Chicken, not as their King, but, because he knew so well how to speak, to go as their messenger, to ask Mankind to share that thing with them. Chicken left the Forest, and started on his journey, and came to the towns of Men.

He found so much food lying around, and it tasted so good because it had been touched by that bright thing which he heard people call "Fire," that he delayed the delivery of his message. And Men were pleased with his usefulness in awaking them in the morning, as he called them to get up and make their fires. The situation was so comfortable, as Mankind allowed him to walk in and out of their houses at will, that he forgot his errand, and chose to stay with Men, and never went back to the Forest.

The birds, having no one else who united both audacity to act and ability to speak, never sent another messenger on that errand, and they remain without fire to this day.

"NJIWO DIED OF SLEEP": A PROVERB

Persons
Njiwo (A Species of Antelope)   Nyare (Ox)

NOTE

An event (the supposed death of the red antelope) is traced to its first cause (sleep) back of the immediate causes (the people who actually sought to kill him). Whence the proverb, "Eziwo a juwi na Antyâvinâ." "Eziwo" is a familiar way of pronouncing Njiwo.

Antelope and Ox went to a town to dance Bweti (a certain spirit-dance). After the dance, Antelope, exhausted with the exercise, fell asleep in the Bweti-house. While he was there, certain persons made a plot to kill him. Ox heard of it, and came to warn him, calling gently, (lest he should be overheard and himself seized), "Njiwo! Eziwo!" But antelope did not hear, and Ox made no further effort, and ran away to his home in fear for his own life.

Then came Antelope's wife, while he still slept, and loudly called him. He, only half-awake, grumbled, "What do you call me for? Let me rest. I'm tired by the dancing." She persisted, "I call you because certain persons want to kill you." But, he, still heavy with sleep, did not understand, and was not willing to rise, and went on sleeping. Then his wife, unable to arouse him, went to call other people to help her.

While she was away, his enemies came and tied him with ropes, and left him there tied, still sleeping, alone in the house. They locked the house, and went away, intending to return and kill him when he should awake. Before they came back, his wife returned with aid; and, with machetes and knives, they cut open the door, and found him with his limbs tied, and still sleeping. They roughly shook him, and he, half-conscious, asked, "What do you want here?" His wife replied, "I have come to carry you away." So, she untied the ropes, and they lifted him and carried him away, still too sleepy to walk himself.

While all this was going on, the people of the town to which Ox had fled, asked him, "There were two of you who went to dance Bweti. You are here, but where is the other?" Ox, assuming that Antelope was dead, and not knowing what Antelope's wife had done, told how he had been unable to waken him, and said, "Eziwo was killed while asleep." Then the village people said regretfully, "Eh! Eziwo! Sleep has killed him!"

In the meantime, Antelope and his wife had reached the town, where the news of his death had preceded them; and the people wondered, saying, "Nyare reported that you were cut to pieces!" Then Antelope's wife explained that he would have been killed, because Ox had not made every effort to arouse him from his deep sleep.

So the friendship of Ox and Antelope ended. And the proverb came, that, "Eziwo died of sleep."

WHICH IS THE FATTEST?

Persons

King Ra-Mborakinda   Ngowa (Hog; Pl. Ingowa)

Manga (Manatus)   Arandi (Oyster)

NOTE

Accept no challenge whose test you know you cannot endure. Oyster, without fat, accepted the challenge of the fat Hog and the fatter Manatus.

The fat of the Manatus, or dugong seal, is delicious and very abundant.

Ra-Mborakinda was dwelling in his Town, with his people and the glory of his Kingdom. There were gathered there the Manatus, the Oyster and the Hog, waiting to be assigned their kingdoms. To pass the time, while waiting until the King should summon them for their assignments, Oyster said, "You, Manga, and Ngowa, let us have a dance!" And they went to exhibit before the King. They danced and danced, each one dancing his own special dance.

After that they made a fire, each one at his own fire-place, and sat down to rest. Then Hog proposed a new entertainment. He said, "You, Arandi, and Manga, we all three shall test ourselves by fire, to see who has the most fat." And they all three went into their respective fire-places, Hog into his, and Manatus into his, and Oyster into its. Under the influence of the heat, the fat in their bodies began to melt.

Then the King announced, "To the one who shall prove to have the most fat, I will give a great extent of country as its kingdom." So, they all three tried to show much fat, in their effort to win the prize.

Presently, the fat of Hog began to cease exuding, for he had not a great deal. As to Oyster, it had no fat. What it produced was not fat at all, but water; and that was in such quantity that it put out its fire.

These facts about the Hog and Oyster were reported to the King, and when he inquired how Manatus was getting on, lo! it was found that she had such abundance of fat, that the oil flowing from her had burst into flame and had set the town on fire.

At this, the King wondered, and exclaimed, "This Manga, that lives in the water, has yet enough fat to set the town afire!"

Then Manatus with Hog and Oyster went and sat together in the open court before the King's house, to await what would be his decision. When he was ready, he sent two heralds to summon not only those three, but all the Tribes of the Beasts of the Forest, and of the Fishes of the Sea; and the town was full of these visitors. But, Hog and all his tribe had become impatient of waiting, and had gone off for a walk. All the other animals that had been summoned, came into the King's presence, and he, having ascended his throne, said, "I am ready now to speak with these three persons; but, I see that the Ingowa are not here. So, because of their disrespect in going off to amuse themselves with a walk instead of waiting for me, I condemn that they shall no longer wear any horns."

Then the King announced that, as Manatus had the most fat, her promised territory should be the Sea, and of it she should be ruler. But, Manatus said, "I do not want to live in the Sea, lest I be killed there." The King asked, "Then, where will you prefer to live?" She answered, "In such rivers as I shall like."

That is the reason that the Manatus lives only in rivers and bays. For, one day she and her children had floated with the tide to the mouth of a river and into the Sea; and some of them had been killed there by sharks and other big fish. So, the Manatus is never now found near the Sea on ordinary tides, but only when high tides have swept it down.

Just as the King had made his announcement, the company of Hogs returned and entered the Assembly. They explained, "We have just come back from our walk, and we wish to resume our horns which we left here." But the King refused, and kept possession of the horns. Hog begged, "Please! let me have my horns!" But the King swore an oath, saying, "O savi! (By the Blessing!) wherever you go, and whatever you be, you shall have no horns." So the Hogs departed.

Now Oyster stood up, and said, "I wish to go to my place. Where shall it be?" The King said, "I will give you no other place than what you already have had. I do not wish to put you into the fresh-water springs and brooks with Manga. You shall go into the salty waters." So Oyster went; and its race lives on the edge of the rivers, near the Sea, in brackish waters. And the King said to Oyster, "All the tribes of Mankind, by the Sea, when they fail to obtain other fish, shall be allowed to eat you."

All knew that this was a punishment given by the King to Oyster, for having dared the test by fire, pretending that it had fat, the while it had none.

WHY MOSQUITOES BUZZ

Persons
Mbo (Mosquito)   Aga (Hands)
Oroi (Ear)

NOTE

It is a practice of African natives, after taking a bath, to anoint their bodies with some oil or grease.

In the time of Long-ago, in Njambi's Town, Mosquito and Ear went out to take a bath together. After taking her bath, Ear began to rub an oily substance over herself; while Mosquito did not. So Ear said to Mosquito, "Why do you leave your skin so rough? It is better to rub on a little oil." Mosquito replied, "I have none." So Ear said, "Indeed! I did not know that. I will give you part of mine, as I have plenty." Mosquito had to wait the while that Ear was rubbing the soft wax over herself. But, as soon as Ear had finished, she put back the wax into her ear where she usually kept it, and did not fulfill her promise to Mosquito.

When Mosquito saw this, that the wax was put away, he came near to the door, and said, "I want the oil you promised for rubbing on my body." But Ear took no notice of him, except to call on Hands to drive Mosquito away.

So, to this day, Mosquito is not willing to cease making his claim for the unfulfilled promise; and is always coming to our ears, and buzzing and crying. Always Mosquito comes and says, "I want my oil, Bz-z-z-z." But Ear remains silent, and gives no answer. And Mosquito keeps on grumbling and complaining, and gets angry and bites.

UNKIND CRITICISM

Persons

Tyema (A Black Monkey)   Ekaga (Tortoise)

NOTE

This story is probably of comparatively recent origin though known at least fifty years ago. It seems to point to the time when white men began to taunt negroes because of their color, the common insult by an angry white master being "You black monkey!" The tale cannot antedate the first coming of white men to West Africa three hundred years ago; for, no native would have invented this insult, though they do now imitate white men, when, in a quarrel, they wish to taunt an opponent.

The Black Monkey, up a tree, saw Tortoise passing beneath, slowly and awkwardly moving step by step. Monkey laughed at the dull manner and appearance of Tortoise; and, to tease one whom he thought stupid and unable to resent insult, he jumped down onto the back of Tortoise. There, safely perched, he jeered at Tortoise, saying many unkind things. Tortoise was unable to throw off his tormentor; nor could he reach him. His short hands and feet could not touch Monkey. So, Tortoise was compelled to carry Monkey on the way, the while that the latter was taunting him. Finally, the patience of Tortoise was exhausted, and, his indignation being aroused, he stopped, and said angrily, "Get off of my back, you black monkey!"

Monkey was sensitive about his color; and, at that word "black," he slipped off, and went away ashamed. But he was angry also, and determined to have some revenge.

Some time after this, Monkey made a feast, and invited a number of beasts, among the rest Tortoise. But Monkey purposely placed all the dishes up high, so that Tortoise, unable to reach to them, could get no food, as he vainly went around and around the table. All the while, Monkey was sarcastically urging him to come and help himself and eat. Tortoise bore it without complaint; and at the end of the feast, he went away hungry. But he also determined to have his revenge.

On another day, Tortoise made a feast, and invited the same persons who had seen his humiliation at the house of Monkey. Monkey came to the feast. But Tortoise had prepared the food in only one dish, around which the company were to sit on the ground, and from which they were to eat with their hands. Before calling them to eat, Tortoise had provided water and soap for them to wash their hands previous to their putting them into the same dish. As Monkey was about to put his, Tortoise reminded him that it was black, and that he should first wash it. He said, "Here is water, and the soap by which white people keep their hands from getting black."

Monkey was ashamed, and lathered the soap over his hands until they were white with foam. "Now," said Tortoise, "put your hand into the water to remove the foam." Monkey did so; and his hands were still black.

The rest of the company objected to his black hand going into their food. And he went away ashamed and hungry.

THE SUITORS OF PRINCESS GORILLA

Place

Njambi's Country

Persons

King Njina (Gorilla) and His Daughter	Ngowa (Hog)
	Njɛgâ (Leopard)
Njâgu (Elephant)	Telinga (a very small Mon-
Nguwu (Hippopotamus)	key)
Bejaka (Fishes: Sing. Ejaka)	

NOTE

This story evidently dates back to the first introduction of Rum into Africa. Gorilla's "new kind of water" was Rum.

Telinga's cheating did not finally succeed in obtaining him the wife; but was the cause of his now living only in trees; whereas formerly he lived in the long grass. The Telinga are very numerous, and they all look so alike that one cannot be distinguished from another. In the story, he had arranged with all his companions to help him drink.

In the Gorilla Country there are no lions, and there he is readily called the King of Beasts, because of the fearful length and strength of his arms.

How absurd that so horribly ugly a caricature of a human being should be supposed to have a beautiful daughter!

King Gorilla had a daughter, whose beauty had been much praised. She being of marriageable age, he announced to all the tribes that he would give her in marriage to any one who could accomplish a certain task. He said he would not take any of the goods usually given in payment for a wife, as dowry. But, that he had a new kind of water, such as had never before been seen; and, whoever could drink an entire barrelful of it, should have the prize that had been coveted by many.

So, all the tribes came together one day in the forest country of the King, to compete for the young woman, and the paths were crowded with the expectant suitors on their way to the King's Court.

First, because of his size, Elephant stepped forward. He walked with his solemn dignity, his ponderous feet sounding, tubu, tubu, as he strode toward where the barrel stood. He could, however, scarcely suppress his indignation, in the presence of the King, at what he considered the insultingly small test to which he was about to be subjected. He thought in his heart, "That barrelful of water! Why! I, Njâgu, when I take my daily bath, I spurt from my trunk many barrelfuls over my whole body, and I drink half a barrelful at every meal. And this! Why! I'll swallow it down in two gulps!" He thrust his proboscis into the barrel to draw up a big mouthful. But, he instantly withdrew it, before he began to suck up any of it. "The new water" stung him. He lifted his trunk, and trumpeting with rage, declared that the task was impossible.

Many in the company, who had feared that the big elephant

would leave no chance for them, secretly rejoiced at his failure; and began to hope for themselves.

Then Hippopotamus blundered forward. He was in haste, for he was sure he would succeed. He was not as big or heavy as Elephant, though he was more awkward. But he did not hesitate to boast aloud what he could do. "You, Njâgu, with your big body, afraid of that little barrel of water! Why! I live in water half of the time. And when I begin to drink in a river, I cause the Bejaka to be frightened." So he came bellowing and roaring, in order to impress the young woman with his importance. But his mouth had not sunk into the barrel as he thrust his nose in, before he jerked his head up with a bigger bellow of pain and disgust at the new water. Without making even a bow to the King, he shambled off to a river to wash his mouth.

Next came Hog. He said to Gorilla, "King Gorilla, I do not boast like those two other fellows, nor will I insult you as they have done, even if I fail. But, I do not think I shall fail. I am accustomed to putting my nose into all sorts of dirty places; so I shall try." He did try, slowly and carefully. But, even he, used to all sorts of filth and bad smells, turned from the barrel in disgust, and went away grunting.

Then Leopard came bounding forward, boasting and jumping from side to side to show his beautiful skin to the young woman. He derided the other three who had preceded him. "O! you fellows! You had no chance at all, even if you had drunk up that water. The woman would not look at you, nor live with such blundering, awkward gawks as you. Look at my graceful body and tail! These strong but soft paws of mine! And, as to that barrel, you shall see in a few minutes. Though we of the Cat Tribe do not like to wet our feet, I will do it for the sake of the woman. I'm the dandy of the Forest, and I shall go at it more gracefully than you." He leaped onto the barrel. But, its very fumes sickened him. He made one vain effort. And with limp tail between his legs he crawled away to hide his shame.

One after another of the various Beasts attempted. And all failed. Finally, there crept forward the little Telinga. He had left the hundreds of his Tribe of little Monkeys hidden out in the grass field. As he advanced, there was a murmur of surprise from the unsuccessful spectators. Even King Gorilla could not refrain from saying, "Well! my little fellow! what do you want?" Telinga replied, "Your Majesty, did not you send word to all the Tribes that any one might compete?" "Yes, I did," he answered. And Telinga said, "Then I, Telinga, small as I am, I shall try." The King replied, "I will keep my royal word. You may try." "But, Your Majesty," asked Telinga, "is it required that the barrel must be drank at one draught? May I not, between each mouthful, take a very short rest out in the grass?" Said Gorilla, "Certainly, just so you drink it today."

So Telinga took a sip, and leaped off into the grass. And, apparently, he immediately returned, and took another sip and leaped back into the grass; and, apparently, immediately returned again. And apparently—(They were his companions who had come one by one to help him!) Thus the barrelful of firewater was rapidly sipped away.

King Gorilla announced Telinga as the winner of the prize.

What the young woman thought of the loss of her graceful lovers, the Antelopes and others, is not known. For, when Telinga advanced to take her, Leopard and others dashed at him, shouting, "You miserable little snip of a fellow! You've won her; but if we can't have her you shan't. There! take that! and that! and that!" as they began to beat and kick and bite him.

In terror, he jumped into the trees, abandoning his bride.

And he and his tribe have remained in the trees ever since, afraid to come down to the ground.

Robert Hamill Nassau

TALE 15
LEOPARD OF THE FINE SKIN

Place
Town of King Mborakinda
Persons

King Mborakinda	Njǒgâ (Leopard)
Ilâmbe, His Daughter	Kabala (A Magic Horse)
Ra-Marânge, A Doctor	Ogula-Ya-Mpazya-Vazya, A Sorcerer
And Other People	

NOTE

Leopards can swim if compelled to, but they do not like to enter water, or wet their feet in any way.

At the town of Ra-Mborakinda, where he lived with his wives and his children and his glory, this occurred.

He had a beloved daughter, by name Ilâmbe. He loved her much; and sought to please her in many ways, and gave her many servants to serve her. When she grew up to womanhood, she said that she did not wish any one to come to ask her in marriage; that she herself would choose a husband. "Moreover, I will never marry any man who has any, even a little bit of, blotch on his skin."

Her father did not like her to speak in that way; nevertheless, he did not forbid her.

When men began to come to the father and say, "I desire your daughter Ilâmbe for a wife," he would say, "Go, and ask herself." Then when the man went to Ilâmbe's house, and would say, "I have come to ask you in marriage," her only reply was a question, "Have you a clear skin, and no blotches on your body?" If he answered, "Yes," Ilâmbe would say, "But, I must see for myself; come into my room." There she required the man to take off all his clothing. And if, on examination, she saw the slightest pimple or scar, she would point toward it, and say, "That! I do not want you." Then perhaps he would begin to plead, "All my skin is right, except—." But she would interrupt him, "No! for even that little mark I do not want you."

So it went on with all who came, she finding fault with even a small pimple or scar. And all suitors were rejected. The news spread abroad that Ra-Mborakinda had a beautiful daughter, but that no one was able to obtain her, because of what she said about diseases of the skin.

Still, many tried to obtain her. Even animals changed themselves to human form, and sought her, in vain.

At last, Leopard said, "Ah! this beautiful woman! I hear about her beauty, and that no one is able to get her. I think I better take my turn, and try. But, first I will go to Ra-Marânge." He went to that magic-doctor, and told his story about Ra-Mborakinda's fine daughter, and how no man could get her because of her fastidiousness about skins. Ra-Marânge told him, "I am too old. I do not now do those things about medicines. Go to Ogula-ya-mpazya-vazya."

So, Leopard went to him. As usual, the sorcerer Ogula jumped into his fire; and coming out with power, directed Leopard to tell what he wanted. So he told the whole story again, and asked how he should obtain the clean body of a man. The sorcerer prepared for him a great "medicine" by which to give him a human body, tall, graceful, strong and clean. Leopard then went back to his town, told his people his plans, and prepared their bodies also for a change if needed. Having taken also a human name, Ogula, he then went to Ra-Mborakinda, saying, "I wish your daughter Ilâmbe for wife."

On his arrival, at Ra-Mborakinda's, the people admired the stranger, and felt sure that Ilâmbe would accept this suitor, exclaiming, "This fine-looking man! his face! and his gait! and his body!" When he had made his request of Ra-Mborakinda, he was told, as usual, to go to Ilâmbe and see whether she would like him. When he went to her house, he looked so handsomely, that Ilâmbe was at once pleased with him. He told her, "I love you; and I come to marry you. You have refused many. I know the reason why, but I think you will be satisfied with me." She replied, "I think you have heard from others the reason for which I refuse men. I will see whether you have what I want." And she added, "Let us go into the room; and let me see your skin."

They entered the room; and Ogula-Njᵢgâ removed his fine clothing. Ilâmbe examined with close scrutiny from his head to his feet. She found not the slightest scratch or mark; his skin was like a babe's. Then she said, "Yes! this is my man! truly! I love you, and will marry you!" She was so pleased with her acquisition, that she remained in the room enjoying again a minute examination of her husband's beautiful skin. Then she went out, and ordered her servants to cook food, prepare water, etc., for him; and he did not go out of the house, nor have a longing to go back to his town, for he found that he was loved.

On the third day, he went to tell the father, Ra-Mborakinda, that he was ready to take his wife off to his town. Ra-Mborakinda consented. All that day, they prepared food for the marriage-feast. But, all the while that this man-beast, Ogula-Nj⊠gâ was there, Ra-Mborakinda, by his okove (a magic fetish) knew that some evil would come out of this marriage. However, as Ilâmbe had insisted on choosing her own way, he did not interfere.

After the marriage was over, and the feast eaten, Ra-Mborakinda called his daughter, and said, "Ilâmbe, mine, now you are going off on your journey." She said, "Yes; for I love my husband." The father asked, "Do you love him truly?" She answered "Yes." Then he told her, "As you are married now, you need a present from me, as your ozendo (bridal gift)." So, he gave her a few presents, and told her, "Go to that house," indicating a certain house in the town; and he gave her the key of the house, and told her to go and open the door. That was the house where he kept all his charms for war, and fetishes of all kinds. He told her, "When you go in, you will see two Kabala, standing side by side. The one that will look a little dull, with its eyes directed to the ground, take it; and leave the brighter looking one. When you are coming with it, you will see that it walks a little lame. Nevertheless, take it." She objected, "But, father, why do you not give me the finer one, and not the weak one?" But he said, "No!" and made a knowing smile, as he repeated, "Go, and take the one I tell you." He had reason for giving this one. The finer-looking one had only fine looks; but this other one would some day save her by its intelligence.

She went and took Horse, and returned to her father; and the journey was prepared. The father sent with her, servants to carry the baggage, and to remain with and work for her at the town of her marriage. She and her husband arranged all their things, and said good-bye, and off they went, both of them sitting on Horse's back.

They journeyed and they journeyed. On the way, Ogula-Njⵘgâ, though changed as to his form and skin, possessed all his old tastes. Having been so many days without tasting blood or uncooked meats, as they passed through the forest of wild beasts, the longing came on him. They emerged onto a great prairie, and journeyed across it toward another forest. Before they had entirely crossed the prairie, the longing for his prey so overcame him that he said, "Wife, you with your Kabala and the servants stay here while I go rapidly ahead; and wait for me until I come again." So he went off, entered the forest, and changed himself back to Leopard. He hunted for prey, caught a small animal, and ate it; and another, and ate it. After being satisfied, he washed his hands and mouth in a brook; and, changing again to human form, he returned on the prairie to his wife.

She observed him closely, and saw a hard, strange look on his face. She said, "But, all this while! What have you been doing?" He made an excuse. They went on.

And the next day, it was the same, he leaving her, and telling her to wait till he returned; and hunting and eating as a Leopard. All this that was going on, Ilâmbe was ignorant of. But Horse knew. He would speak after awhile, but was not ready yet.

So it went on, until they came to Leopard's town. Before they reached it, Ogula-Njⵘgâ, by the preparations he had first made, had changed his mother into a human form in which to welcome his wife. Also the few people of the town, all with human forms, welcomed her. But, they did not sit much with her. They stayed in their own houses; and Ogula-Njⵘgâ and his wife stayed in theirs. For a few days, Leopard tried to be a pleasant Ogula, deceiving his wife. But his taste for blood was still in his heart. He began to say, "I am going to another town; I have business there." And off he would go, hunting as a leopard; when he returned, it would be late in the day. So he did on other days.

After a time, Ilâmbe wished to make a food-plantation, and sent her men-servants to clear the ground. Ogula-Njᴁgâ would go around in the forest on the edge of the plantation; and catching one of the men, there would return that day one servant less.

One by one, all the men-servants were thus missing; and it was not known what became of them, except that Leopard's people knew. One night Ogula-Njᴁgâ was out; and, meeting one of the female servants, she too was reported missing.

Sometimes, when Ogula-Njᴁgâ was away, Ilâmbe, feeling lonesome, would go and pet Horse. After the loss of this maid-servant, Horse thought it was time to warn Ilâmbe of what was going on. While she was petting him, he said, "Eh! Ilâmbe! you do not see the trouble that is coming to you!" She asked, "What trouble?" He exclaimed, "What trouble? If your father had not sent me with you, what would have become of you? Where are all your servants that you brought with you? You do not know where they go to, but I know. Do you think that they disappear without a reason? I will tell you where they go. It is your man who eats them; it is he who wastes them!" She could not believe it, and argued, "Why should he destroy them?" Horse replied, "If you doubt it, wait for the day when your last remaining servant is gone."

Two days after that, at night, another maid-servant disappeared. Another day passed. On another day, Ogula-Njᴁgâ went off to hunt beasts, with the intention that, if he failed to get any, at night he would eat his wife.

When he had gone, Ilâmbe, in her loneliness, went to fondle Horse. He said to her, "Did I not tell you? The last maid is gone.

You yourself will be the next one. I will give you counsel. When you have opportunity this night, prepare yourself ready to run away. Get yourself a large gourd, and fill it with ground-nuts; another with gourd-seeds; and another with water." He told her to bring these things to him, and he would know the best time to start.

While they were talking, Leopard's mother was out in the street, and heard the two voices. She said to herself, "Ilâmbe, wife of my son, does she talk with Kabala as if it was a person?" But, she said nothing to Ilâmbe, nor asked her about it.

Night came on; and Ogula-Njⓧgâ returned. He said nothing; but his face looked hard and bad. Ilâmbe was troubled and somewhat frightened at his ugly looks. So, at night, on retiring, she began to ask him, "But why? Has anything displeased you?" He answered, "No; I am not troubled about anything. Why do you ask questions?" "Because I see it in your face that your countenance is not pleasant." "No; there's no matter. Everything is right. Only, about my business, I think I must start very early." Ogula-Njⓧgâ had begun to think, "Now she is suspecting me. I think I will not eat her this night, but will put it off until next night."

That night, Ilâmbe did not sleep. In the morning, Leopard said that he would go to his business, but would come back soon. When he was gone away to his hunting work, Ilâmbe felt lonesome, and went to Horse. He, thinking this a good time to run away, they started at once, without letting any one in the village know, and taking with them the three gourds. Horse said that they must go quickly; for, Leopard, when he discovered them gone, would rapidly pursue. So they went fast and faster, Horse looking back from time to time, to see whether Leopard was pursuing.

After they had been gone quite a while, Ogula-Njᵭgâ returned from his business to his village, went into his house, and did not see Ilâmbe. He called to his mother, "Where is Ilâmbe?" His mother answered, "I saw Ilâmbe with her Kabala, talking together; they have been at it for two days." Ogula-Njᵭgâ began to search; and, seeing the hoof-prints, he exclaimed, "Mi asaiya (shame for me). Ilâmbe has run away. I and she shall meet today!"

He instantly turned from his human form back to that of leopard, and went out, and pursued, and pursued, and pursued. But, it took some time before he came in sight of the fugitives. As Horse turned to watch, he saw Leopard, his body stretched low and long in rapid leaps. Horse said to Ilâmbe, "Did I not tell you? There he is, coming!" Horse hasted, with foam dropping from his lips. When he saw that Leopard was gaining on them, he told Ilâmbe to take the gourd of peanuts from his back, and scatter them along behind on the ground. Leopards like peanuts; and when Ogula-Njᵭgâ came to these nuts, he stopped to eat them. While he was eating, Horse gained time to get ahead. As soon as Leopard had finished the nuts, he started on in pursuit again, and soon began to overtake. When he approached, Horse told Ilâmbe to throw out the gourd-seeds. She did so. Leopard delayed to eat these seeds also. This gave Horse time to again get ahead. Thus they went on.

Leopard, having finished the gourd-seeds, again went leaping in pursuit; and, for the third time, came near. Horse told Ilâmbe to throw the gourd of water behind, with force so that it might crash and break on the ground. As soon as she had done so, the water was turned to a stream of a deep wide river, between them and Leopard. Then he was at a loss. So, he shouted, "Ah! Ilâmbe! Mi asaiya! If I only had a chance to catch you!" So, he had to turn back.

Then Horse said, "We do not know what he may do yet; perhaps he may go around and across ahead of us. As there is a town which I know near here, we had better stay there a day or two while he may be searching for us." He added to her, "Mind! this town where we are going, no woman is allowed to be there, only men. So, I will change your face and dress like a man's. Be very careful how you behave when you take your bath, lest you die." Ilâmbe promised; and Horse changed her appearance. So, a fine-looking young man was seen riding into the street of the village. There were exclamations in the street, "This is a stranger! Hail! stranger; hail! Who showed you the way to come here?" This young man answered, "Myself; I was out riding; I saw an open path; and I came in." He entered a house, and was welcomed; and they told him their times of eating, and of play, etc. But, on the second day, as this young man went out privately, one of the men observed, and said to the other, "He acts like a woman!" The others asked, "Really! you think so?" He asserted, "Yes! I am sure!" So, that day Ilâmbe was to meet with some trouble; for, to prove her, the men had said to her, "Tomorrow we all go bathing in the river, and you shall go with us." She went to ask Horse what she should do. He rebuked her, "I warned you, and you have not been careful. But, do not be troubled; I will change you into a man."

That night, Ilâmbe went to Horse; and he changed her. He also told her, "I warn you again. Tomorrow you go to bathe with the others, and you may take off your clothes; for, you are now a man. But, it is only for a short time, because we stay here only a day and a night more, and then we must go."

The next morning all the town went to play, and after that to bathe. When they went into the water, the other men were all expecting to see a woman revealed; but they saw that their visitor was a man. They admired his wonderfully fine physique.

On emerging from the water, the men said to the one who had informed on Ilâmbe, "Did you not tell us that this was a woman? See, how great a man he is!" As soon as they said that, the young man Ilâmbe was vexed with him, and began to berate him, saying, "Eh! you said I was a woman?" And she chased him and struck him. Then they all went back to the town.

In the evening, Horse told Ilâmbe, "I tell you what to do tomorrow. In the morning, you take your gun, and shoot me dead. After you have shot me, these men will find fault with you, saying 'Ah! you shoot your horse, and did not care for it?' But, do not say anything in reply. Cut me in pieces, and burn the pieces in the fire. After this, carefully gather all the black ashes; and, very early in the following morning, in the dark before any one is up, go out of the village gateway, scatter the ashes, and you will see what will happen."

The young man did all this. On scattering the ashes, he instantly found himself changed again to a woman, and sitting on Horse's back; and they were running rapidly away.

That same day, in the afternoon, they came to the town of the father Ra-Mborakinda. On their arrival there, they (but especially Horse) told their whole story. Ilâmbe was somewhat ashamed of herself; for, she had brought these troubles on herself by insisting on having a husband with a perfectly fine skin. So, her father said, "Ilâmbe, my child, you see the trouble you have brought on yourself. For you, a woman, to make such a demand was too much. Had I not sent Kabala with you, what would have become of you?" The people gave Ilâmbe a glad welcome. And she went to her house, and said nothing more about fine skins.

WHY THE PLANTAIN-STALK BEARS BUT ONE BUNCH

Persons

Oyila (Oil-Palm Tree)   Akândâ (Plantain-Stalk)

Mbindi (Wild Goat)

NOTE

According to native law of hospitality, duty to a guest requires almost any sacrifice. This is oriental. (See Genesis Chap. 19, vs. 8.) A plantain-stalk bears but one bunch. Therefore, to gather the fruit, the stalk with apparent ruthlessness is cut down. But, there are always from two to five young sprouts at the base, from 2 feet to 5 feet in height, which, in succession, take the place of the parent stem.

Observe the Cannibalism. All African tribes were formerly Cannibals. Many interior tribes still are. This story is a marked illustration of the characteristic impossibilities in native tales, "Plantain" being at one and the same time a plant and a human being!

Palm-tree produced Plantain tree.

Then there stood up an animal called Wild Goat, and it went

to seek marriage with Palm-tree's daughter Plantain. It was so arranged; and the marriage was held.

As Goat and his wife were about departing to his own town, Palm-tree gave some parting advice to her daughter Plantain; "When you shall be about to become a mother, come back and stay with me."

Not long after this, Plantain was to become a mother; and people went to Palm-tree to inform her of the fact. This daughter Plantain did not obey her mother's directions, but remained in the town until her child was born. This was told to mother Palm-tree, who was dissatisfied, and said, "Eh! I told Akândâ to have her child born with me!"

The reason that Palm-tree had given this direction to Plantain was, that, as her own custom, in bearing her palm-nuts, was to have several bunches in sight at one time, and ripening in succession, she wished her daughter to have the same habit.

After Plantain had borne her child, it grew well and became very strong. One day, strangers came to the town on a visit; and, when the villagers looked for food for the visitors, to their shame, they found they had none. Then one of the women of the village said, "Well! let us cut down this Akândâ, and cook it and eat it." So, a machete was seized, and Plantain's stalk was slashed, and Palm-tree's child Plantain was taken and cooked and eaten. At this, people went and told Palm-tree, saying, "Your child is cut down, and is cooked and eaten." The mother Palm-tree helplessly replied, "What can I do?"

All this while, the husband Goat had been away on a journey. When he returned, and came to his town, and found that his wife, Palm-tree's child, was not there, he asked, "My wife; is she dead?" The people answered him, "Yes!" "But," he asked, "for what reason did she die?" They answered, "Because the people of the town had no food for their guests." Mbindi complained further, saying, "So! when Akândâ was cooked, you gave your guests only plantains; were you so inhospitable as to give them also no meat or fish?"

At this the people were vexed, and they said, "Well then! let this husband be killed and eaten as the meat!" So they killed and ate him.

This news, people also carried to Palm-tree, telling her that Plantain's husband was also killed and eaten.

Then Palm-tree came to the town to speak about the death of Plantain. The people justified themselves, saying, "But, what else could we do? It was necessary to provide for the guests."

Palm-tree submitted, "Truly, had Akândâ obeyed me and come to me and borne her child in my presence, she would have had abundance, and would not have died."

PART SECOND
BENGA TRIBE

FOREWORD

The tales of this second part had their source with narrators of Benga-speaking tribes of Corisco Island, the region of the Bonito River, and Batanga. Nos. 1, 2, 3 and 4 were written in Benga by the pioneer missionaries, Rev. Messrs. Mackey and Clemens, from the dictation in Benga by natives of Corisco, more than 40 years ago; and were printed as reading-lessons in the Primer used in their schools.

I have translated them into English. They having thus passed twice through foreign thought, have lost most of their native idioms. Tale 4 was independently re-told me at Batanga within the past few years, by a narrator living there. It differs from the version printed in the Primer, and I have combined the two.

The remaining thirty tales were given me at Batanga; by three adult narrators, all of them civilized men. They spoke them with me alone, or in the presence of one or two silent attendants, sentence by sentence, in their Bapuku dialect of the Benga language. I rapidly made notes in an English translation of their principal words. This was always at night, in order to leave the narrator at that ease which he would naturally feel if he was telling the story to an audience in the street, as he is accustomed to do in the evenings. For that purpose also, I shaded my lamp, using its light only for my pencil; he therefore spoke unrestrainedly. Next morning, with my memory still fresh of the night's story, I filled out the sentences. This set of the tales therefore is more native, in the preservation of its idioms, than any other part.

TALE 1
SWINE TALKING

Persons
Ingowa (Hogs)

NOTE

Unlike other native legends based on "they say," the native narrator, now more than 40 years ago, gave the name and family name of the man who is stated to have reported that he heard Swine talking with human speech.

There was a certain man in the time long ago, by name Bokona, whose family name was Bodikito. He went to the depths of the forest to do some business. When he was about to return in the afternoon to go to his village, he heard in advance of him, a noise of conversation. He thought that perhaps they were people (of whose presence he was not aware; for, there were no villages in that part of the forest). But, when he had approached the spot, he did not see people; but only a herd of Hogs speaking with the voices of people. He was thus perfectly sure that they speak the language of Mankind.

Robert Hamill Nassau

TALE 2
CROCODILE

Persons

Ngando (Crocodile)   Two Children, and Towns-People

Two children were bathing in a river; and a crocodile came where they were. It seized one, and, grasping it with its teeth, went with it to its hole in the river bank. It did not kill him, but said to him, "I leave you here, and I go straight back to bring the other one who remained." After the crocodile had left, the one thus put into the hole, turning his eyes about, saw it full of living fish (kept on hand by the crocodile as its food-supply). He saw also that there was another opening in the cavity, above, just over his head. Climbing up and jumping through it, he rapidly went straight away to his village. He related all this incident to the people. Then they gladly fired guns, for welcome of the child.

When the crocodile reached the bathing-place on its return, it did not see the one whom it had left there; and it was angry. While it was thus angry, the people shot at it with guns, but their shots could not even wound it; and it went back again to its hole to seek for and eat the child whom it had seized.

When it again entered into the hole and searched, and did not find him, it was very angry, and pursued him, going up to the very middle of the village. For three days it was there barking in the village, and trying to kill some one.

ORIGIN OF THE ELEPHANT

Persons

Uhâdwe, Bokume and Njâku Sons of   Towns-People, Sailors
Njambi the Creator   and Others

NOTE

I have never seen the place; but, intelligent natives, (though they did not believe in the legend itself) told me there was the likeness to a human foot-print in a rock on the beach of the north shore of Corisco Bay. Doubtless a fossil.

Uhâdwe, Bokume, and Njâku were human beings, all three born of one mother. (Afterwards Bokume was called "Njâp⊠.")

As time went on, Uhâdwe called his brethren, Bokume and Njâku, and said, "My brothers! Let us separate; myself, I am going to the Great Sea; you, Bokume go to the Forest; you, Njâku, also go to the Forest."

Bokume went to the forest and grew up there, and became the valuable mahogany tree (Okume).

Njâku departed; but he went in anger, saying, "I will not remain in the forest, I am going to build with the towns-people." He came striding back to the town. As he emerged there from the forest, his feet swelled and swelled, and became elephant feet. His ear extended 'way down. His teeth spreading, this one grew to a tusk, and that one grew to a tusk. The towns-people began to hoot at him. And he turned back to the forest. But, as he went, he said to them, "In my going now to the Forest, I and whatever plants you shall plant in the forest shall journey together," (*i.e.*, that their plantations should be destroyed by him). So Njâku went; and their food went.

When Uhâdwe had gone thence and emerged at the Sea, from the place where he emerged there grew the stem of "bush-rope" (the Calamus palm); and the staff he held became a mangrove forest. The footprints where he and his dog trod are there on the beach of Corisco Bay until this day. He created a sand-bank from where he stood, extending through the ocean, by which he crossed over to the Land of the Great Sea. When he reached that Land, he prepared a ship. He put into it every production by which white people obtain wealth, and he said to the crew, "Go ye and take for me my brother."

The ship came to Africa and put down anchor; but, for four days the crew did not find any person coming from shore to set foot on the ship, or to go from the ship to set foot ashore, the natives being destitute of canoes.

Finally, Uhâdwe came and appeared to the towns-people in a dream, and said, "Go ye to the forest and cut down Njâpⵉ, dig out a canoe, and go alongside the ship."

Early next morning they went to the forest, and came to the Okume trees; they cut one down, and hacked it into shape. They launched it on the sea, and said to their young men, "Go!" Four young men went into the canoe to go alongside the ship. When they had nearly reached it, looking hither and thither they feared, and they stopped and ceased paddling. The white men on the ship made repeated signs to them. Then the young men, having come close, spoke to the white men in the native language. A white man answered also in the same language. That white man said, "I have come to buy the tusks of the beast which is here in the forest with big feet and tusks and great ears, that is called Njâku." They said, "Yes! a good thing!" When they were about leaving, the white man advancing to them, deposited with them four bunches of tobacco, four bales of prints, four caps, and other things.

When they reached the shore, they told the others, "The white men want Njâku's tusks; and also they have things by which to kill his tribe."

The next morning, they went to the white men; they were trusted with guns and bullets and powder; they went to the forest, and fought with the elephants. In two days the ship was loaded, and it departed.

This continues to happen so until this day, in the Ivory-Trade.

LEOPARD'S MARRIAGE JOURNEY

Persons

Njambi (Chief of a Town)	Vyâdu (Antelope)
Njâ (Leopard)	Ehibo (Red Antelope)
Etoli (House-Rat)	Ihⵉli (Gazelle)
Mbindi (Wild Goat)	Ekwⵉdikwⵉdi (Fire-Fly)

Leopard wanted to marry, and he sought a betrothal at Njambi's town. Secretly, Njambi had arranged with Leopard that he should bring him no goods in payment of the "Dowry," but only the bodies of animals.

Leopard agreed, and said to Njambi's daughter, "I will dowry you only with animals." He returned to his home for a few days; and then he called Rat to escort him to the town of his prospective father-in-law. Rat consented. And they started on their journey.

On their way, they came to a wide river; and Leopard said to Rat, "Before one crosses this river, he must throw his knife into it." Rat threw his knife; and so (apparently) did Leopard. They crossed; went on their way, and came to a Kuda tree; and they stopped, and began to gather the nuts. Leopard drew his knife from its sheath, and splitting the nut-shells and eating the kernels, said derisively to Rat, "One who has no knife will not be able to eat kuda." Rat, in his helplessness, made no protest. And they went on. They came to a certain "Medicine" tree; and Leopard said, "Etoli, if I shall fall sick on the way, and I tell you to go back and get the bark of a certain tree for medicine, see! this is the tree." Finally, they came to the town of the woman whom Leopard was to marry. There, food was cooked for them. Just before they were to sit down to eat, Leopard exclaimed, "Etoli! I am sick! Go, and get that medicine for me!" While Rat was gone, Leopard ate up almost all the food, leaving only a few scraps for Rat.

At night, inside of the entrance of the house where the two strangers were to sleep, was a pit already dug. Leopard knew of it, and jumped over it; but Rat fell into it. Leopard shouted to the town's-people, "This is the animal I brought to pay on my Dowry! Come, and take him!" The people came, caught Rat, and ate him.

The next morning, Leopard's father-in-law had food prepared for him; he ate; and returned to his town. There, the relatives of Rat asked him, "Where is the little one you took to escort you?" Leopard replied, "He refused to return, staying there with the woman."

Again, Leopard prepared gifts of dried fish and tobacco for his mother-in-law, and arranged for another journey. He called to his relative, "Brother" Wild-Goat, "Come, escort me to the town of my marriage." Wild Goat consented; and they started. They came to the River; and, as in the case of Rat, Leopard said to Goat, "You will first throw away your knife, before you can cross this river." Goat actually did so; Leopard pretending to do so. Continuing their journey, they came to that Kuda tree. Leopard was careful to stand on a side of the tree opposite to Goat, as they gathered the nuts. But, he said provokingly, "One can not eat kuda without a knife." Wild Goat innocently replied, "But, you, Njâ, you are eating nuts! Did you bring two knives?" They journeyed on, and came to the Medicine tree. And Leopard gave to Goat the same directions about it as he had given to Rat.

When they reached the marriage town, food was set before them. But Leopard immediately began to groan and scream, "I'm dead! I'm dead! I'm dead with pain!" Wild Goat sympathisingly inquired, "What shall I do to help you?" Leopard replied, as in the case of Rat, "Go back to that tree, and get its bark as a medicine for me." Wild Goat went; and while he was away, Leopard ate the food, leaving very little of it. On his return, Wild Goat protested at so little being given him. Leopard explained, "In my great suffering from tooth-ache, I ate nothing. Perhaps it was the town's-people who ate up the food, leaving you only these pieces."

After they had eaten, they were called to the reception-house, and spent the evening in conversation with the people of the town. Then, they were shown to the house in which they were to sleep. It was the one with the pit-fall inside the door-way. Leopard, of course, jumped over it; but Wild Goat fell into it. And, as in the case of Rat, Leopard called out, "People of the town! This is your dowry-goods! I have brought it to you!" The next morning, Leopard took his journey, and came back home. When the people of his town asked him, as in the case of Rat, "Where is the friend you took with you?" he made the same reply, "Don't ask me! He is entangled off there with women."

On a third journey, Leopard called Antelope to accompany him. Antelope agreed. They came to the River; and as before Leopard told how that river could not be crossed by travelers unless their knives were thrown away. This, Antelope did.

Then, they came to the Kuda tree. There, Antelope heard Leopard splitting the nuts, and asked him. "Did you not throw away your knife? Do you travel with two?" Leopard answered,

"Yes! I always travel with two." Then, they came to the Medicine tree. And Leopard explained about its bark being the cure for his frequent tooth-aches, when eating at his father-in-law's town.

They came to the town. And when food was brought to them, Leopard cried out, "O! my tooth! my tooth!" Antelope asked, "Where is your medicine that you said you use?" Leopard answered, "At the tree which I showed you on the way. Go, and get it." While Antelope was gone, Leopard ate up almost all the food. On returning, Antelope exclaimed "What! only this little food for me?" Leopard explained, "With my great tooth-ache, I ate none. Nothing happened, except that the town's-people came, and were eating up the food; and I, in my kindness for you, begged them to leave at least a little for you." Antelope handed him the medicine, and Leopard said, "Put it down there"; and he threw it away, while Antelope's back was turned.

After they had eaten, they went to their room for the night. Leopard, as usual, jumped over the pit; but Antelope fell in. And Leopard gave his shout to the people to come and take the Dowry-goods he had brought. The next morning, after breakfast, Leopard again started on his home journey. There, again he was anxiously asked, "But, those whom you take with you don't come back! Why?" He made the same reply, "They know why! Off there are damsels and dancing; and they were unable to return."

For his next journey, Leopard asked Red Antelope, who heartily replied, "Yes, come on! There is nothing to prevent my going on a journey!" They journeyed, and they came to the River. There, Leopard made his statement about the necessity of throwing their knives into the river. Red Antelope wondered a little, but he consented saying, "Yes, but what is that to me?" Said Leopard, "Well, then, shut your eyes, and I will be the first to throw, lest you say I am deceiving you." Said Red Antelope, "Yes." And he shut his eyes tightly. Then Leopard, having a stone in his hand, flung it into the water, saying, "I've thrown mine; throw also yours!" Red Antelope demanded, "But, you must shut your eyes also." Leopard half-closed his eyes, and Red Antelope, knife in hand, flung it into the water. Then, wading across, they went on and on to the base of the Kuda tree. Said Leopard, "Mr. Ehibo, this Kuda is eaten of here only by each person on his own side of the trunk." Red Antelope assented; and they turned, this one to one side, and that one to the other side. There, as Red Antelope was vainly trying to crack the nuts with his teeth, Leopard was deriding him while himself was comfortably using his knife.

Then, Leopard said, "Let us go on; for, the day is declining." Red Antelope agreed. As they went, they came to an Ebwehavu tree. And Leopard said, "Let us climb for Bebwehavu fruits. But, when we climb this particular tree, it is the practice here, to climb, one by one. While the one is climbing, the other has his eyes shut; and, the climbing is done, not by the trunk, but by this adjoining Bongo tree which you see here. But, first, close your eyes, and I will go up." (The Bongo's trunk is covered with hard sharp thorns.) Red Antelope stood, with his eyes tightly closed. Leopard grasped a vine; and, with one swing, he at once was up the tree. Red Antelope began climbing that Bongo, creeping slowly to the top, his whole body spoiled, and nothing on him but blood and blood.

Said Leopard, "This Ebwehavu is accustomed to be plucked only the green unripe, but the dark ripe ones are to be left." That seemed strange to Red Antelope, nevertheless he said, "Yes." But Leopard was plucking the ripe and leaving the green. When they had finished plucking, Leopard said, "Ehibo! shut eyes! that I may descend!" Red Antelope shut his eyes. Leopard grasped the vine; and, with one spring, was on the ground. Then, he said, "Now,

Ehibo, descend." Red Antelope began descending by the Bongo, down, down, landing finally on the ground.

Leopard waited for him; and then said, "Having no fire, how shall we cook those green bebwehavu?" Just then, he saw a Fire-fly passing; and he said. "Mr. Ehibo! Pursue! That's fire passing there!" Red Antelope bent in rapid pursuit. Leopard turned to the base of the tree, gathered dried fire-wood, struck his flint, lighted a fire, cooked his fruits, ate them, finished, and put out his fire. Red Antelope, back again, said, "I did not reach it, I'm tired." Leopard said, "Well, let it go. I chewed mine uncooked. But, let us journey; and, as you go, you chew yours." They went on, and came to the town of the marriage. Food was cooked and set for them in their room. Said Leopard, "Ehibo, sit you on the floor, while I eat at the table. And, while I eat the flesh, you eat the bones." Red Antelope had become so utterly wearied and humiliated that he did not resent this indignity. They ate. And then Leopard said, "Ehibo, sweep up the scraps, and go and throw them into the back yard." (Immediately on his arrival at the town, Leopard had gone alone to his father-in-law, and said, "I have brought you an animal. But, let another pit, this time, be dug in the back yard of the room where we shall be. And, do you put spears and daggers and all kinds of sharp sticks there. When I shall send him to throw away the sweepings, and he shall fall in, kill ye him.")

Red Antelope swept, and scraped up the sweepings, and threw them into a basket. He turned with them to the back yard, to fling them away. As he was about to do so, he slipped down to the bottom of the pit. Impaled on the spears, he was unable to jump out. When the town's-people arrived, they thrust him through with sharp poles; and he lay dead.

When Leopard returned home, Red Antelope's people asked,

"Where is Ehibo?" Leopard made his former answer, "Ehibo was hindered by the hospitality of that marriage town, with its food and its women; and, he said, 'I won't go back!' "

Thus, with each journey, Leopard called for another animal. They went, over the same route; and the same things happened each time. So, matters went on for a long while. But, Gazelle, a very smart beast, began to suspect, observing that none of Leopard's travel-companions ever came back. In his heart, he thought to himself, "Leopard deceives people!" He determined to find out, by offering to go, and watch for himself. At last, he said, "Uncle Njâ, let me go to escort you to the town of your marriage. When next you go on your journey, call me to go with you." Said Leopard, "I don't want you." (He suspected Gazelle's smartness.) Gazelle insisted, "Uncle, as to these others whom you have invited to go with you, and not the rather me, your relative?"

So, Leopard agreed, "Yes, let us go." By the next morning they started on their journey, going on and on, clear to the big River. There, as usual, Leopard told about knives to be thrown into the river; and he said, "Nephew Ih␣li, you first throw your knife." Said Gazelle, "First, you throw yours, then I will throw mine also." Said Leopard, "Well! shut your eyes!" Gazelle half-closed his hands on his eyes, and was peeping. He saw Leopard seize a chunk of wood and fling it in the water. Then he said, "Shut eyes! Let me also throw mine!" Leopard's eyes shut tight. Gazelle, seizing a stick, flung it into the water. Then, they crossed the river, and went on and on, until they came to the base of the Kuda tree. Leopard made his usual statement about parties eating the nuts on opposite sides of the tree. Gazelle, with apparent obedience, said, "Yes." Leopard, with knife drawn, began to hack and split the nuts, throwing the kernels into his mouth, and making his usual derisive remark, "By the truth! a person without a knife can not eat the kernels of kuda." Gazelle also, hacking his, and throwing them into his mouth, said, "Just exactly so! a person without a knife can not eat the kernel of kuda-nut!" Leopard exclaimed, "What are you doing? Have you two knives?" Gazelle replied, "But, what are *you* doing? Had *you* two knives?" Leopard answered, "Yes, for, I am the senior." Gazelle responded, "And I also carry two knives; for, I also am an adult." Leopard only said, "Ih⬚li! Come on!" They went on, until they came to the Ebwehavu tree. There, Leopard made his usual explanation of climbing only by means of the Bongo tree. Gazelle agreed, and said, "Yes; climb you first." Leopard said, "Shut your eyes." Gazelle stood, with eyes apparently tightly closed. With one swing on a vine, Leopard is up the tree. Said Gazelle, "You also, shut your eyes. Let me go up." Leopard pretended to shut his eyes. And Gazelle, with one swing, was also up the tree. Leopard made his usual statement about plucking only the green fruit. To which, Gazelle seemed to assent.

And they descended the tree, without Leopard attempting to deceive Gazelle about the Bongo tree.

But, Leopard seeing the sun going down, said, "Ih⬚li! Pursue! that's fire that's going there!" But, Gazelle showed he was not deceived, by simply saying, "That's not fire!" So, Leopard gathered fire-wood; and they cooked and ate their bebwehavu.

Then, they resumed their journey, and came to the Medicine tree. There Leopard told his usual story about the bark of that tree being his great cure-all. Gazelle quietly said, "Yes." But, when they left the tree, and had gone a short distance farther, he exclaimed, "O! I forgot my staff! I must go back and get it!" He went back to the tree, stripped bark from it, put it into his traveling-bag, and overtook Leopard. And they came on together to the town. After they had entered their house, Gazelle remarked to Leopard, "Let me go out and see the other fellows, who came with you on your previous journeys, and who, you said, had stayed here with the women." He went out; and returned, saying, "I saw the women, but none of those fellows." Food was cooked for them, and they sat down to eat. But, suddenly, Leopard broke out in groans, "Ihᴻli! I feel a pain in my stomach; go, get bark of that tree I showed you. The medicine! Get the medicine!" Gazelle answered "Yes, but just wait until I finish my plate;" and he continued eating rapidly. Leopard was distressed to see the food disappearing; but, as he had pretended sickness, he did not dare begin to eat. When, finally there was but little food left, Gazelle introduced his hand into his bag, and, handing out the pieces of bark, said, "Here's your medicine! That's it!" Leopard said, "Yes, just leave it there. I do not need the medicine now. The pain has ceased. Let us first eat. We will eat together." After finishing their eating, Gazelle swept up the scraps, and placed them in a basket. Said Leopard, "Come, I will go with you to show you the place where sweepings are to be thrown." Gazelle was about to fling the basket, as Leopard came to push him into the pit. But, Gazelle lightly leaped across to the other side of it, and cried out, "Uncle! what do you want to do to me?" Leopard said, "That's nothing!"

It being night, they went to their sleeping-room, Leopard accompanied by his wife. He and she carefully jumped over the other pit that was inside of the door-way of that house. Gazelle also jumped, with careful observation, the while that people stood outside expecting him to fall into it. They retired for the night, Leopard and his wife on the bed; Gazelle on a mat on the floor. Said Gazelle, "Uncle, if you hear me stertorously snoring, then I am awake; but, if silently, then I am asleep." In a little while, Gazelle feigned gentle snoring. Leopard thinking Gazelle was asleep, took an iron rod, and thrust it into the fire. Gazelle saw what he was doing. When it was red-hot, he removed it, and, stepping softly, was about to stab Gazelle with it; who, quickly moving aside, exclaimed, "Eh! what are you doing?" Leopard coolly replied, "Nothing; I was only brushing away an insect that was biting you." Gazelle thought within himself, "Njâ will surely kill me to-night." So, he took chalk, and secretly marked circles around his eyes, making himself look as if his eyes were open and he awake, even if he should actually be asleep. After a while, Leopard slept, sound asleep with his wife. Then Gazelle passed over to Leopard's bed, and lifting the woman (unconscious in her sleep) to his mat on the floor, laid down in her place, beside Leopard in the bed. During the night, Leopard awoke, and, not noticing, in the darkness, the change at his side, went with the rod, to the mat where he supposed Gazelle was sleeping, and stabbed the woman to death.

Then Gazelle (who had remained awake) cried out, "Eh! you kill another person? You are killing your wife!" Leopard exclaimed, "Umph! Is that you? I said to myself that this was you!" Gazelle said, "Yes! what did you go to my bed for? So, then! I am the one you wanted to kill!" Leopard confessed, "It is true that I came here to kill you, thinking this was you. But, as the matter is thus, say no more about it. Let us cut up and eat this woman. Come, cut up!" But, Gazelle said, "I? When the town's-people hear the chopping, then won't they say, 'What animal has Ihⵗli killed in his brother-in-law's town, that he is cutting it up at night?' Yourself, cut her to pieces."

So, Leopard said, "Well, leave the work on the body of the woman to me; but, do you attend to the cooking." Said Gazelle, "I? When the town's people shall hear the kettle boiling, then will they say, 'Whom has Ihⵗli killed in the town of his brother-in-law, that he cooks at night?' "

Leopard boiled the kettle. It was cooked; and he said to Gazelle, "Go, cut down a bunch of plantains, out there in the back-yard." (This he said, hoping that Gazelle would fall into that pit, either in going out or coming in.) But, Gazelle said, "I? When the town's people hear the strokes of the machete, and the crash of the fall of the bunch, then, will they not suspect me, and say, 'What meat has Ihⓧli killed, that he is cutting down a plantain at night?' Cut it yourself." Leopard went and cut down a bunch of plantains, and said to Gazelle, "Now, come and peel the plantains, and cook them." Gazelle refused, "No; do you peel and cook. I'm in bed. I'll eat only greens." Then Leopard said (making a last effort to get Gazelle into the pit), "Well, go to the back-yard, and pluck pepper for the soup." Gazelle again refused, "No; when the town's-people hear the plucking of the pods, will they not say, 'What animal has Ihⓧli killed that he is gathering pepper for the soup?' "

Finally, Leopard, having done all the work, and finished cooking, and set the table, said, "Come, Ihⓧli, I have finished all. Come, and eat." Gazelle came, but said, "First, put out all the lights." Leopard did so. And Gazelle added, "We will understand that whichever, at the close of the meal, has the largest pile of bones by his plate, shall be known as the one who killed the woman." Leopard agreed. The light having been extinguished, they ate in darkness. But, while they were eating, Gazelle chose only the bony pieces that had little meat; and, having picked them, he quietly laid the bones by Leopard's plate. When they had finished eating, the torches were re-lighted, and Gazelle cried out at Leopard's big pile of bones. They were counted. And Gazelle said, "Did you not say that whoever had the most bones would prove himself the murderer? So! indeed! you are the one who killed another person's child!"

Leopard evaded, and said, "But, Ihⓧli, take a broom and

sweep up the scraps from the floor, and throw them into the yard." (Making thus a final effort to get Gazelle into that pit.) But, Gazelle, refused, "No; yourself do it. When the town's-people hear the bones falling as they are thrown in the yard, will they not suspect me, and say, 'What animal has Ih⊠li killed at night, that he is clearing away the scraps?' " Leopard swept up the floor and table, and threw the pieces into the backyard. As they were finishing, day began to dawn. Gazelle said, "Njâ, the day is breaking; let us seek hiding-places; for, when the people come in, in the morning, and find that their daughter is dead, lest they kill us." So, they began to look around for hiding-places. Gazelle said, "I shall hide in this big box on the floor." But, Leopard objected, "No; that traveling-box befits me; and, as the elder, I shall take it." Gazelle said, then, "Well, I'll hide under the bed." But, Leopard again objected (hoping to leave Gazelle without a place). "No; that also is my place; it suits me." Gazelle protested, "You are claiming this and that place! Where shall I go? Well! I see! I'll hide over the door." "Yes" said Leopard, "that's the hiding-place for a young person like you." (This he said, still thinking of the pit near the door.) Gazelle agreed, saying, "I am here, by the door. You get into that box, and I'll tie it with a string, as if no one was in it." Leopard objected, "But, the string will hinder my breaking out." "No," replied Gazelle, "it shall be a weak twine. You can easily burst it, when you fling up the lid, and jump out, and run away."

Leopard got into the box, and Gazelle began to tie it with a heavy chain. Leopard hearing the clanking, exclaimed, "With a chain, Ih⊠li?" Gazelle had the chain fast; and he coolly replied, "It's only a little one." Then he piled heavy stones on the box. As day broke, he took his stand among a bundle of dried plantain-leaves that was over the door-way. The towns-people sent a child to open the door of the strangers' house, to call them to eat. As the child was about to enter, Gazelle struck him a blow on the head; and the child went away wailing with pain. The child's father said to his family that he would go to see what was the matter. As he pushed wide open the door of the strangers' house, Gazelle slid down, sprang out, and ran rapidly away, shouting, "Njâ is there! Njâ is in that box! He it is who has killed your woman!" And the towns-people shouted after him, "Is that so? Well, you're off, Ih◼li! Go!"

Leopard, when he heard that, made desperate efforts to get out of the box. The town's-men entered the house and found the box with Leopard tied in it. They fired their guns at him, and killed him. As they did so, they reproached him, "Why did you kill our daughter, whom you came to marry?" Then they gathered together a great pile of fire-wood in the street, thrust on to it the dead body of Leopard, and burned him there. Gazelle went back to the town of Beasts, and they asked him, "Where is he with whom you went on your journey?" Gazelle told them, "He is dead. He it was who killed the other Beasts who went with him. And he is now killed by the relatives of the woman whom he was to marry, but whom also he had murdered."

For this reason, that Gazelle informed on Leopard in the box, the relatives of Leopard since then have no friendship with Gazelle, and always pursue and try to kill him. The entire Leopard tribe have kept up that feud with the Gazelle tribe, saying, "You caused our father's death." And they carry on their revenge.

TORTOISE IN A RACE

Persons
Kudu (Tortoise)   Mbalanga (Antelope)

NOTE

Discussions about seniority are common causes of quarrel in Africa. The reason assigned why tortoises are so spread everywhere is that the antelope tribe, in public-meeting, recognized their superiority. At Batanga, Gaboon, Ogowe, and everywhere on the equatorial west coast, there are tortoises even in places where there are no other animals. On account of this, the tortoise is given many names; and has many nicknames in the native tribes, *e.g.*, "Manyima," and "Evosolo."

Tortoise had formerly lived in the same town with several other animals. But, after awhile, they had decided to separate, and each built his own village.

One day, Tortoise decided to roam. So he started, and went on an excursion; leaving his wife and two children in the village. On his way, he came to the village of Antelope. The latter welcomed him, killed a fowl, and prepared food for him; and they sat at the table, eating.

When they had finished eating, Antelope asked, "Kudu! My friend, what is your journey for?"

Tortoise answered, "I have come to inquire of you, as to you and me, which is the elder?" Antelope replied, "Kudu! I am older than you!" But Tortoise responded, "No! I am the elder!" Then Antelope said, "Show me the reason why you are older than I!" Tortoise said, continuing the discussion, "I will show you a sign of seniority. Let us have a race, as a test of speed." Antelope replied derisively, "Aiye! how shall I know to test speed with Kudu? Does Kudu race?" However, he agreed, and said, "Well! in three days the race shall be made."

Tortoise spoke audaciously, "You, Mbalanga, cannot surpass me in a race!" Antelope laughed, having accepted the challenge; while Tortoise pretended to sneer, and said, "I am the one who will overcome!"

The course chosen, beginning on the beach south of Batanga, was more than seventy miles from the Campo River northward to the Balimba Country.

Then Tortoise went away, going everywhere to give directions, and returned to his village. He sent word secretly to all the Tortoise Tribe to call them. When they had come very many of them together, he told them, "I have called my friend Mbalanga for a race. I know that he can surpass me in this race, unless you all help me in my plan. He will follow the sea-beach. You all must line yourselves among the bushes at the top of the beach along the entire route all the way from Campo to Balimba. When Mbalanga, coming along, at any point, looks around to see whether I am following, and calls out, 'Kudu! where are you?' the one of you who is nearest that spot must step out from his place, and answer for me, 'Here!'"

Thus he located all the other tortoises in the bushes on the entire route. Also, he placed a colored mark on all the tortoises,

132

making the face of every one alike. He stationed them clear on to the place where he expected that Antelope would be exhausted. Then he ended, taking his own place there.

Antelope also arranged for himself, and said, to his wife, "My wife! make me food; for, Kudu and I have agreed on a race; and it begins at seven o'clock in the morning."

When all was ready, Antelope said, to (the one whom he supposed was) Kudu, "Come! let us race!" They started. Antelope ran on and on, and came as far as about ten miles to the town of Ub◻nji, among the Igara people. At various spots on the way Tortoise apparently was lost behind; but as constantly he seemed to re-appear, saying, "I'm here!"

At once, Antelope raced forward rapidly, pu! pu! pu! to a town named Ip◻ny◻ny◻. Then he looked around and said, "Where is Kudu?" A tortoise stepped out of the bushes, saying "Here I am! You haven't raced."

Antelope raced on until he reached the town of Beyâ. Again looking around, he said, "Where is Kudu?" A tortoise stepped out, replying, "I'm here!"

Antelope again raced, until he reached the town Lolabe. Again he asked, "Where is Kudu?" A tortoise saying to himself, "He hasn't heard anything," replied, "Here I am!"

Again Antelope raced on as far as from there to a rocky point by the sea named Ilale-ja-moto; and then he called, "Wherever is Kudu?" A tortoise ready answered, "Here I am!"

From thence, he came on in the race another stretch of about ten miles, clear to the town of Bongah◻li of the Batanga people. At each place on the route, when Antelope, losing sight of Tortoise, called, "Kudu! where are you?" promptly the tortoise on guard at that spot replied, "I'm here!"

Then on he went, steadily going, going, another stretch of about twenty miles to Plantation Beach. Still the prompt reply to Antelope's call, "Kudu, where are you?" was, "I'm here!"

As he started away from Plantation, the wearied Antelope began to feel his legs tired. However, he pressed on to Small Batanga, hoping for victory over his despised contestant. But, on his reaching the edge of Balimba, the tortoise was there ready with his, "I'm here!"

Finally, on reaching the end of the Balimba settlement, Antelope fell down, dying, froth coming from his mouth, and lay dead, being utterly exhausted with running. But, when Tortoise arrived, he took a magic-medicine, and restored Antelope to life; and then exulted over him by beating him, and saying, "Don't you show me your audacity another day by daring to run with me! I have surpassed you!"

So, they returned separately to their homes on the Campo River. Tortoise called together the Tortoise Tribe; and Antelope called all the Antelope Tribe. And they met in a Council of all the Animals. Then Tortoise rose and spoke—"All you Kudu Tribe! Mbalanga said I would not surpass him in a race. But, this day I have surpassed!"

So the Antelope Tribe had to acknowledge, "Yes, you, Kudu, have surpassed our champion. It's a great shame to us; for, we had not supposed that a slow fellow such as we thought you to be, could possibly do it, or be able to out-run a Mbalanga."

So the Council decided that, of all the tribes of animals,

Tortoise was to be held as greatest; for, that it had out-run Antelope. And the Animals gave Tortoise the power to rule.

GOAT'S TOURNAMENT

Persons
Tomba (Goat)   Njâ (Leopard)

NOTE

The reason why leopards wander everywhere, and fight all other animals, is their shame at being overcome by a goat. Their ancestor had said, "I did not know that a Goat could overcome me."

The Tribe of Goats sent a message to the Tribe of Leopards, saying, "Let us have a Wrestling Match, in an effort to see which is the stronger." Then Leopard took counsel with his Tribe, "This Tribe of Goats! I do not see that they have any strength. Let us agree to the contest; for, they can do nothing to me."

So, the Goat Tribe gathered all together; and the Leopard Tribe all together; and they met in a street of a town, to engage in the drumming and dancing and singing usually preceding such contests.

For the wrestling, they joined in thirty pairs, one from each tribe. The first pair wrestled; and the representative of the Leopards was overcome and thrown to the ground. Another pair joined; and again the Leopard champion was overcome. A third pair joined and wrestled, contesting desperately; the Leopard in shame, and the Goat in exultation. Again the Leopard was overcome.

There was, during all this time, drumming by the adherents of both parties. The Leopard drum was now beaten fiercely to encourage their side, as they had already been overcome three times in succession.

Then, on the fourth effort, the Leopard succeeded in overcoming. Again a pair fought; and Leopard overcame a second time. The sixth pair joined; and Leopard said, "Today we wrestle to settle that doubt as to which of us is the stronger."

So, pair after pair wrestled, until all of the thirty arranged pairs had contested. Of these, the Leopard tribe were victors ten times; and the Goat Tribe twenty times.

Then the Leopard tribe said, "We are ashamed that the report should go out among all the animals that we beat only ten times, and the Tomba twenty times. So, we will not stay any longer here, with their and our towns near together:" for they knew that their Leopard tribe would always be angry when they should see a company of Goats passing, remembering how often they were beaten. So, they moved away into the forest distant from their hated rivals. In their cherished anger at being beaten, and to cover their shame, Leopard attacks a Goat when he meets him alone, or any other single beast known to be friendly to the Goats, *e.g.*, Oxen or Antelopes.

TALE 7
WHY GOATS BECAME DOMESTIC

Persons

Tomba-Ya-Taba (Goat)

With Etoli, plural Betoli (Rat)

Vyâdu (Antelope, plural Lâdu)

Njâ (Leopard)

Ko (Wild-Rat)

Njâku (Elephant)

Mankind

Nyati (Ox)

Goat and his mother lived alone in their village. He said to her, "I have here a magic-medicine to strengthen one in wrestling. There is no one who can overcome me, or cast me down; I can overcome any other person."

The other Beasts heard of this boast; and they took up the challenge. First, house-Rats, hundreds of them, came to Goat's village, to test him. And they began the wrestling. He overcame them, one by one, to the number of two hundred. So, the Rats went back to their places, admitting that they were not able to overcome him.

Then, forest-Rat came to wrestle with Goat. He overcame them also, all of them. And they went back to their own place defeated.

Then, the Antelope came to wrestle with Goat. He overcame all the Antelopes, every one of them; not one was able to withstand him. And they also went back to their places.

Also, Elephant with all the elephants, came on that same challenge. Goat overcame all the Elephants; and they too, went back to their place.

Thus, all the Beasts came, in the same way, and were overcome in the same way, and went back in the same way.

But, there still remained one Beast, only one, Leopard, who had not made the attempt. So he said he would go; as he was sure he could overcome. He came. Goat overcame him also. So, it was proved that not a single beast could withstand Goat.

Then the Father of All-the-Leopards said, "I am ashamed that this Beast should overcome me. I will kill him!" And he made a plan to do so. He went to the spring where Mankind got their drinking-water. And he stood, hiding at the spring. Men of the town went to the spring to get water; Leopard killed two of them. The people went to tell Goat, "Go away from here, for Leopard is killing Mankind on your account." The Mother of Goat said to him, "If that is so, let us go to my brother Vyâdu." So they both went to go to Uncle Antelope. And they came to his village. When they told him their errand, he bravely said, "Remain here! Let me see Njâ come here with his audacity!"

They were then at Antelope's village, about two days. On the third day, about eight o'clock in the morning, Leopard came there as if for a walk. When Antelope saw him, Goat and his mother hid themselves; and Antelope asked Leopard, "What is your anger? Why are you angry with my nephew?"

At that very moment while Antelope was speaking, Leopard seized him on the ear. Antelope cried out, "What are you killing me for?" Leopard replied, "Show me the place where Tomba-Taba and his mother are." So, Antelope being afraid said, "Come tonight, and I will show you where they sleep. And you kill them; but don't kill me."

While he was saying this, Goat overheard, and said to his mother, "We must flee, lest Njâ kill us." So, at sun-down, that evening, Goat and his mother fled to the village of Elephant. About midnight, Leopard came to Antelope's village, according to appointment, and looked for Goat, but did not find him. Leopard went to all the houses of the village, and when he came to Antelope's own, in his disappointment, he killed him.

Leopard kept up his search, and followed to find where Goat had gone. Following the tracks, he came to the village of Elephant. When he arrived there, Elephant demanded, "What's the matter?" And the same conversation was held, as at Antelope's village, and the incidents happened as at that village, ending with Elephant's being killed by Leopard. For, Goat and his mother had fled, and had gone to the village of Ox.

Leopard followed, and came to Ox's village. There all the same things were said and done, as in the other villages, and ending with Goat and his mother fleeing, and Ox being killed.

Then, the mother, wearying of flight, and sorry at causing their entertainers to be killed, said, "My child! if we continue to flee to the villages of other beasts, Njâ will follow, and will kill them. Let us flee to the homes of Mankind."

So, they fled again, and came to the town of Man, and told him their story. He received them kindly. He took Goat and his mother as guests, and gave them a house to live in.

One time, at night, Leopard came to the town of Man, in pursuit of Goat. But Man said to Leopard, "Those Beasts whom you killed, failed to find a way in which to kill you. But, if you come here, we will find a way." So, that night, Leopard went back to his village.

On another day, Mankind began to make a big trap, with two rooms in it. They took Goat and put him in one room of the trap. Night came. Leopard left his village, still going to seek for Goat; and he came again to the town of Man. Leopard stood still, listened, and sniffed the air. He smelled the odor of Goat, and was glad, and said, "So! this night I will kill him!"

He saw an open way to a small house. He thought it was a door. He entered, and was caught in the trap. He could see Goat through the cracks in the wall, but could not get at him. Goat jeered at him, "My friend! you were about to kill me, but you are unable."

Daybreak came. And people of Man's town found Leopard in the trap, caught fast. They took machetes and guns, and killed him. Then Man said to Goat, "You shall not go back to the Forest; remain here always."

This is the reason that Goats like to live with mankind, through fear of Leopards.

IGWANA'S FORKED TONGUE

Persons

Ngâmbi (Igwana)   Vyâdu (Antelope)

Njâ (Leopard)   Ihᵫli (Gazelle)

Betoli (Rats)   Ehibo (Red Antelope)

NOTE

Natives believe that the Igwana kills with its long tongue. This story assigns the fear of leopards as a reason why Igwanas like to live near water. Igwanas swim readily, while leopards (as all the cat-tribe) do not like even to wet their feet.

There were two friends, Igwana and Leopard, living in the same village, one at each end. Igwana had six wives; Leopard also had six. Leopard begot twenty children; Igwana had eight. One time, at night, they were sitting with their wives and children in the street, in a conversation. Leopard said to Igwana, "Ngâmbi! I have a word to say to you." Igwana said, "Speak."

Then Leopard said, "I wish you and me to have our food together." Igwana agreed, "Well." And Leopard arranged, "For two months, you shall come and eat in my house; and then, for two months, I at your house."

And they separated, to go to their houses for sleep.

Soon the night passed, and day broke.

Leopard went to the forest and killed an Antelope. He and Igwana and their families spent four days in eating it.

On another day, Leopard went to the forest and killed a Gazelle. It also was finished in four days.

And again, Leopard went to the forest, and killed a Red Antelope. They were occupied in eating it also four days.

So, they continued all the two months. Then Leopard said, "Ngâmbi! it is your time to begin the food." Igwana replied, "I have no wild meat, only vegetables."

On the following day, Igwana got ready his food and sent word for Leopard to come to eat. He came and ate, there being on the table only vegetables and salt. Then the day darkened; and, in the evening they all came together in one place, as usual. Leopard said to Igwana, "I began my turn with meats in my house, and you ate them. I cannot eat only vegetables and salt." Igwana explained, "I do not know the arts for killing beasts." Leopard told him, "Begin now to try the art of how to catch beasts." Igwana replied, "If I begin a plan for catching Beasts, that plan will be a dreadful one." Leopard exclaimed, "Good! begin!"

Igwana promised, "Tomorrow I will begin."

And they all went to their houses to sleep their sleep. The night passed, and day broke.

Igwana started out very early in the morning. On the way, he came to a big tree. He stood at its base, and, with a cord, he loosely tied his own hands and feet around the tree. Then he began to squeak as if in pain, "Hwa! hwa! hwa!" three times.

At that same time, a child of Leopard had gone wandering out into the forest. He found Igwana tied to the tree and crying. Igwana said to him, "Ah! my child! come near me, and untie me."

The child of Leopard came near to him; and then Igwana thrust his forked tongue into the nostrils of young leopard, and pulled his brains out, so that the child died. Then Igwana untied himself, skinned the young leopard, divided it, tied the pieces in a big bundle of leaves, and took them and the skin to the village. There he gave the meat to his wife, who put it in a pot. And he went to his house, and left the skin hanging in his bedroom.

Then when the meat was cooked, he sent word for Leopard to come and eat. Leopard came and sat down at the table, and they ate. As they were eating, Leopard said, "Ah! my friend! You said you did not know how to catch beasts! What is this fine meat?"

Igwana replied, "I am unable to tell you. Just you eat it." So, they ate, and finished eating. Igwana continued that way for two weeks, killing the young leopards.

At that Leopard said to himself, "I had begotten twenty children, but now I find only ten. Where are the other ten?" He asked his children where their brothers were. They answered that they did not know, "Perhaps they were lost in the forest." The while that Igwana was killing the young leopards, he had hidden their skins all in his bedroom.

On another day, Leopard and Igwana began a journey together to a place about forty miles distant. Before he started, Igwana closed his house, and said to his children, "Njâ and I are going on a journey; while I am away, do not let any one enter into my bedroom." And they two went together on their journey. They reached their journey's end, and were there for the duration of seven days. While they were gone, there was no one to get meat for their people, and there came on their village a great njangu (hunger for meat).

One of those days, in the village, so great was that famine that the children of Leopard were searching for rats for food. The rats ran away to the house of Igwana that was shut up; and the children of Leopard pursued. But the children of Igwana said to them, "Do not enter the house! Our father forbade it! Stop at the door-way!"

But the young leopards replied, "No! all the Betoli have run in there. We must follow." So, they broke down the door. There they found skins of young leopards, and they exclaimed, "So! indeed! Ngâmbi kills our brothers!" And two days later, the two fathers came back to the village.

The young igwanas told their father that the young leopards had broken the door, and found leopard-skins hanging inside. Igwana asked them, "Really? They saw?" The young igwanas answered, "Yes! they saw!" Then Igwana said, "Be on your guard! For, Njâ will be angry with me."

Also, the young leopards said to their father, "Paia! so it is that Ngâmbi killed our brothers. We saw their skins in his bedroom." Leopard asked, "Truly?" They answered, "Yes! we saw!" He said only, "Well, let it be."

On another day, Leopard said, "This night I will go to Ngâmbi to kill him and all his children." The wife of Igwana heard this, and told him, "Tonight, Njâ will come to kill you and our children." At this, Igwana said to himself "But! we must flee, I, and my children, and my wives!" So, they all went and hid in the water of a small stream.

Leopard came, in the dark of the morning, to Igwana's house, and entered it; but he saw no people, only the skins of his children. So he exclaimed, "At whatever place I shall see Ngâmbi, I will kill and eat him. We, he and I, have no more friendship!"

TALE 9
WHAT CAUSED THEIR DEATHS?

Persons
Mbwa (Dog)   Mbala (Squirrel)
Kudu (Tortoise)

NOTE

Dog and squirrel were of the same age, and they met with the same end. They each had an object of their special liking, the excessive use of which finally was the cause of their death.

Dog, Squirrel, Tortoise and others were living in one town. They all, at that time, ate of the same kind of food. But, they were at peace in that village during only two weeks. Then Squirrel and Dog said to Tortoise, "Let us divide, and have peace each at our separate villages. You, Kudu, and the others can stay at this spot if you like."

Squirrel said he would remove to a place about three miles distant north. Dog went about three miles in the opposite direction. So, each had his own little hamlet.

On another day, Squirrel said to his wife, "I am going on a journey to see my friend Mbwa." He started, came to Dog's place, and entered the house. Dog welcomed him, played with him, and killed a fowl for their dinner. With Squirrel had come one of his wives.

While the women were cooking inside the house, Dog and Squirrel were sitting in the ikenga (reception-room). They were conversing there. After awhile, Dog said to Squirrel "Excuse me, I will go to see about the food." He went inside, and lay down near the fire, and Squirrel was left alone.

Dog stayed there inside the house, until the food was cooked. Then he came out to his friend, and began to set the table, while the women came in with the food, and put it on the table. Dog drew up by the table ready to eat; and Squirrel also; and Squirrel's wife, and Dog's wife also, making four at the table.

During the eating, Squirrel said to Dog, "My friend! when you left me here in the ikenga, where did you go to, the while that the women were cooking the food?" Dog answered, "Ah! my friend, you know that I like fire very much. While we were talking here, you and I, cold seized me."

Then Squirrel said, "Ah! my friend, you like fire too much; I think you will die of fire some day."

They finished the food; and after that, Squirrel prepared his return journey to his village. And he said to Dog, "My friend Mbwa, how many days before you shall come to my place?" Dog answered, "In two days, then will I come."

So, Squirrel returned to his village. His wives and children told him the daily news of what had occurred in the village while he was away. And he told them about what he had seen at Dog's. And he added, "But, there is one thing I noticed; my friend Mbwa likes fire very much."

He waited the two days; Dog came on his visit; and Squirrel killed a fowl for his guest. And he bade his woman cook the fowl. In the meanwhile, Dog and Squirrel sat in the ikenga conversing.

Presently Squirrel said to Dog, "Excuse me, I am going. I will return."

Squirrel went out into his garden, and climbed up a banana stalk, and began eating the ripe fruit at the top of the bunch. After awhile, he came down again. And he went into the ikenga to prepare the table for the food. When it was ready, Dog sat up at the table. With him were his wife, and Squirrel and Squirrel's wife.

Presently, Dog inquired of Squirrel, "My friend! when you left me sitting here alone, where did you go to?" Squirrel answered, "My friend! you know I like to eat bananas. So, I was up the tree," Then Dog said, "My friend! you love bananas too much; some day, you will die with them."

When they had finished their food, Dog said, "I am on my return to my village." So he returned thither. But he was arrived there only two days when he happened to fall into the fire-place. And he died in the fire. The news was carried to his friend Squirrel, "Your friend Mbwa is dead by fire." Squirrel replied, "Yes, I said so; for he loved fire too much."

On another day, in Man's town, a person went to look for food at his banana tree. And he saw that the fruit was eaten at the top, by some animal. So, that Man made a snare at the Banana tree. On the next day, Squirrel said to himself, "I'm going to eat my banana food wherever I shall find it."

He came to the town of Man, and climbed the tree. The snare caught and killed him; and he died there. The Man came and found the body of Squirrel; and he exclaimed "Good!"

The news was carried to the village of Squirrel's children, "Your father is dead, at a banana tree."

And they said, "Yes; for our father loved bananas very much.

He had said that Mbwa would die by fire because he loved fire. And himself also loved bananas."

A QUARREL ABOUT SENIORITY

Persons

Ihendi (Squirrel)	Pe (Viper)
And 2 children	A Hunter
Ikundu (Vengeance)	
Ihana (Help)	

NOTE

This story suggests that when a neighbor flatters another, suspicion is raised that he is plotting some evil. Squirrel and the Adder professed great friendship; but their friendship was soon broken.

Claims of seniority are a constant cause of native quarrels.

A certain fetish-charm or "medicine" (generally poisonous) is supposed to be able to decide, on its being drunk by accused parties, as to their guilt or innocence.

There is a common belief in premonitions by unusual beats of the heart, or twitching of any muscle.

Squirrel and Adder were great friends, living in the same town. Each of them had two wives.

One day, in the afternoon, Squirrel and one of his wives went into the house of Adder. The latter said to his wife, "Make ready food." So, she made a great deal of food. Then he said to his friend

Squirrel, "Come, eat!" But Squirrel said, "I won't eat alone without my wife." So he called his wife to eat. His wife came and ate at the table. Then he said to Adder, "Also, you call your wife to eat with us." So Adder's wife came. And Squirrel said to Adder, "Now let us eat; for, everything is right." So they began to eat.

While they were eating, Adder said, "I have a word to say about you, Ihendi." Squirrel replied, "Speak your word; I will listen." Then Adder asked, "You, Ihendi, and I, Pe; which is the elder? And your wife and my wife; also which is the elder?" Squirrel replied, "I am the elder, and my wife is older than your wife." But Adder said, "No! I am the elder; and my wife is older than yours." Squirrel responded, "I will give you my answer tomorrow in my own house." This occurred in the evening.

Then the day darkened, and Squirrel went to his house to lie down. Adder also went to lie down in his bedroom.

In the night, Squirrel remarked to his wife, "My wife! what sort of a word is this that Pe has spoken about so to me? I don't know about his birth, and he does not know of mine. We have no other person in the town who is able to decide which of us is the elder, and which the younger. This question has some affair behind it." His wife replied "I think that Pe wants to get up a quarrel in order to kill you or our children." Squirrel had two children, one named Vengeance and the other Help. Squirrel replied to his wife, "No! I will have no discussion with Pe; but tomorrow there shall be only a test of Medicine."

Soon the day broke. Squirrel sent word to Pe, "Chum! you and I will have today nothing else but a medicine-test and no quarrel. For, you and I profess to love each other. I do this to prove both yourself and myself, lest you get up some affair against me, even though we love each other very much." Adder consented, "Yes; get the Medicine. I will know then what I shall say."

Squirrel went to the forest to get leaves and bark of a certain tree for the kwai (test). On his return, he said to Adder, "Here is the test; let us drink of it." Adder replied, "The Medicine is of your getting. You first drink of it." Squirrel agreed, "Yes, I will drink first."

So, Squirrel, conscious of his innocence, drank the test and swore an oath, "If I meet Pe's mother, it shall be only in peace. Or his father, only peace; or his children, only peace." Squirrel added, "I have finished speaking for my part." And he sat down on the ground.

Then Adder arose from his seat and stood up. And he exclaimed, "Yes! let it be so!" He took up the medicine from the ground; and he drank of it greedily. And he swore, "If I meet with the children of Ihende, it will be only to swallow them. Or, father of Ihende, only to eat him; or mother of Ihende, only to eat her!" Then he sat down.

But, Squirrel exclaimed, "Ha! my friend! you saw how I drank my share of the medicine, and I have not spoken thus as you. For what reason have you thus spoken?" Adder answered, "Yes! I said so; and I will not alter my words."

They dispersed from the medicine ordeal, and went each to his house. Then that day darkened into night. And they all went to their sleep.

Soon the next day broke. Squirrel and his wife prepared for a journey to the forest to seek food. He said to his wife, "Leave the children in the house." So the woman shut them in, and closed the doors tight. And he and she went off to the forest.

Later on in the morning, Adder arose from his place, and he said to himself, "I'm going to stroll over to the house of my friend Ihende." So he came to Squirrel's house, and found no one there. He tried to break in the door; finally, he succeeded in opening it; and he entered the house. He found the two children of Squirrel lying together asleep. He shook them, and they awoke. He asked them, "Where is my friend?" They answered, "Our father and mother have gone to the forest."

Then Adder suddenly joined the two children together and swallowed them. (They were both of them lads.) Then he went out of the house, and closed the door. His stomach being distended with what he had swallowed, he went back to his house, and laid down on his bed.

Off in the forest, Squirrel said to his wife, "My heart beats so strangely! I have eaten nothing here; what should disturb my heart?" His wife replied, "Well! let us hasten back to town. Perhaps some affair has happened in our house!"

They hastily gathered their food, to go back rapidly to town. On their arrival, they went at once to their house. Looking at the door, the wife exclaimed, "I did not leave this door so! Who has been at it?" Her husband urged, "Quickly! Open the door! Let us enter at once!" They opened the door; and found no one in the house.

Then Squirrel, fearing evil, said to her, "Stay you here! I will go over to Pe's house. I know that fellow!" He came to Adder's house, and found him distended with this stomach. Squirrel asked him, "Chum! have you been at my house?" Adder answered, "Yes, I went to your house; but I have done nothing there." Squirrel asked him, feeling sure of his guilt, "But, where then are my children? Why did you not leave even one of them? Ah! my friend!" Adder replied, "When we drank the Test, did I not swear the truth that if I met with your children, I would swallow them?" Squirrel answered, "Yes! and you have kept your word well! But you shall see something just now and here!" Adder laughed, and said, "What can you do? You have no strength like mine."

Close by the house of Adder (which was only a hole in the ground) was a large tree. Squirrel went out of the house, and climbed to the top of the tree. There he began to wail for his dead, and cried out, "Ikundu ja mâ! Ikundu ja mâ!" (A play on words: either an apostrophe to the name of one of his children, or a prayer for vengeance.) Another squirrel, that was a mile or two away, heard the wailing; and it came to where Squirrel was. Also his wife followed Squirrel to that tree; and she wailed too. And other squirrels came; about twenty.

A hunter, living in the town of Mankind, started from his town to go hunting. Coming along the path, he heard Squirrel crying. Looking up, he exclaimed, "O! how many squirrels!" He thought to himself, "Why do these animals make this noise, and keep looking down at the foot of this big tree?"

He approached near to the tree; and they dispersed among the branches. He then said to himself, "I will look around here at the bottom; for, as those squirrels continue their cry, they keep looking down here." Searching at the foot of the tree, he saw a hole, like the home of some beast. Looking in, he saw the Adder sluggish in his distention. The hunter killed it with his machete. And he took the dead adder with him to the town of Mankind.

Squirrel, from the tree-top, shouted after dead Adder, "You have seen my promised Ikundu." (Another play on words; either—"You saw my child;" or, "You see my Vengeance.")

TALE 11
THE MAGIC DRUM

Persons

Kudu (Tortoise)   Njâ (Leopard)

King Maseni, A Man   Ngâmâ (A Magic Drum)

NOTE

The reason is here given why the turtle tribe of tortoises likes to live only in water; viz., their fear of the vengeance of the descendants of Leopard the King, because of the whipping to which he was subjected by the trick of the ancestor of the tortoises.

In the Ancient days, there were Mankind and all the Tribes of the Animals living together in one country. They built their towns, and they dwelt together in one place. In the country of King Maseni, Tortoise and Leopard occupied the same town; the one at one end of the street, and the other at the other.

Leopard married two women; Tortoise also his two.

It happened that a time of famine came, and a very great hunger fell on the Tribes covering that whole region of country. So, King Maseni issued a law, thus:—"Any person who shall be found having a piece of food, he shall he brought to me." (That is, for the equal distribution of that food.) And he appointed police as watchmen to look after that whole region.

The famine increased. People sat down hopelessly, and died of hunger. Just as, even today, it destroys the poor; not only of Africa, but also in the lands of Manga-Man☒ne (White Man's Land). And, as the days passed, people continued sitting in their hopelessness.

One day, Tortoise went out early, going, going and entering into the jungles, to seek for his special food, mushrooms. He had said to his wife, "I am going to stroll on the beach off down toward the south." As he journeyed and journeyed, he came to a river. It was a large one, several hundred feet in width. There he saw a coco-nut tree growing on the river-bank. When he reached the foot of the tree, and looked up at its top, he discovered that it was full of very many nuts. He said to himself. "I'm going up there, to gather nuts; for, hunger has seized me." He laid aside his travel-ing-bag, leaving it on the ground, and at once climbed the tree, expecting to gather many of the nuts. He plucked two, and threw them to the ground. Plucking another, and attempting to throw it, it slipped from his hand, and fell into the stream running below.

Then he exclaimed, "I've come here in hunger; and does my coco-nut fall into the water to be lost?" He said to himself, "I'll leave here, and drop into the water, and follow the nut." So, he plunged down, splash! into the water. He dove down to where the nut had sunk, to get it. And he was carried away by the current. Following the nut where the current had carried it, he came to the landing-place of a strange Town, where was a large House. People were there in it. And other people were outside, playing. They called to him. From the House, he heard a Voice, saying "Take me! take me! take me!" (It was a Drum that spoke.)

At the landing-place was a woman washing a child. The woman said to him, "What is it that brought you here? And, Kudu, where are you going?" He replied, "There is great hunger in our town. So, on my way, I came seeking for my mushrooms.

Then it was that I saw a coco tree; and I climbed it; for, I am hungry and have nothing to eat. I threw down the nuts. One fell into the river. I followed it; and I came hither." Then the woman said, "Now then, you are saved." And she added, "Kudu! go to that House over there. You will see a Thing there. That Thing is a Drum. Start, and go at once to where the Drums are."

Others of those people called out to him, "There are many such Things there. But, the kind that you will see which says, 'Take me! take me!' do not take it. But, the Drum which is silent and does not speak, but only echoes, 'wo-wo-wo,' without any real words, you must take it. Carry it with you, and tie it to that coco tree. Then you must say to the Drum, 'Ngâmâ! speak as they told to you!' " So, Tortoise went on, and on, to the House, and took the Drum, and, carrying it, came back to the river bank where the Woman was. She said to him, "You must first try to learn how to use it. Beat it!" He beat it. And, a table appeared with all kinds of food! And, when he had eaten, he said to the Drum, "Put it back!" And the table disappeared.

He carried the Drum with him clear back to the foot of the coco tree. He tied it with a rattan to the tree, and then said to the Drum, "Ngâmâ! do as they said!" Instantly, the Drum set out a long table, and put on all sorts of food. Tortoise felt very glad and happy for the abundance of food. So he ate and ate, and was satisfied. Again he said, "Ngâmâ! do as they said!" And Drum took back the table and the food to itself up the tree, leaving a little food at the foot; and then came back to the hand of Tortoise. He put this little food in his traveling-bag, and gathered from the ground the coco-nuts he had left lying there in the morning, and started to go back to his town. He stopped at a spot a short distance in the rear of the town. So delighted was he with his Drum that he tested it again. He stood it up, and with the palm of his hand struck it, tomu! A table at once stood there, with all kinds of food. Again he ate, and also filled his traveling-bag. Then he said to a tree that was standing near by, "Bend down!" It bowed; and he tied the Drum to its branch; and went off into the town. The coco-nuts and the mushrooms he handed to his women and children. After he had entered his house, his chief wife said to him, "Where have you been all this long while since the morning?" He replied evasively, "I went wandering clear down to the beach to gather coco-nuts. And, this day I saw a very fine thing. You, my wife, shall see it!" Then he drew out the food from the bag, potatoes, and rice, and beef. And he said, "The while that we eat this food, no one must show any of it to Njâ." So, they two, and his other wife and their family of children ate.

Soon day darkened; and they all went to go to sleep. And soon another day began to break. At day-break, Tortoise started to go off to the place where was the Drum. Arrived there, he went to the tree, and said to the Drum, "Ngâmâ! do as they said!" The Drum came rapidly down to the ground, and put out the table all covered with food. Tortoise took a part, and ate, and was satisfied. Then he also filled the bag. Then said he to the Drum, "Do as you did!" And Drum took back the things, and went up the tree. On another day, at day-break, he went to the tree and did the same way.

On another day, as he was going, his eldest son, curious to find out where his father obtained so much food, secretly followed him. Tortoise went to where the Drum was. The child hid himself, and stood still. He heard his father say to the tree, "Bend!" And its top bent down. The child saw the whole process, as Tortoise took the Drum, stood it up, and with the palm of his hand, struck it, v⊠! saying, "Do as you have been told to do!" At once a table stood prepared, at which Tortoise sat down and ate. And then, when he had finished, saying, "Tree! bend down," it bent over for Drum to be tied to it. He returned Drum to the branch; and the tree stood erect.

On other days, Tortoise came to the tree, and did the same way, eating; and returning to his house; on all such occasions, bringing food for his family. One day, the son, who had seen how to do all those things, came to the tree, and said to it, "Bow down." It bowed; and he did as his father had done. So Drum spread the table. The child ate, and finished eating. Then said he to Drum, "Put them away!" And the table disappeared. Then he took up the Drum, instead of fastening it to the tree, and secretly carried it to town to his own house. He went to call privately his brothers, and his father's women, and other members of the family. When they had come together in his house, at his command, the Drum did as usual; and they ate. And when he said to the Drum, "Put away the things!" it put them away.

Tortoise came that day from the forest where he had been searching for the loved mushrooms for his family. He said to himself, "Before going into the town, I will first go to the tree to eat." As he approached the tree, when only a short distance from it, the tree was standing as usual, but the Drum was not there! He exclaimed, "Truly, now, what is this joke of the tree?" As he neared the foot of the tree, still there was no Drum to be seen! He said to the tree, "Bow down!" There was no response! He passed on to the town, took his axe, and returned at once to the tree, in anger saying, "Lest I cut you down, bend!" The tree stood still. Tortoise began at once with his axe chopping, Ko! ko! The tree fell, toppling to the ground, tomu! He said to it, "You! produce the Drum, lest I cut you in pieces!" He split the tree all into pieces; but he did not see the Drum. He returned to the town; and, as he went, he walked anxiously saying to himself, "Who has done this thing?" When he reached his house, he was so displeased that he declined to speak. Then his eldest son came to him, and said, "O! my father! why is it that you are silent and do not speak? What have you done in the forest? What is it?" He replied, "I don't want to talk." The son said, "Ah! my father! you were satisfied when you used to come and eat, and you brought us mushrooms. I am the one who took the Drum." Tortoise said to him, "My child, now bring out to us the Drum." He brought it out of an inner room. Then Tortoise and the son called together all their people privately, and assembled them in the house. They commanded the Drum. It did as it usually did. They ate. Their little children took their scraps of potatoes and meat of wild-animals, and, in their excitement, forgot orders, and went out eating their food in the open street. Other children saw them, and begged of them. They gave to them. Among them were children of Leopard, who went and showed the meat to their father.

All suddenly, Leopard came to the house of Tortoise, and found him and his family feasting. Leopard said, "Ah! Chum! you have done me evil. You are eating; and I and my family are dying with hunger!" Tortoise replied, "Yes, not today, but tomorrow you shall eat." So, Leopard returned to his house.

After that, the day darkened. And they all went to lie down in sleep. Then, the next day broke.

Early in the morning, Tortoise, out in the street, announced, "From my house to Njâ's there will be no strolling into the forest today. Today, only food."

Tortoise then went off by himself to the coco tree (whither he had secretly during the night carried the Drum). Arrived at the foot of the tree, he desired to test whether its power had been lost by the use of it in his town. So, he gave the usual orders; and they were, as usually obeyed. Tortoise then went off with the Drum, carrying it openly on his shoulder, into the town, and directly to the house of Leopard, and said to him, "Call all your people! Let them come!" They all came into the house; and the people of Tortoise also. He gave the usual commands. At once, Drum produced abundance of food, and a table for it. So, they all ate, and were satisfied. And Drum took back the table to itself. Drum remained in the house of Leopard for about two weeks. It ended its supply of food, being displeased at Leopard's rough usage of itself; and there was no more food. Leopard went to Tortoise, and told him, "Drum has no more food. Go, and get another." Tortoise was provoked at the abuse of his Drum, but he took it, and hung it up in his house.

At this time, the watchmen heard of the supply of food at Leopard's house, and they asked him about it. He denied having any. They asked him, "Where then did you get this food which we saw your children eating?" He said, "From the children of Kudu." The officers went at once to King Maseni, and reported, "We saw a person who has food." He inquired, "Who is he?" They replied, "Kudu." The King ordered "Go ye, and summon Kudu." They went and told Tortoise, "The King summons you." Tortoise asked, "What have I done to the King? Since the King and I have been living in this country, he has not summoned me." Nevertheless, he obeyed and journeyed to the King's house. The King said to him, "You are keeping food, while all the Tribes are dying of hunger? You! bring all those foods!" Tortoise replied, "Please excuse me! I will not come again today with them. But, tomorrow, you must call for all the tribes."

The next morning, the King had his bell rung, and an order announced, "Any person whatever, old or young, come to eat!" The whole community assembled at the King's house. Tortoise also came from his town, holding his Drum in his hand. The distant members of that Tribe, (not knowing and not having heard what that Drum had been doing) twitted him, "Is it for a dance?"

Entering into the King's house, Tortoise stood up the Drum; with his palm he struck it, v⊠! saying, "Let every kind of food appear!" It appeared. The town was like a table, covered with every variety of food. The entire community ate, and were satisfied; and they dispersed. Tortoise took the Drum, and journeyed back to his town. He spoke to his hungry family, "Come ye!" They came. They struck the Drum; it was motionless; and nothing came from it! They struck it again. Silent! (It was indignant at having been used by other hands than those of Tortoise.) So, they sat down with hunger.

The next day, Tortoise went rapidly off to the coco tree, climbed it, gathered two nuts, threw one into the river, dropped into the stream, and followed the nut as he had done before. He came as before to that landing-place, and to the Woman, and told her about the failure of the Drum. She told him that she knew of it, and directed him to go and take another. He went on to that House, and to those People. And they, as before, asked him, "Kudu! whither goest thou?" He replied, "You know I have come to take my coco-nut." But they said, "No! leave the nut, and take a Drum." And, as before, they advised him to take a silent one. So, he came to the House of Drums. These called to him, "Take me! take me!" Then, he thought to himself, "Yes! I'll take one of those Drums that talk. Perhaps they will have even better things than the other." So, he took one, and came out of the House, and told those People "I have taken. And, now, for my journey."

He started from the landing-place, and on up the river, to the foot of the coco-tree. He tied the Drum to the tree with a cord, as before, set it up, and gave it a slap, v⊠! And a table stood there! He said, "Ngâmâ! do as you usually do!" Instantly, there were thrown down on the table, mbwâ! whips instead of food. Tortoise, surprised, said, "As usual!" The Drum picked up one of the whips, and beat Tortoise, v⊠! He cried out with pain, and said to the Drum, "But, now do also as you do. Take these things away." And Drum returned the table and whips to itself. Tortoise regretfully said to himself, "Those People told me not to take a Drum that talked; but my heart deceived me."

However, a plan occurred to him by which to obtain a revenge on Leopard and the King for the trouble he had been put to.

So, taking up the Drum, he came to his own town, and went at once to the house of Leopard. To whom he said, "To-morrow come with your people and mine to the town of King Maseni." Leopard rejoiced at the thought, "This is the Drum of food!"

Then Tortoise journeyed to the King's town, and said, "I have found food, according to your order. Call the people tomorrow."

In the morning, the King's bell was rung, and his people, accompanied by those of Tortoise and Leopard, came to his house. Tortoise privately spoke to his own people, "No one of you must follow me into the house. Remain outside of the window."

Tortoise said to the King, "The food of today must be eaten only inside of your house." So, the King's people, with those of Leopard, entered into the house. There, Tortoise said, "We shall eat this food only if all the doors and windows are fastened." So, they were fastened (excepting one which Tortoise kept open near himself). Then, the Drum was sounded, and Tortoise commanded it, "Do as you have said." And, the tables appeared. But, instead of food, were whips. The people wondered, "Ah! what do these mean? Where do they come from?" Tortoise stationed himself by the open window, and commanded the Drum, "As usual!" Instantly the whips flew about the room, lashing everybody, even the King, and especially Leopard. The thrashing was great, and Leopard and his people were crying with pain. Their bodies were injured, being covered with cuts.

But, Tortoise had promptly jumped out of the window. And, standing outside, he ordered, "Ngâmâ! do as you do!" And the whips and tables returned to it, and the whipping ceased. But, Tortoise knew that the angry crowd would try to seize and kill him. So, taking advantage of the confusion in the house, he and his people fled to the water of the river, and scattered, hiding among the logs and roots in the stream. As he was disappearing, Leopard shouted after him, "You and I shall not see each other! If we do, it will be you who will be killed!"

TALE 12
THE LIES OF TORTOISE

Persons

Njâ (Leopard)   Ihᵭli (Gazelle)

Kudu (Tortoise)   Ngando (Crocodile)

Etoli (Rat)   Ngomba (Porcupine)

Embonda (Prairie Antelope)

NOTE

African natives climb the palm-tree, cut out a cavity in the heart at the leafy top, and fasten a vessel below the cavity, to catch the sweet, milky juice that exudes. This is unintoxicating. But, like cider, it becomes intoxicating if kept a few days. The cutting destroys the tree in two or three months.

The beginning of this tale is that Leopard went to the forest, to cut an itutu tree (bamboo-palm) for palm-wine. After he had fastened the bowl at the cavity he had cut at the top in the heart of the tree, then he came back to town.

Tortoise came along to that palm-wine tree; and he climbed to the top. There he found that the sap had already collected in the bowl. And he drank three tumblerfuls. Excited by his success, he shouted out aloud, "I'm drunk! I'm drunk!"

Off in the forest, Wild Rat heard his voice, and, following the sound, came to the place. To Tortoise, Rat said, "Whose wine-tree is this?" Tortoise replied, "My own!" So, Rat begged of him, "Give me a glassful!" Tortoise told him "Climb up! Of what are you afraid?" So, Rat climbed up the tree. He also drank two glassfuls.

Presently, Tortoise heard Leopard coming, and he said to Rat. "Await me here, I'm just going down to the ground." When he reached the ground, Tortoise hid his body in a hole at the base of the tree.

In a very little while, Leopard arrived at the tree. He lifted up his eyes to the top and saw Rat there. To him Leopard said, "Who owns this palm-tree?" Rat replied, "My Chum, Kudu." But, Leopard asked, "This Kudu, where is he?" Then Leopard flung one of his claws at Rat. It stuck in him, and Rat fell dead.

Leopard took Rat's body and went away with it to his town. And he said to his wife, "Cook this; this is our meat."

Soon after Leopard had gone from the tree, Tortoise came out of his hiding, and climbed the tree a second time. Then, having drank again, he shouted, as before, "I'm drunk! I'm drunk!"

In his hole off among the rocks, Porcupine heard Tortoise shouting; and he came to the tree, and asked for a drink. Tortoise told him to climb; adding, "What are you afraid of?" So, Porcupine followed Tortoise up the tree, and drank two glassfuls of the wine.

Again Tortoise heard Leopard coming, recognizing the thud of his steps as he leaped on the way. So, Tortoise cried out, as if in pain, "O! my stomach hurts me! I'm going down!" At the base, he hid himself again in the cavity of the tree.

In a little while, Leopard appeared standing at the foot of the tree. Looking up, he saw Porcupine there. And he inquired, "Ngomba! who owns this tree?" Porcupine answered, "Chum Kudu!" Leopard asked, "This Kudu, who is he? I want to see him."

Porcupine replied, "Kudu has gone off, his stomach paining him." Then Leopard exclaimed, "So! indeed! you are the ones who use up all my wine here!" And he added, "What day I shall meet Kudu I do not know. But, that day we will meet in fight." While he was saying all this, Tortoise, in the hole at the tree, heard.

Then Leopard threw a claw at Porcupine. Porcupine fell down to the ground a corpse. Leopard taking it, went away with it to his town, and said to his wife, "Cook this meat, and let us eat it."

After Leopard had left the tree, Tortoise emerged from his hiding-place. He climbed the tree a third time, and took a cup, and drank two glassfuls. Again he shouted, "I, Kudu, I'm drunk! I, Kudu, I'm drunk!"

Out on a prairie, Antelope heard the shouting; and he came to the tree. Seeing Tortoise, he said, "Chum, give me a glass of wine!" Tortoise directed him, "Climb up! Of what are you afraid?" So, Antelope went up the tree, and drank.

Soon Tortoise heard Leopard coming, bounding through the forest. And Tortoise said to Antelope, "Chum! my bowels pain me; I'll soon return." He descended, and hid his body as before. Leopard arrived as before. And he spoke to Antelope; and then killed it with another of his claws. He took its carcass to his town, and bade his wife cook it, as had been done with the others.

After Leopard had gone from the tree, Tortoise climbed the tree a fourth time, again he drank; and again he shouted, changing his words slightly, "I've drank! I've drank!"

In the jungle, Gazelle heard, and came to the base of the tree, but said nothing. Tortoise spoke first, "O! my nephew! the wine is finished!" Gazelle asked, "Who owns this tree?" Tortoise answered, "It's my own, and not another's."

When he came from the jungle, Gazelle had brought with him a bag. As Gazelle still stood at the foot of the tree, Tortoise said to him, "Come up here! What do you fear?" So, Gazelle climbed; but went up only half-way.

While the two were thus apart, and before Gazelle had drunk any of the wine, Tortoise heard Leopard coming, leaping through the bushes. Then Tortoise said to Gazelle, "Ah! nephew! let me pass! My stomach hurts me!" But Gazelle said, "No! uncle, let us stay and drink." Tortoise heard Leopard nearing the tree; and he said to Gazelle, "Ah! Hurry! Let me pass! How my stomach hurts!" Gazelle said, "No! uncle, we'll go down together."

While they were thus talking, Leopard reached the foot of the tree. Then Gazelle took Tortoise and hid him in the bag. Leopard exclaimed, "Ihⱥli! who owns this tree?" Gazelle replied, "This is the palm-wine tree of my uncle." Leopard asked, "Who is your uncle?" Gazelle answered, "Kudu."

So, Leopard began to prepare to climb the tree, in order to fight with Gazelle. Then Gazelle put his hand into the bag, and drew out Tortoise, tightly grasped in his hand. And he flung Tortoise violently into Leopard's face. Leopard fell to the ground, dazed with the blow, while Gazelle leaped to the ground, and fled off in the forest.

When Leopard rose from the earth, he found Tortoise sprawling helpless on its back. Leopard tied a string to him, and went away with him to town. And he said to his wife, "My wife! this is the person who drinks at my wine-tree!" So he suspended him by the string, waiting to kill him next day.

The day began to darken towards night; and they went to their sleep.

Then came the daylight of next morning.

Leopard said to his wife, "I'm going to a palaver (council) at a place three miles distant. Take Kudu and cook him with udika (gravy of kernels of wild mango). When I come back, let me find the food all ready to be eaten at once."

So, Leopard went on his journey. And his wife remained to do her work. But, she exclaimed, "Ah! I forget what my husband told me!" Tortoise, overhearing her said, "Your husband said, 'Take the dried Etoli from the shelf, and cook it with udika; give it to Kudu, and let him eat it; and then take Kudu and wash him in the water of the brook.' " The woman gladly listened, and said, "Eh! Kudu! you remember well what my husband said to me!"

So, she did about the food as Tortoise had reported, and gave it to him to eat. When Tortoise had finished eating, the woman went with him to wash him in the water at the edge of the brook. While she was doing this, Tortoise asked, "Throw me off into the water where it is deep." The woman did so. And Tortoise shouted, "So! you will die this day by your husband's hands!" The woman began to see her mistake, and she begged Tortoise, "Come! let us go back to town." But Tortoise said, "I shan't come! I'm here safe in my place down in the bottom of the stream."

Then the woman went back to her town; and as she went, she went crying.

Late in the day, Leopard returned from the discussions of the Council. And he said to his wife, "O! my wife! I'm just dying of hunger!" She told him, "Ah! my husband! Kudu has run away!" Leopard, in his anger, flung a claw at her; and she died on the spot.

Tortoise, in the meanwhile, went as fast as he could under the water of the stream. And he came to the house of Crocodile, and crept into the doorway. Crocodile, in tears, met him with the words, "Ah! Kudu! I'm just dying here with grief and crying." Tortoise asked her, "What is the matter?" She told him, "I've laid a hundred eggs, but none of them had children in them." Tortoise replied, "That's my work, the causing of eggs to have children. Shall I do it?" Crocodile consented, "Yes, I've here three hundred other eggs; you may make them have children." Tortoise told her, "I'm the only one to do that thing." So, Crocodile said, "Go into this room, and do it."

Tortoise went into the room, found the eggs there; and said to Crocodile, "Give me here a kettle, also firewood and water. Give me my food here. For, I will not go out of this house; I will go out only at the time when I shall have caused the eggs to have children." Crocodile agreed, saying, "Yes, I am willing. It is well." And she gave direction to her people, "Give Kudu all the things he has asked for there."

Then Tortoise locked all the doors, and stayed inside the room. He began to arrange the fire-wood, and set the kettle and put water in it. In the afternoon, he took twenty eggs, and cooked, and ate them with his food.

At night, all went to sleep.

At daybreak, he cooked twenty more eggs, and ate them; at noon he cooked and ate more; and at evening supper, he cooked and ate some more. So, he spent about seven days in eating all the eggs. Then he called out to Crocodile "Do you want to hear the little crocodiles talk?" Crocodile replied, "Yes! I want to hear!" Tortoise took two pieces of broken plates, and scraped one across the other, making a rasping sound. Crocodile and the people of the town heard the squeaking sounds, and they exclaimed in joy. "So! So, So!" They replied to Tortoise, "We hear the little ones talking!" Tortoise also told them, "Tomorrow, then, I will make a Medicine to cause them to talk loudly." But Crocodile began to have some doubts. And day darkened to night.

Very early in the next morning, Crocodile's doubts having increased, she rose up without calling her people. And she went slowly alone to peep through a crack into the room of Tortoise. She saw only the piles of egg-shells; and she wondered, "Where are the little ones?" Then she went softly back to her own room; and she told the townspeople, "Get up! Let us open the room of Kudu!"

They all got up, and they went to the house. They broke the room door by force; and they found Tortoise sitting among the scattered shells of the eggs. The Crocodile exclaimed, "Kudu! have you deceived me? Your life too ends today!"

They tied Tortoise, and put him in the kettle; and they killed him there. They divided his flesh onto their plates. And Crocodile and her people ate Tortoise.

This is the end of the lies of Tortoise.

Robert Hamill Nassau

"DEATH BEGINS BY SOME ONE PERSON": A PROVERB

Persons

Kâ (A Very Big Snail)	Lonâni (Birds)
Ngâmbi (Igwana)	Kema (Monkeys)
Kudu (Tortoise)	A Man

NOTE

Trouble came to all these animals, even to the innocent, through the noise of some of them. Igwanas are supposed, by the natives, to be deaf.

Snail, Igwana and Tortoise all lived together in one village. One day, Tortoise went to roam in the forest. There he found a large tree called Evenga. He said to himself, "I will stay at the foot of this tree, and wait for the fruit to fall." During two days, he remained there alone.

On the third day, Igwana said to Snail, "I must go and search for our Chum Kudu, wherever he is." So, Igwana went; and he found Tortoise in a hole at the foot of that tree. Igwana said to him, "Chum! for two days I haven't seen you!" Tortoise replied, "I shan't go back to the village; I will remain here." Then Igwana said to him, "Well, then; let us sit here together in the same spot."

Tortoise objected, "No!" So Igwana climbed up the trunk a very short distance, and clung there.

After two days, Snail, who had been left alone, said to himself, "I must follow my friends, and find where they are."

So, Snail journeyed, and found Tortoise and Igwana there at that tree. Looking at the tree, he exclaimed, "Ah! what a fine tree under which to sit!" The others replied, "Yes; stay here!" So Snail said to Igwana, "I will stay near you, Chum Ngâmbi, where you are." But Igwana objected, "No!"

There was a vine hanging down from the treetop to the ground, and Snail climbed up the vine. Thus the three friends were arranged; Tortoise in the hole at the foot of the tree, Igwana up the trunk a short way, and Snail on the vine half-way to the top.

Igwana held on where he was, close to the bark of the tree. He was partly deaf, and did not hear well.

After two days, the tree put forth a great abundance of fruit. The fruit all ripened. Very many small Birds came to the tree-top to eat the fruit. And very many small Monkeys too, at the top. Also big monkeys. And also big birds. All crowded at the top. They all began to eat the fruit. As they ate, they played, and made a great deal of noise.

Tortoise hearing this noise, and dreading that it might attract the notice of some enemy, called to Igwana, "Ngâmbi! tell Kâ to say to those people there at the top of the tree, to eat quietly, and not with so much noise."

Tortoise himself did not call to Snail, lest his shout should add to the noise. He only spoke in a low voice to Igwana. But, to confirm his words, he quoted a proverb, "Iwedo a yalak⬛ndi na moto umbaka" (death begins by one person). This meant that they all should be watchful, lest Danger come to them all by the indiscretion of a few. But Igwana did not hear; and was silent.

Tortoise called again, "Ngâmbi! tell Kâ to tell those people to eat quietly, and without noise." Igwana was silent, and made no answer. A third and a fourth time, Tortoise called out thus to Igwana; but he did not hear. So, Tortoise said to himself, "I won't say any more!"

A man from Njambo's Town had gone out to hunt, having with him bow and arrow, a machete, and a gun. In his wandering, he happened to come to that tree. Hearing the noise of voices, he looked up and saw the many monkeys and birds on the tree. He exclaimed to himself, "Ah! how very many on one tree, more than I have ever seen!"

He shot his arrow; and three monkeys fell. He fired his gun, and killed seven birds. Then the Birds and the Monkeys all scattered and fled in fear. The Man also looked at the foot of the tree, and saw Tortoise in the hole. He drew him out, and thrust him into his hunting-bag. Then he looked on the other side of the tree, and saw Igwana within reach. He rejoiced in his success, "Oh! Igwana here too!" He struck him with the machete; and Igwana died.

Observing the vine, the Man gave it a pull. And down fell Snail! The Man exclaimed, "So! this is Snail!"

As the Man started homeward carrying his load of animals, Tortoise in the bag, mourning over his fate, said to the dead Igwana and the others, "I told you to call to Kâ to warn Kema and Lonani; and, now death has come to us all! If you, Kema and Lonani, in the beginning, on the tree-top, had not made such a noise, Man would not have come to kill us. This all comes from you."

And Man took all these animals to his town, and divided them among his people.

TORTOISE AND THE BOJABI TREE

Place

Country of All-The-Beasts

Persons

Mbâmâ (Boa Constrictor)	Ih◻li (Gazelle)
Kudu (Tortoise)	Ngomba (Porcupine)
Etoli (House Rat)	Nyati (Ox)
Vyâdu (Antelope)	And the Bojabi Tree
Njâku (Elephant)	

NOTE

African natives hesitate to eat of an unknown fruit or vegetable, unless they see it first partaken of by some lower animal.

All the tribes of Beasts were living in one region, except one beast, which was staying in its separate place. Its name was Boa Constrictor. His place was about thirty miles away from the others.

In the region of all those Beasts, there was a very large tree. Its name was Bojabi. But none of those beasts knew that that was its name.

There fell a great famine on that Country-of-all-the-Beasts. In their search for food, they looked at that tree; and they said, "This tree has fine-looking fruit; but, we do not know its name. How then shall we know whether it is fit to be eaten?" After some discussion, they said, "We think our Father Mbâmâ will be able to know this tree's name." So they agreed, "Let us send a person to Mbâmâ to cause us to know the name of the tree." They selected Rat, and said to him, "You, Etoli, are young; go you, and inquire." They also decided that, "Whoever goes shall not go by land along the beach, but by sea." (This they said, in order to prove the messenger's strength and perseverance; whether he would dally by the way ashore, or paddle steadily by sea.) Also, they told Rat that, in going, he should take one of the fruits of the tree in his hand, so that Boa might know it. So, Rat took the Bojabi fruit, stepped into a canoe, and began to paddle. He started about sun-rise in the morning. In the middle of the afternoon, he arrived at his journey's end.

He entered into the reception-room of Boa's house, and found him sitting there. Boa welcomed him, and said to his wife, "Prepare food for our guest, Etoli!" And he said to Rat, "Stranger! eat! And then you will tell me what is the message you have brought."

Rat ate and finished, and began to tell his message thus:—He said, "In our country we have nothing there but hunger. But there is there a tree, and this is its fruit. Whether it is fit to be eaten or not, you will tell us." Boa replied, "That tree is Bojabi; this fruit is Njabi; and it is to be eaten."

Then the day darkened to night. And they slept their sleep.

And then the next day broke.

And Boa said to Rat, "Begin your journey, Etoli! The name of the tree is Bojabi. Do not forget it!"

Rat stepped into his canoe, and began to paddle. He reached his country late in the afternoon. He landed. And he remained a little while on the beach, dragging the canoe ashore. So occupied was he in doing this, that he forgot the tree's name. Then he went up into the town. The tribes of All-the-Beasts met him, exclaiming, "Tell us! tell us!" Rat confessed, "I have forgotten the name just this very now." Then, in their disappointment, they all beat him.

On another day, they said to Porcupine, "Ngomba! go you!" But they warned Rat, "If Ngomba brings the name, you, Etoli, shall not eat of the fruit."

Porcupine made his journey also by sea, and came to the town of Boa. When Porcupine had stated his errand, Boa told him, "The tree's name is Bojabi. Now, go!"

Porcupine returned by sea, and kept the name in his memory, until he was actually entering the town of his home; and, then, he suddenly forgot it. The tribes of All-the-Beasts called out to him, as they saw him coming, "Ngomba! tell us! tell us!" When he informed them that he had forgotten it, they beat him, as they had done to Rat.

They had also in that country, another plant which was thought not proper to be eaten. They did not know that its leaves were really good for food.

On another day, they said to Antelope, "Go you; and tell Mbâmâ, and ask him which shall we eat, this fruit or these leaves. What shall we Beasts do?"

Antelope went by sea; and came to Boa's town. And he asked Boa, "What do you here eat? Tell us." Boa replied, "I eat leaves of the plants, and I drink water; that is all I do. And the name of the tree that bears that fruit is Bojabi. You, all the Beasts, what are you to eat? I have told you."

Antelope slept there that night. And the next day, he started on his return journey. At his journey's end, as he was about to land on the beach, a wave upset the canoe, and he fell into the sea. In the excitement, he forgot the name. The anxious tribes of All-the-Beasts had come down to the beach to meet him, and were asking, "What is the name? Tell us!" He replied, "Had I not fallen into the water, I would not have forgotten the name." Then, in their anger, they beat him.

Almost all the beasts were thus tried for that journey; and they all failed in the same way, with the name forgotten, even the big beasts like Ox and Elephant. There was no one of them who had succeeded in bringing home the name.

But there was left still, one who had not been tried. That was Tortoise. So, he said, "Let me try to go." They were all vexed with him, at what they thought his audacity and presumption. They began to beat him, saying, "Even the less for us, and more so for you! You will not be able!" But Gazelle interposed, saying, "Let Kudu alone! Why do you beat him? Let him go on the errand. We all have failed; and it is well that he should fail too."

Tortoise went to his mother's hut, and said to her, "I'm going! How shall I do it?" His mother told him, "In your going on this journey, do not drink any water while at sea, only while ashore. Also, do not eat any food on the way, but only in the town. Do not perform any call of Nature at sea, only ashore. For, if you do any of these things on the way, you will be unable to return with the name. For, all those who did these things on the way, forgot the name." So Tortoise promised, "Yes, my mother, I shall not do them."

On another day, Tortoise began his journey to Boa, early. He paddled and he paddled, not stopping to eat or drink, until he had gone about two-thirds of the way. Then hunger and thirst and calls of Nature seized him. But he restrained himself, and went on paddling harder and faster. These feelings had seized him about noon; and they ceased an hour later. He continued the journey; and, before four o'clock in the afternoon, had arrived at Boa's. There Tortoise entered Boa's house, and found him sitting. Boa saluted, and said, "Legs rest; but the mouth will not. Wife! bring food for Kudu!" The wife brought food, and Tortoise ate.

Then Boa said to Tortoise, "Tell me what the journey is about." Tortoise told him, "A great hunger is in our place. There also we have two plants; the one,—this is its fruit; and this grass,—the leaves. Are they eaten?" Boa replied, "The tree of this fruit, its name is Bojabi; and it is eaten. But, I, Mbâmâ, here, I eat leaves and drink water; and that is enough for me. These things are the food for All-us Beasts. We have no other food. Go and tell All-the-Beasts so." Tortoise replied, "Yes; it is well."

Then the day darkened, and they slept.

And another day came. And Tortoise began his journey of return to his home. As he went, he sang this song, to help remember the name:—"Njâku! Jaka Njabi. De! De! De!" (Elephant! eat the Bojabi fruit. Straight! Straight! Straight!) The chorus was "Bojabi," And, in each repetition of the line, he changed the name of the animal, thus:—"Nyati! jaka njabi. De! De! De. Bojabi" (Ox! eat the Bojabi fruit. Straight! straight! straight! Bojabi!)

He thus nerved himself to keep straight on in his journey. And, as he went, he kept repeating the chorus. "Bojabi, bojabi! bojabi!"

He had gone about one-third of the way, when a large wave came and upset the canoe, and threw him, pwim! into the water. He clung to the canoe, and the wave carried it and him clear ashore, he still repeating the word, "Bojabi! bojabi!" Ashore, he began to mend the canoe; but, all the while, he continued singing,

"Bojabi!" When he had repaired the canoe, he started the journey again, and went on his way, still crying out, "Bojabi!"

By that time, All-the-Beasts had gathered on the beach to wait the coming of Tortoise. He came on and on, through the surf near to the landing-place of the town. As he was about to land, a great wave caught him, njim! and the canoe. But, he still was shouting, "Bojabi!" Though All-the-Beasts heard the word, they did not know what it meant, or why Tortoise was saying it. They ran into the surf, and carried the canoe and Tortoise himself up to the top of the beach. And they, all in a hurry, begged, "Tell us!" He replied, "I will tell you only when in the town." In gladness, they carried him on their shoulders up into the town. Then he said, "Before I tell you, let me take my share of these fruits lying out there in the yard." They agreed; and he carried a large number, hundreds of them, into his house. Then he stated, "Mbâmâ said, 'Its name is Bojabi.'" And All-the-Beasts shouted in unison, "Yes! Bojabi!"

Then they all began to scramble with each other in gathering the fruit; so that Tortoise would have been unable to get any, had he not first taken his share to his mother, whose advice had brought him success.

He also reported to them, "Mbâmâ told me to tell you that himself eats leaves and grass, and drinks water, and is satisfied. For, that is the food of All-the-Beasts."

Had it not been for Boa, the Beasts would not have known about eating leaves. But, though that is so, the diligence and skill, in this affair, was of Tortoise.

So, All-the-Beasts agreed:—"We shall have two Kings, Kudu and Mbâmâ, each at his end of the country. For, the one with his wisdom told what was fit to be eaten; and, the other, with his skill, brought the news."

THE SUITORS OF NJAMBO'S DAUGHTER

Place

In Njambo's Town

Persons

Njambo and His Daughter Ndenga	Nyati (Ox)
Etoli (House Rat)	Kudu (Tortoise)
Njâ (Leopard)	Njâku (Elephant)
Ko (Forest Rat)	

NOTE

Africans cut down trees, not at the base, but some 12 or 20 feet up where the diameter is less. They sit in the circle of a rope enclosing the tree and their own body, the rope resting against their backbone at the loins, and their feet braced against the tree trunk.

The reason why Tortoise lives in brooks is his fear of Leopard.

All the Beasts were living long ago in one place, separate from the towns of Mankind; but they had friendship for and married with each other.

Among the towns of Mankind was living a man named Njambo. There was born to him a female child named Ndenga. In the town, at one end of it, there was a very large tree.

Njambo said of his daughter, "This child shall be married only with Beasts." So when the Beasts heard of that one of them, House-Rat, said, "I'm going to marry that woman!" So he went to the father to arrange what things he should pay on the dowry. Njambo said to him, "I do not want goods. But, if any one shall be able to hew down this tree, he shall marry my child."

At once, Rat took the axe that Njambo handed him, and began to hack at the Tree. He tried and tried, but was not able to make the axe enter at all. At last, he wearied of trying and stopped. He said to himself, "If I go to Njambo, and tell him I am unable to do the task, he will kill me." So, he left the axe, at the foot of the tree, and fled to his town.

Njambo waited a while, but seeing no signs of Rat's coming to him to report, himself came to the Tree, and found only the axe, but saw no person. He took up the axe, and went with it back to his house.

Off in the Forest, all-Beasts saw Rat returning, and were surprised that he came alone. They asked him, "Where is the woman?" Rat answered, "I wearied of trying to get the woman, by reason of the greatness of the task of cutting down a tree. So, I gave up the work, and fled, and have come home."

Then all the Beasts derided him, saying, "You like to live in another person's house, and scramble around, and nibble at other people's food, but you are not able to marry a wife!"

Then Forest-Rat said, "I will marry that woman!" So he went to Njambo for the marriage, and came to the town. Njambo said to him, "I do not object to anybody for the marriage, but, I will only test you by that Tree off yonder. If you are willing to hew the Tree, you may marry this woman!"

This Forest-Rat replied, "Yes! I shall wait here today; and will cut down the Tree early tomorrow morning." That day darkened. And Njambo's people cooked food for Forest-Rat as their guest. They all ate; and then they went to lie down to sleep.

Then after awhile, the light of another day began to break.

They arose. And they gave Forest-Rat an axe. He took it, and went to the foot of the Tree. He fastened two cords, with which to climb up to where the Tree was at half its thickness. There he tried to cut the Tree. But he was unable to cut away even the smallest chip. At last he exclaimed, "Ah! brother Etoli is justified! I am not able to cut this tree, because of its hardness."

So, he came down the Tree, and left the axe at the foot, saying, "If I go back to the house of this Man, he will kill me. No! I am fleeing."

When he arrived at his town, the other people asked him, "Where's the woman?" He answered, "The woman is a thing easy to marry, but the Tree was a hard thing to cut."

After waiting awhile for the Forest-Rat, Njambo came to the foot of the Tree; and, seeing the axe lying, took it, and went with it to his House.

Then Leopard tried for the woman; and failed in the same way as the two who preceded him.

Next, Elephant tried, and failed in the same way.

So did Ox in the same way.

And all the other Beasts, one after another, in the same way, wearied of the task for obtaining this woman.

But, there was left still one Beast, Tortoise, that had not made the attempt at the marriage. He stood up, and said, "I will go; and

I shall marry that woman at Njambo's town!" Ox heard Tortoise say that; and struck him, saying, "Why! even more so we; and the less so you, to attempt to obtain her!" But Elephant said to Ox, "Let Kudu alone! Let us see him marry the woman!"

So, Tortoise made his journey to Njambo's town, and came there late in the afternoon. He said to Njambo, "I have come to marry your child." Njambo replied, "Well! let it be so!"

Tortoise said to Njambo, "First, call your daughter, to see if she shall like me." When she entered the room, Tortoise asked her, "Do you love me?" She answered, "Yes! I love you with all my heart." This made Tortoise glad; for the woman was very beautiful to look upon. Then Njambo told him, "Kudu, I want no goods for her; only the cutting of the Tree." Tortoise assented, "Yes! I will try."

So they all went to sleep that night.

And then the next day broke.

An hour after sunrise, Njambo called Tortoise, and, showing him the axe, said, "This is the axe for the tree." Tortoise took the axe, and went to the foot of the Tree. He looked at its sides closely, and saw there was a difference in them. He also looked very steadily at the top of the tree. Then he took rattan ropes, and mounted to the middle of the thickness of the Tree. He chose also the side opposite that at which the others had cut. He found it soft when he began to cut; and, at once the chips began to fall to the ground. He had begun the chopping early, and by the middle of the morning, the Tree began to fall. And it fell to the ground with a great crash, nji-i!

Njambo heard the fall of the tree, and he came to see it. And he said to Tortoise, "You have done well, because you have cut down the Tree. But, finish the job by cutting off the top end with its branches. That will leave the trunk clear." Tortoise asked Njambo, "What will you do with the log?" Njambo answered him, "To make a canoe."

So, Tortoise cut off also the end of the Tree with its branches.

Then Njambo told him, "Come on, into the town, to take your wife; because you have cut down the tree; that is the price I asked." The two came to the house in the town; and Njambo brought his daughter to Tortoise, saying, "This is your wife. And I give with the woman these other things." Those things were only different kinds of food.

Tortoise made his journey with his wife towards his town. He journeyed, going, going on, until he had reached half of the way. Then he said to his wife, "What shall I do? For, Njâ is ahead in the way?" The wife replied, "No! go on! I think Njâ will do nothing to us."

Shortly afterward, they met with Leopard in the path. Leopard said to Tortoise, "Ah! Chum! this wife is not proper for you to marry, only with me, Njâ." Tortoise said "No!" But Leopard insisted, "No! I take this one! I will give you another wife in her place." So, he snatched the woman from Tortoise, and ran away with her to his town.

Tortoise went on his way, as he went, crying, till he came to his own village. There Elephant asked him, "Why do you cry as you go? Has Njambo struck you about the affair of the marriage? For, we had heard the news that you had cut down the tree, and had taken the woman. What then is the reason?"

Tortoise answered, "Yes! I married the woman, because I had cut down the Tree. But Njâ took the woman away."

Then Elephant called all the Beasts together to take counsel. He said to them, "What shall we do, because Njâ has taken away the wife of Kudu?" They all replied, "We are all afraid of Njâ. None of us can dare to say anything to him. For, he kills us people. So, our decision is: Let Kudu give up his wife to Njâ."

But Tortoise said, "I am unable to leave her. If it be death, I will die because of my wife."

So, they all dispersed from the house of Tortoise, and went to their own houses.

At that time, Leopard had eight wives.

Tortoise removed from the Town-of-all-the-Beasts, and built a village for himself, about one-and-a-half miles away. He built on the public highway, where passed by all people. He put a very large stone in front of his door-yard, large enough for one to sit down on it. He made also a bench near the stone. And he put a plate with water in it on the ground by the stone. Then he placed a certain magic-medicine on the seat of the bench. And he uttered a Charm: "Let any one else who sits on this seat go free from it. But, if it be Njâ, let him not go from it."

He finished all these things late in the afternoon. The day darkened, and he went to his house, and slept his sleep.

Soon the day broke.

That day, Elephant said, "I'm going to the forest, and my wives with me." As he came on his way, he passed by the street of Tortoise's House. He observed the stone and the bench and the water. He exclaimed, "Ah! I'll sharpen my machete here!" So, he sat down on the bench, and sharpened his machete. Then, went on his way into the forest with his wives.

After a while, Ox came on his journey, and saw the stone and water. He also sat down on the bench, and sharpened his machete. And then went on his way into the forest with his wives.

Soon afterward, Leopard journeyed along with all his eight, and the new one, the ninth, the wife of Tortoise. He came to the house of Tortoise. Looking into the door-yard, he exclaimed, "Ah! good! and fine! that Kudu has prepared these things."

Tortoise was in the house; he saw Leopard coming, and he rejoiced, "Very good! indeed! for the coming of this person." Leopard sat down on the bench, and sharpened his machete on the stone with the water of the plate. His women standing by, waited for him to finish the sharpening. When he had finished, he said, "I will get up, and start the journey again." But, he stuck fast to the bench. He exclaimed, "My women! I am unable to rise! What shall I do?"

The "medicine" on the bench began to sting him like bees. And he cried out, "Ah! I'm dead! For, I am unable to rise!"

Tortoise, coming out into the yard, said to Leopard, "I am the one who caused you this. You will not move thence until you give me back my wife. If you do not, you will remain there a whole month, a whole year."

At this, Leopard felt very much grieved; and he inquired of his women, "The wife of Kudu is here in this company?" The woman answered, "Yes! I'm here." Then Leopard said, "Please, Kudu, take your wife, and remove me from this bench. It hurts me." So, Tortoise took his wife. And he added, "I want also my food you took from us in the path."

Leopard sent a child back to his town in haste to cut plantains. The child went; and the plantains were brought. Tortoise took them, and said, "Njâ! you are done, for your part. I have taken all

I owned. But, if I release you, you will kill me, and take again my wife. You shall be released only after I have fled."

So, Tortoise fled with his wife and all his goods into a stream of water. When safely there, he shouted, "Let Njâ remove from that seat!"

At once, Leopard stood up, and was free. And he went back to his town, giving up his intended journey into the forest.

TORTOISE, DOG, LEOPARD AND THE NJABI FRUIT

Persons

Njâ (Leopard)	Inâni (A Bird)
Mbwa (Dog)	And Other Beasts
Kudu (Tortoise)	

NOTE

Observe the cannibalism of the human-animals.

At first, all Animals were living in one region. Of these, Tortoise and Dog lived together in one place, and built a town by themselves. But, all the others, Leopard, Hippopotamus, Elephant, Ox, etc., lived together in another place.

After some time, a great famine fell on the part of the country where Tortoise and Dog lived; and they had to seek for any kind of food.

One day Tortoise said to Dog, "I'm going awalking into the forest." So, early at daybreak, he started off to seek for mushrooms. All those other Beasts that were living together had a kind of tree called Bojabi, bearing a very large heavy fruit called Njabi. And they had all agreed, "There are no other Animals, but our own companies, who shall eat of the fruit of this Tree." They were accustomed, whenever they had eaten of this fruit, to go to an adjacent prairie, to play.

So that day, on his journey, Tortoise happened to come to the foot of that Tree. The ripe fruit were falling from it, and quantities were lying on the ground. He exclaimed "Em⊠! (indeed!), Ib⊠⊠! (splendid), Em⊠! Abundance of food!" He gathered, and ate, and stayed a while gathering others, which he would carry back to his town.

While doing this, a fruit fell from the branch above, and struck him hard on the back. The blow hurt him; but he only said, "Ah! the back of an aged person!" (My back feels like that of an aged person.) This he said because of the pain it gave him; but he made no out-cry.

He had with him a bag, into which he put food on a journey. So, he filled it with the fruits, and resumed his journey to go back to his town. On his arrival at his house, his wife said to him, "Why did you delay so long?" He replied, "I found a Tree belonging to the Tribes-of-All-the-Beasts. Had they seen me, they would have killed me." And, he drew the fruits from the bag, and gave his wife and children, saying, "Eat ye!" But, he added, "While you eat of it, do not allow Mbwa to see it."

One of the children ran out into the street, with the fruit grasped in his hand. Just then, Dog happened to meet the child in the street, and asked him, "Who gave you this fruit, child of Kudu?" The child answered, "My father came from the forest, and brought this fruit with him." In the evening, when the day had darkened, Dog came and said to Tortoise, "My friend! you are a bad fellow; for, we live together in one place, and you do not share with me! Chum! is it possible that you eat such good things here? Where did you discover them?" Tortoise then gave Dog and his children a share. But, he was not willing to tell the place of that Tree. He evaded, by saying, "As I went, I forced my way through the jungle of the forest. But, I did not find any mushrooms; they are about done. Also, we are not allowed to go to the place where this fruit grows." So it went on for some time.

On another evening, Tortoise remarked, in conversation with Dog, that he would be going into the forest next day. Dog said nothing, but went back to his house, as if to sleep; while Tortoise remained in his house, and went to bed.

Tortoise had left his hunting-bag hanging in the public reception-room by his house. At night, Dog arose from his house, and slowly and stealthily went to the house of Tortoise, clear into that room. Entering it secretly, and finding the bag, he threw ashes into its mouth and then, with his knife, made holes in it at the lower end. For, he said to himself, "When Tortoise shall go out early, then I will follow him." Then he went back to his house, and laid down again.

When day-light began to break, early in the morning, Tortoise arose, took the bag, and started on a journey to that forest tree which belonged to the Beasts. As he went the ashes sifted through the holes in the bottom of the bag, and fell on the path. He finally arrived at the tree.

Dog also arose early, and found which way Tortoise had gone, by the dropping of the ashes; for, as he went, Dog was looking out for the marks on the way; and, following the signs, they clearly showed him the route, until he reached the tree, soon after Tortoise had arrived.

Tortoise exclaimed, "Ah! Chum! What have you come here to do? Who called you, you with your loud howling? Do you know who own this Tree? Can you endure if one of these fruits should fall down on you? For, if you cry out in pain, then the owners of this Tree will catch both you and me. If they seize me, who am Kudu, what shall I do? For, I, Kudu, do not know how to run rapidly." Then Dog said, "If they come to seize you, I will come to take you from their hands." At this, Tortoise laughed out aloud, "Those beasts of strength! When they seize me, you will come and take me from them? Really?"

Just then while they were thus speaking, two of the fruits fell on Tortoise's back, at the same time, with a thud, ndu! ndu! Though in pain, he only unconcernedly remarked, "The hardened skin of an aged person! Ah! the back of an old man!" and went on eating.

Dog exclaimed, "O! Chum! that big thing struck you, and you were able to refrain from crying!" Tortoise replied, "Wait till yours also!"

Presently a very small fruit thus fell, and hit Dog on the head. He howled lustily, "Ow! ow! ow! ow!" Tortoise said to him, "Did I not tell you so!"

There came down another fruit, and fell on Tortoise; he quietly disregarded it. Another then fell on Dog with a thump, ngomu! And he ran off howling, "mwâ! mwâ!"

All this while, Leopard had been up the Tree. It was he who had flung the fruit at Dog and Tortoise.

When Dog ran, Leopard instantly descended the Tree, and, disregarding Tortoise, chased Dog; but could not overtake him. Had he caught Dog, seizing him tightly, he would have killed him with one blow of his paw, ndi! and would have eaten him on the spot. While Leopard was away, Tortoise was in fear and did not know what to do, for he knew that he could not run from

Leopard. A Bird whistled, "Pu! pu! pu! Chum Kudu, Hide! hide!" So Tortoise went into a hole at the base of the tree, and hid there.

Leopard, on his return, sought for Tortoise, but could not find him. So, he climbed the Tree again, and gathered his fruits, and went off towards the town of the Beasts. But, he met those Beasts coming; for, they had heard the howls of Dog, and had shouted at him, "He! e. e.! Wait for us! Don't be afraid!"

All those People-of-the-Tree came and gathered about its trunk. They searched; and presently they saw Tortoise. They exclaimed, "So! you are the one who eats for us the fruit of this tree! You shall die!"

They tied him, and took him with them to their town. There they suspended him from the roof of a house, saying, "To-morrow, you will be eaten!" Off at his town, the wife of Tortoise asked Dog, "Where is my husband?" Dog answered, "I think that the Tribes-of-all-the-Beasts have caught him." After a while, Dog, thinking, said to himself, "I remember my word that I said to Kudu, 'If they seize you, I will come to take you.' " So, Dog went and gathered shells of a very large snail named Kâ. He took a large number, pierced each one with a hole, and strung them all on a string. These he placed about his neck; and, as he went along, he wriggled his body, and the shells struck together like little bells. Then said he to himself, "The time is fulfilled for taking away my friend." So, he went rapidly to where the Tribes-of-the-Beasts had a spring for their drinking-water. Those Beasts had sent one of their lads to get water with which to cook Tortoise. The lad came to the spring. Dog jingled the shells; and, the lad ran back to town screaming, "There's some Thing at the spring, which kills!"

Then the Tribes sent a young man stronger than the lad, and said to him, "Go you, and get water at the spring." When the young man came near the spring, Dog jingled the shells, as before. And, the young man fled in fear. So, the people of the town said, "Let us all go to the spring together; for, that Thing can not hurt us all."

So they came to the spring. Dog seeing that all were coming, left the spring, and ran around to their town by another path, to take Tortoise away. Dog found Tortoise suspended by a rope. He bit through the rope, and, with Tortoise on his back, he ran rapidly to their town.

Those of the Tribes who first arrived at the spring, searched, inquiring, "Where is It? Where is It? Where is It?" Discovering nothing, they returned to the town. Then, they could not find Tortoise. And they said, "Let be! Kudu has slipped away."

One day after this, the wife of Dog and the wife of Tortoise went into the forest to their gardens to seek for food. And their children went out on the prairie, to play. Dog and Tortoise both remained in the town. Notwithstanding that Dog had saved his life, Tortoise was still angry at him for having spoiled their going to the Njabi Tree. Tortoise came to Dog's end of the town and said to him, "Let us shave our foreheads." Dog was pleased, and said, "Kudu, you first do me; then I will do you."

So Tortoise took the razor, and he shaved away Dog's front locks.

Then Tortoise said to Dog, "Let me shave also your neck." Dog bent down his head. Tortoise slashed the entire neck, cutting Dog's head off. And Dog fell down a corpse.

Tortoise cut up the body, and put the pieces in a kettle of water on the fire. Also, he gathered pepper pods, and ground them for the seasoning. He looked for salt, and saw it was up on top of a shelf. So, he took three chairs, putting them on top of one another, by which to climb up. As he was creeping up, the chairs fell over on the ground. As they fell, he tumbled also down, almost into the kettle of hot water, where were boiling the pieces of Dog. But, Tortoise scrambled away, and went off to his end of the town.

After a while the children of Dog came back from their play, and not finding their father in his house, they came to the house of his friend Tortoise, and asked, "Where is our father?" Tortoise replied, "As for me, where I was, I did not see him. When he went from here, who sent for him?"

When the two women returned, Dog's wife found, but did not recognize, the pieces of meat in her kettle. She wailed and mourned for him as dead. When, by the next day, the people of Dog did not find him, they said, "He is dead." But they suspected Tortoise. The wife of Tortoise also doubted him, and deserting him, returned to the house of her father. So, Tortoise left them all, and went to another place, fearing they would charge him with the death of Dog.

A JOURNEY FOR SALT

Persons

Njâbu (Civet)   Kudu (Tortoise)

Mbâmâ (Boa)   A Man, and Hunters

Ngweya (Hog)

NOTE

Interior tribes formerly obtained their salt from sea-water evaporated by the coast tribes in large shallow brass pans, called "neptunes," imported by foreign traders.

All these four Beasts were neighbors, living together in one town.

One time, in the evening, about an hour after the regular six o'clock sunset, they all, were sitting conversing in the street. Then Tortoise said to the others, "Here! I have something to say! I wish to talk with you. Tomorrow, let us go on a journey, to take a walk through the forest down to the Sea, to buy salt." They all assented, "Yes! so let it be!"

Late at night, they dispersed to their houses, to lie down for sleep.

After awhile, the day began to break.

Early in the morning, they prepared for their journey. And Tortoise said to them, "I have here another thing to say; my last word. That is: As we go, no one of us is to start any new affair on the way; only steadily down to the Seacoast." They all said, "Yes! we are agreed."

So, they started through the forest, going on their journey. They went, and they went, on and on, expecting to go a long way, until they should by evening come to their camping-place for the night. But, on the way, Civet began to say, "Ah! my stomach aches! Ah! my stomach aches!" Tortoise asked, "What do you mean by 'stomach-ache?' " Civet answered, " 'Stomach-ache' means that my bowels trouble me, and that I need to go."

Tortoise said, "Well! go! step aside from the path into the bushes, and we will wait for you here." But Civet said, "No! not in the bushes; for, I must go back to the kitchen-garden of my mother in our town." Tortoise exclaimed, "By no means! When we arranged for this journey, what did I say in the town?" They all admitted, "You said that none of us should start any affair on the way." Therefore Tortoise said, "But, you, Njâbu, have begun a new matter on the way. If so, this journey is going to end in trouble!"

Nevertheless, Civet ran rapidly back before night to his mother's kitchen-garden in his town, at the place where he usually went, while the three others sat down in the path to await his return. After a long time, Civet, having relieved himself, came again by night to his companions, saying, "I am feeling very well."

The next day, they all rose, saying, "Now! Let us resume our journey!" and they started again.

They walked, and they walked, until Boa cried, "O! my stomach! O! my stomach aches!" Then Tortoise asked him, "What is 'stomach ache'?" Boa replied, "It means that hunger has seized me." So Tortoise said, "Yes, that's right. We have with us food for the journey ready. So, come, all of you, let us all eat." But Boa said, "No! not this food. I must go and seek other food." Tortoise inquired, "What other kind of food?" Boa said, "Let me go over yonder a little way; and I shall return."

As he was going, he came in sight of a red Antelope. Boa curled his body in folds, according to his manner of crushing his prey. The Antelope happened along; and Boa seized and killed it. He covered it with saliva very much, as is its manner in swallowing its prey. And, carrying it to their camp, Boa lay down with it. Tortoise said, "We will all eat together of it." But Boa replied, "We do not give each other in the town; shall we give each other on the journey?" Then he swallowed the entire carcass. Presently he called the other three; and they went to him. And he said to them, "I have finished eating, and I am satisfied."

So, Tortoise said, "Come on, then; let us continue our journey." But Boa said, "No! I shall leave this place only when this Beast I have eaten dissolves." Tortoise expostulated, "Indeed! Chum! I said in the town, 'Let no one begin any matter on the way,' yet, first Njâbu began his affair; and now you, Mbâmâ, begin yours!"

However, they all sat down, and waited for Boa's food to digest. For an entire month they waited there, delaying while that food was being digested. Finally, Boa said, "Now, we will journey, but first I will go to the river to drink." He drank a very great deal of water, which acted as a purgative to relieve his bowels of the bones of the Antelope. Then he reported to the others, "I am feeling very well. Let us go."

They went, and they went. And they came to a large tree so recently fallen across the path that its leaves were still green. Hog jumped over to the other side of it. Also, Boa crawled over it. And Civet leaped over it. They called to Tortoise, who was vainly trying to climb over it, "Come on! Let us go ahead! Jump!"

But, Tortoise being vexed, said, "No! I won't go! You know I have no long legs. What can I do! So, I shall leave this spot only when this tree has rotted through, giving me an open way!" They all wondered, and said, "No! this tree is new and fresh. It will rot in how many days?"

Tortoise replied, "Not me! you! For, had not you two, Njâbu and Mbâmâ, delayed us, we would already have passed this spot long before this tree fell. You, Njâbu, first began a matter; soon, you, Mbâmâ, began your matter; now, this is my matter. Now wait for me." So, they waited and waited.

But, while waiting, the other three went out sometimes by early daylight in the morning to an adjacent plantation, and found there corn, yams, plantains, and all kinds of food. Civet and Hog said, "We must eat!" They ate up the corn, and finished the plantains.

One day, a Man of another town, was wandering in the forest. As he journeyed, he was looking from side to side on the way, peering for what he might find. And he saw many tracks of Beasts. Examining them closely, he said, "This track looks like that of a tortoise! Yes, and this like a hog's! And, here, O! this other is of a civet! And, ha! ha! a trail of a boa is this!" He exclaimed, "How many Beasts this place has! I will call the townspeople to come and kill these Beasts; for, there must be many." So, he hurried rapidly back, and arrived at the town.

When there, he shouted, "Come on, men! Come to the forest! I've found many Beasts!" The owner of the Plantation came along. His people took their guns; and some took machetes; and some, spears and knives. Others took nets. And they all went together at once. They also had with them, dogs, to whose necks they tied little bells.

When they came to that place where the four Beasts were, the dogs barked and shook their bells as they raced. And the men began to shout "Hâ! hâ!" to drive the Beasts into the net. They first came upon Hog, fired a gun at him, and he died. Next, they came upon Civet, and pierced him with a spear. They killed also Boa, who was lying dormant by the log. And they saw the other Beast, Tortoise, on one side of the log, trying to conceal itself among the decayed leaves, and seized it. Having the three dead bodies, they kept Tortoise alive, and tied him with a cord.

They had begun the killing of these Beasts late in the afternoon, and they reached their town about sunset. And they said, "Put all the carcasses in one house; but suspend Tortoise from the roof." They consulted, "We shall eat those Beasts only tomorrow; for, the evening is too late to cut them up and cook them." So, they all went to sleep.

Near midnight, Tortoise, after a long effort, wriggled out of the coils of the cord. He came to the corner of the room where were the bodies of the other three Beasts. He said over Civet's body, "Did I not say to you, 'Begin no new matter on the way?' And now you are a corpse." And over Boa, he said, "You too; I told you not to begin a matter; and now you are a dead body. Had we not begun these matters on the way, we would have finished our journey safely."

Then he scratched a hole under the wall of the house, and escaped to the forest.

After that, the day broke. And the townspeople said among themselves, "Bring the Beasts outside of the house; let us cut them up." They did so with the three dead bodies. And they told a lad, "Bring the Kudu that is suspended from the rafters."

The lad looked and reported, "I have seen no Kudu." They all went to look for it, and could see nothing of it. So, they said, "Let us eat these. Let the other go; for, it has run away."

A PLEA FOR MERCY

Persons

Njâbu (Civet)   Vyâdu (Antelope)

Uhingi (Genet)   Kudu (Tortoise)

Kuba (Chicken) Ivenga, A Woman and Her Husband Njambo

NOTE

This Tale seems to be a version of No. 17. The plea of Tortoise that he did not spoil the fruits of plantations is true; it does not injure the gardens of the natives.

These four Beasts were living in one town; Civet, in his own house; Tortoise in his; Antelope also in his; Genet too in his own. But their four houses opened on to one long street.

One day, in the afternoon, they all were in that street, sitting down in conversation. Tortoise said to them, "I have here a word to say." They replied "Well! Speak!"

At that time, their town had a great famine. So, Tortoise said, "Tomorrow, we will go to seek food." They replied, "Good! just as soon as the day, at its first break."

Then they scattered, and went to their houses to lie down for sleep. Soon, the day broke. And they all got up, and were ready by sunrise at six o'clock.

They all went on their journey to find food. They searched as they walked a distance of several miles. Then they came to a plantation of Njambo's wife Ivenga. It was distant from Njambo's town about one hour's walk. It had a great deal of sugar-cane; also of yams and cassava. It had also a quantity of sweet potatoes. There also, the chickens of Njambo were accustomed to go to scratch for worms among the plants.

At once, Civet exclaimed, "I'll go no further! I like to eat sugar-cane!" So he went to the plot of cane.

Antelope also said, "I too! I'll not go any further. I like to eat leaves of potato and cassava." So he went to the plot of cassava.

And Genet said, "Yes! I see Kuba here! I like to eat Kuba! I'll go no further!" So, he went after the chickens.

But first, the three had asked Tortoise, "Kudu! what will you do? Have you nothing to eat?" Tortoise answered, "I have nothing to eat. But, I shall await you even two days, and will not complain." So, Civet remarked, "Yes! I will not soon leave here, till I eat up all this cane. Then I will go back to town." Antelope also said, "Yes! the same. I will remain here with the potato leaves till I finish them, before I go back." Genet also said, "Yes! I see many Kuba here. I will stay and finish them."

Tortoise only said, "I have nothing to say."

In that plantation was a large tree; and Tortoise went to lie down at its foot.

They were all there about four days, eating and eating. On the fifth day, Njambo's wife Ivenga in the town said to herself, "I'll go today, and see about my plantation, how it is."

She came to the plantation, and when she saw the condition in which it was, she lifted up her voice, and began to wail a lamentation. She saw that but little cane was left, and not much of potatoes. Looking in another part of the plantation, she saw lying there, very many feathers of chickens.

She ran back rapidly to town to tell her husband. But, she was so excited she could scarcely speak. He asked her, "What's the matter, Ivenga?" She answered, "I have no words to tell you. For, the Plantation is left with no food." Then, the Man called twenty men of the town; and he said to them, "Take four nets!" They took the nets, and also four dogs, with small bells tied to the necks of the dogs. The men had also guns and spears and machetes in their hands. They followed into the forest; and they came on to three of the Beasts. They came first upon Antelope, with their dogs; and they shot him dead. Then the dogs came on Genet, and they followed him; and soon he was shot with a gun. They came also on Civet, and killed him.

Taking up the carcasses, they said to each other, "Let us go back to town." On the way, they came to the big Tree, and found Tortoise lying at the base. They took him also, and then went on to their town.

Arrived there, Njambo ordered, "Put Kudu in a house and suspend him from the roof." Also he ordered, "Take off the skin of Vyâdu and hang it in the house where Kudu is." He added, "Take off also the skin of Njâbu." They did so, and they put it into that house. He directed that Genet should also be skinned, and his skin hung in that same house. So, there was left of these beasts in the street, only the flesh of their bodies. These the men cut up and divided among themselves. And they feasted for several days.

On the fourth day afterward, Njambo said to his wife, "I'm going on a visit to a town about three miles away. Do you, while I am away, kill Kudu, and prepare him with ngândâ for me, by my return." The woman got ready the ngândâ seeds (gourd) for the pudding, and then went into the room to take Tortoise. In the dim light, she lifted up her hand, and found the string that suspended Tortoise.

But, before she untied it, Tortoise said, "Just wait a little." The woman took away her hand, and stood waiting. Tortoise asked her, "This skin there looks like what?" The woman replied, "A skin of Vyâdu." And Tortoise inquired, "What did Vyâdu do?" The woman answered, "Vyâdu ate my potatoes in the Plantation, and my husband killed him for it." Tortoise said, "That is well."

Then Tortoise again asked, "This other skin is of what animal?" The woman replied, "Of Uhingi." Tortoise inquired, "What did Uhingi do?" The woman answered, "Uhingi killed and ate my and my husband's Kuba; and he was killed for that." Then Tortoise said, "Very good reason!"

Again Tortoise asked the woman, "This other skin?" She answered, "Of Njâbu." Tortoise asked, "Njâbu, what did he do?" She answered, "Njâbu ate my sugar-cane, and my husband killed him." Tortoise said, "A proper reason! But, you, you are going to kill me and cook me with ngândâ-pudding. What have I done?" The woman had no reason to give. So she left Tortoise alive, and began to cook the gourd-seeds with fish.

Soon, Njambo himself came back, and his wife set before him the ngândâ and fish. But he objected, "Ah! my wife! I told you to cook Kudu; and you have cooked me fish. Why?" The woman told him, "My husband! first finish this food, and then you and I will go to see about Kudu." So, Njambo finished eating, and Ivenga removed the plates from the table. Then they two went into the room where Tortoise was suspended.

The woman sat, but Njambo was standing ready to pluck

down Tortoise. Then Tortoise said to Njambo, "You, Man! just wait!" The woman also said to Njambo, "My husband! listen to what Kudu says to you."

Tortoise asked, "You, Man, what skin is this?" Njambo answered, "Of Vyâdu. I killed him on account of this eating my Plantation." Then Tortoise asked, "And that skin?" Njambo answered, "Of Uhingi; and I killed him for eating my Kuba." Tortoise again asked, "And this other?" Njambo answered, "Of Njâbu; for eating my sugar-cane."

Then Tortoise said, "There were four of us in the Plantation. What have I eaten? Tell me. If I have eaten, then I should die." Njambo told him, "I've found no reason against you." Tortoise then asked, "Then, why should I die?" So, Njambo untied Tortoise from the roof, and said to Ivenga, "Let Kudu go; for, I find no reason against him. Let him go as he pleases."

So, Ivenga set Tortoise free; and he hasted back to his town in peace.

THE DECEPTIONS OF TORTOISE

Persons

Njâ (Leopard)	Mbâmâ (Boa)
Kudu (Tortoise)	Ngando (Crocodile)
Ngâmbi (Igwana)	With Men, A Woman, and Child

NOTE

A portion of this Tale seems to be a version of No. 12.

Leopard and Tortoise built together a large town. Leopard said to Tortoise, "I will live with you, but I shall not be able to eat with you; for, I am a great man, and I eat alone."

Some time after this, Tortoise went away, and married a wife. One day, his wife being hungry, he went off into the forest to seek food for her. And he found mushrooms. He gathered them; took them and returned with them to the town. There he said to his wife, "Eat!" and she ate.

Some time after this, the woman was about to become a mother. And, on another day, Tortoise went again into the forest to find food for his wife. As before, he gathered mushrooms. But, when he brought them to his wife, she said to him, "I don't like these things; the same every day!"

So, Tortoise went off again to seek food in the forest. He came near a strange town, and heard voices of Mankind talking. In fear, he hid himself, and watched what would happen. He observed that there were Men going off into the forest, with implements of search for wild animals. He saw them, but kept himself closely hidden.

When they had gone, he came out of his hiding, and went into one of these houses of Men, and sat down there. Then he walked into the rooms. On the shelves of the kitchen, he saw a large quantity of wild meat drying. He took of that meat, and went away with it to his own town.

He found on his arrival that his wife had already borne her child, the little tortoise. When Tortoise showed her the meat, she asked him, "Where did you get all this meat?" He replied evasively, "You told me to get you meat; so I went; and I have come with it." The woman was glad, and said, "Do so every day!"

So, another time, Tortoise again went off into the forest. And he came to the town of those Men. They were not there; for, they had gone off on their hunting. He went again into their house; took of their meat, and returned to his place. On giving the food to his wife, he said to her, "Do not show Njâ this meat!"

After this, little Tortoise grew, and began to go by itself, walking about the town. Tortoise told the child, "Do not show Njâ the things you eat." But, the child did not obey. One day, it went off toward Leopard's house, having in its hand the flesh of the wild animal it was eating. Tortoise saw his child going and called him back, but, he ran rapidly away to Leopard's; who, seeing the child with food in its hand, cried out, "Come here!" Leopard took hold of the child's hand to see what meat he was eating, and said to him, "Your father has no gun; where does he get all this meat?" The child was silent, not knowing whence the meat came, and did not answer; and he returned to his father's house.

So, Leopard said to himself, "Kudu and I must have a talk." He told his wife to make ready their food. She did so. Then he told one of his children, "Go! call Kudu to come and eat with me." The child went and told as he was bidden. Tortoise sent word, "I can't come." His wife, however, said to him, "Go!" Tortoise objected to her, saying, "I'm afraid of that man!" Still his wife said to him, "Go!" So, he went.

Leopard set out the food that had been prepared. Then he asked Tortoise, "Where did you get the meat which I saw with your child?" Tortoise replied, "I picked it up." Leopard said, "No! don't tell lies!" They changed the conversation, and went on eating. When they were done, Tortoise went back to his house.

Next day, Leopard said to his people, "I'm going to visit Kudu." So he went, and entered into the house of the wife of Tortoise. There he saw much dried wild meat. He exclaimed, "O! Kudu! you told me falsely! You and I living in the same town, can't you let me know what happens?"

Then Leopard went back to his house. That evening he said to his children, "Go to the house of Kudu. If you see a hunting-bag hanging there, take hold of it; with a knife pierce holes in the bottom; and fill the bag with ashes." They did so, putting in much ashes. They returned to their father, and told him what they had done. He replied, "Very good!"

That night, Tortoise said to his wife, "Tomorrow, I shall not go out hunting." But, she said, "Yes! Go! and kill me some animal." So, he consented.

Then day began to break. Tortoise went into the entrance-room; thence he took his hunting-bag; but, in the dark of the morning, he saw nothing wrong about it. And he went on his way.

Soon, also, Leopard came out of his house; and, going to the house of Tortoise, he inquired, "Kudu is in the house?" The wife of Tortoise from her bed-room, replied, "Kudu is not here." Then Leopard went into the entrance-room of Tortoise; and looking about, he saw that the bag was not there. So, he followed after Tortoise; and, as he walked, he looked out for marks of the ashes. He followed, and he followed; and finally overtook Tortoise.

Tortoise, as soon as he saw Leopard coming, said to him, "I'm going back to town!" Leopard asked, "Why? Don't go! Why do you go?" Tortoise, remembering his having said he was "a great man," answered, "Because you are proud." But, Leopard insisted, "No! go on where you were going." So, Tortoise consented, "Well, let us go!"

They went, and came to the town of Men. And they found that the men were gone off into the forest. Tortoise observed that the house was closed and locked. Leopard said to him, "Open the house!" But Tortoise replied, "You, Njâ you open the house!" But, Leopard said, "I am a stranger here; you travel here continually; you know the way!" So, Tortoise opened the house; and they both entered.

Leopard saw the bodies of many wild animals drying in the house. Tortoise said to him, "Carry the meat, and let us go!" But, Leopard said, "No! I'm staying here, and will cook some meat here." Tortoise objected, "No! take the meat and let us go. For, here are great Men who kill us people."

However, Leopard insisted, "No! first let me eat." So, Tortoise said, "Very well! I'll carry away my share; for, I'm going." But Leopard still insisted, "No! wait for me." So, Tortoise yielded, and waited for him in the house.

Leopard cooked his meat. While the pot was on the fire-place, and before he had eaten, suddenly the Men returned. Tortoise exclaimed, "The Men of the Town have returned! What shall we do?" For himself, Tortoise said, "I'm going to hide in the bedroom!" But, Leopard said, "No! I'm the elder; the bedroom is the place for me." He went into the bedroom. Tortoise remained in the reception-room, and hid himself in a pile of the women's cassava leaves.

Soon afterward, the Men also came into that room. And a woman said, "I left those leaves here when I was cooking. I must throw them into the back yard." So, she swept the leaves (with Tortoise unseen among them) in a heap, and threw them out doors.

In the bedroom, where Leopard had hidden, there was a child of this woman, sick with a skin-disease. The woman called out to her child, "My child! are you there?" The child replied, "Yes!" The Men in the entrance-room, observing the pot on the fire, asked the woman, "While we were away, did you leave a kettle on the fire-place?" The woman, thinking the pot belonged to someone else who had been cooking, answered, "No." The Men then directed her, "Make food for us!" So, she made them food in that pot which Leopard had left, adding other meat to it.

The child in the bedroom, smelling the odor of cooking, called out, "Mother! I want to eat!" So, the mother made food for him. And she took the plate to him, setting it down in the doorway, (but did not enter the room, and so did not see Leopard).

Leopard took the child's food. The child, in terror, made no out-cry. Leopard ate up all the food. Then the child began to weep. The mother, hearing, asked, "Why do you cry?" The child answered, "For hunger."

She wondered that that plateful had not been sufficient; but, she made him more food. And she brought it to him into the room, but she did not see the Leopard; nor did the child tell her. She left the food there, and went out. The child was about to take the food to eat it, when Leopard again snatched it away. But, even then, the child, in fear, did not scream out. And Leopard ate all the food.

Then the child began to weep out aloud. The mother again asked, "What do you want?" The child answered, "I want food." The mother wondered much, and, hastening into the bedroom, she saw Leopard. Then she shouted, "Men! Here's Njâ!" The men came, and they killed Leopard.

All this while, Tortoise remained hidden in the bushes outside; and he heard all that was happening. He said to himself, "I'm going to town to tell the children of Njâ that he is dead." So, he went back to his town. At first, he told only his wife, "Men have killed Njâ." Then he said, "I must now call the children of Njâ."

So, he called all the people of Leopard. And he said to them, "I will tell you something; but, don't kill me for my evil news. So, I tell you, Njâ is dead!" They all laughed in derision, as if it was not possible, "We will know about that matter tomorrow!"

And that day darkened. In the evening, Tortoise told his wife and children, "We must flee to another place." For, he feared that Leopard's people would charge him with their father's death. So, that night they fled. And they built their town far away at another place.

When the children of Leopard saw that Tortoise had fled, they believed him guilty; and they said, "The day we shall see Kudu, we will kill him."

Tortoise and his family had been living at their new place only about a month, when, one day, he said to his family, "I'm going on a journey to the town of Mbâmâ." So he went to that town. He stayed there visiting about a week. While there, he said to Boa, "If a child of Njâ comes here, hide me." Shortly afterward, a child of Leopard did come. Boa took Tortoise, and set him for safety on a rock in the middle of the river. Tortoise sat there a long time; and, while there, he laid what looked like an egg. Surprised, he threw it into the water; and it floated away. Finally it came ashore at the landing-place of Crocodile's town.

Crocodile saw it, and said, "Go, and seek the person who made this thing." His children went to seek. They journeyed, and found Tortoise, and took him. They brought him to their father, and told him, "This is the person." Crocodile asked Tortoise, "You made this Thing?" Tortoise said "Yes!" Then Crocodile told him, "Make me many of these Things." So Tortoise told him, "Bring me here a great many plantains; and arrange the house in order." Crocodile arranged all the house nicely. Tortoise entered it, and was given an inside room. He remained there in that room all by himself with the plantains.

At last, one day he emerged. And he said to Crocodile, "Send me in company with one of your people across the river." Crocodile told him, "You yourself name the person who shall go with you." Tortoise said he wanted Crocodile's cousin Igwana, who was living there with Crocodile's people.

So Igwana and Tortoise got into a canoe, and started to cross the river. Crocodile then entered the room where Tortoise had been. Searching there, he did not find any of the Things which Tortoise had promised to make. So Crocodile shouted after Tortoise, whose canoe had not yet crossed the river, to come back. Tortoise heard; and he asked Igwana, "Do you hear how

Crocodile is calling to you? Don't you know what he is saying?" (Natives believe the Igwana to be deaf.) Igwana answered, "No! what does he say?" Tortoise said, "He tells you to paddle faster! Don't be so slow!" So, Igwana paddled rapidly; and soon his work was finished; and they reached the other side. There, Tortoise got out of the canoe; and he told Igwana to go back. Igwana did so. And Tortoise went on his way.

After a while, a child of Leopard met with Tortoise on the path. The child asked him, "Is not this Kudu?" Tortoise replied, "Yes, I am he." Then the child of Leopard said to him, "You killed my father! I shall also kill you!" So, he killed Tortoise.

TALE 20
LEOPARD'S HUNTING COMPANIONS

Persons

Njâ (Leopard) and His Nephew	Njâku (Elephant)
Etoli (House-Rat)	Ko (Wild-Rat)
Ngomba (Porcupine)	Kudu (Tortoise)
Ihᵫli (Gazelle)	Indondobe (Wagtail)
Nyati (Ox)	

Leopard and other Beasts, with a son of Leopard's sister, were residing in the same town. One day, Leopard said to the others, "I have here a word to say." They replied, "Tell it." "We must go to kill Beasts (not of our company) for our food, at a place which I will show you a number of miles away." And they made their arrangements.

After two days, he said, "Now, for the journey!" So they finished their preparations. And Leopard said to his nephew, "You stay in the town. I and the others will go to our work."

They began their journey, and had gone only a part of the way, when Leopard exclaimed, "I forgot my spear! Wait for me while I go back to the town." There he found his nephew sitting down, waiting. Leopard said to him, "I have come to tell you that, every day, while we are away, you must come early to where we are killing the animals; and secretly you must take away the meat and bring it here to my house." The nephew heard and promised.

Leopard returned to the others who were awaiting him on the road, and told them to come on. They went, and they arrived at the spot which he had chosen. There they hastily built a small house for their camp. The next day they said, "Now, let us go and make our snares for the animals." They began making snares; and set their traps early in the afternoon. A few hours later, they returned to the camp. Later still, before sunset, they said, "Let us go to examine our snares." They found they had caught an Igwana. They killed it and put it on the drying-frame over the fire in the house.

Then the day darkened. And they went to their sleep.

And then the day broke.

And Leopard said, "While we go to the snares, who shall remain to take care of this house?" They agreed, "Let Etoli stay at the camp." House-Rat assented, "All right." So the others went away together.

The camp had been made near a small stream. At that same hour, Leopard's nephew came to the camp, according to his uncle's directions. He had in his hands a plate and a drum. He came near to the house cautiously. With the plate he twice swept the surface of the water, as if bailing out a canoe. Rat heard the swish of the water, and called out, "Who is splashing water there? Who is dabbling in this water?" The nephew responded, "It is I, a friend." And Rat said, "Well, then come."

The nephew came to the house. After a little conversation, he said to Rat, "I have here a drum, and, while I beat it, you dance for me." Rat was pleased, and said, "Very well." So, the nephew beat the drum, and Rat danced. After a while, the nephew said to Rat, "Go you, out into the front, and dance there, while I beat the drum here." As Rat went out, the nephew snatched the dried meat and ran away with it, suddenly disappearing around a corner of the house. He came to the town, and placed the meat in his own house.

Rat waited a while in the front, and, not hearing the drum came back into the house, and called out, "Chum! where are you?" He looked about, and his eyes falling on the drying-frame, he saw that the dried meat was not there. He began to mourn, "Ah! Leopard will kill me to day, because of the loss of his meat."

While he was thus speaking, the company of trappers, together with Leopard, came back from their morning's work. Leopard told Rat all that had occurred to them in the forest at their traps and snares; and then said, "Now, tell me what you have been doing, and the happenings of this camp." Rat told him, "Some one has come and taken away the dried meat, but I did not see who it was." Leopard said, "You are full of falsehood. Yourself have eaten it while we were away in the forest." So, Leopard gave him a heavy flogging. Then they put on the drying-frame the animal they had trapped that day.

The next day they went again to the forest; and Wild-Rat was left in charge of the camp. The nephew came, as on the day before, with his plate and drum, and did in the same way at the water. And he deceived the Wild-Rat with his drumming, in the same way as he had done to House-Rat.

When Leopard and the others came back from the forest, Wild-Rat told him of the loss of the meat; and said that he had seen no one, and did not know who took it. Leopard said to him,

"You, Ko, have eaten the meat, just as your relative Etoli ate his yesterday."

Thus Leopard and his company went each day to the traps. On the third day, Porcupine was caught; on the fourth Gazelle; on the fifth, Ox; on the sixth, Elephant. Beast after beast was caught, killed and dried; and, day by day, the meat of all was stolen. The last to be thus caught and stolen was Tortoise.

The nephew in Leopard's town, looked with satisfaction on the pile of dried meat that had been collected in his own house. He said to himself, "My uncle told me to gather them; and I have done so. But, I will not put them in Uncle's house."

In the camp, there was left only one animal of Leopard's companions that had not been placed on guard. It was a Bird, a water Wag-tail. It said to Leopard one day, "While you all go on your errand today, I will remain as keeper of the house." Leopard replied, "No! my friend, I don't wish you to remain." (For, Leopard knew that that Bird was very cautious and wise, more so than some other animals.) Nevertheless, they went, leaving the Bird in charge of the house.

The nephew came, as usual, with his plate and drum. He splashed the water of the stream as usual, to see whether there was anyone in the house to respond. And the Bird asked, "Who are you?" The nephew answered, in a humble voice, "I." He came on through the stream, on his way, catching two cray-fish. He entered the house, and he said to the Bird, "Get me some salt, and a leaf in which to tie and roast these cray-fish." When the Bird gave him the leaf, he tied them in it, and laid the small bundle on the coals on the fire-place. But he at once took up the bundle, opened it, and ate the fish, before they were really cooked. The Bird said to him,

"Those fish were not yet cooked. Your stomach is like your Uncle Njâ's. Both you and your Uncle like to eat things raw."

The Bird at once suspected that the nephew was the thief. When the nephew said, "I have here a drum," Bird at once, as if very willing, replied, "Drum! I want to dance." The nephew was standing in the front with his drum, and he said to Bird, "Come and dance out here; for, the drum sounds much better outside." But the Bird said, "I will not dance in the same place with you." The nephew then said, "Well, then; change places; you come here, and I go into the house." But the Bird refused, "No! I stay in the house."

Most of the morning was thus spent by the nephew trying to deceive the Bird, and get into the house alone. Finally, the nephew wearied, and gave up the effort and left.

Soon the company of trappers with Leopard returned from the forest. He told the Bird all the news of their forest work. Looking at the drying-frames, Leopard saw that the dried meat was still there. He thought in his heart, "My nephew has not come today to get this meat."

The Bird then told Leopard all the news of the camp, and how the nephew had been acting. At the last, he exclaimed, "So! it is your nephew who has been coming here every day to take away the dried meat!" And all the animals agreed, "So! so! that's so!" But Leopard replied, "I don't believe it. But, let us adjourn and examine." (He supposed the meat was hidden in his own house, and would not be discovered.)

They all scattered, and hastened to their town. There they entered the nephew's house; and there they found a great pile of dried meat. They proved the theft on Leopard himself, pointing out, "Here is the very meat in the house of one of your own family. We are sure that you yourself made the conspiracy with your nephew for him to do the stealing for you." And they all denounced him, "You are a thief and a liar! You shall not join with us any more in the same town."

Leopard went away in wrath saying, "Do you prove it on me? Well then! all you beasts, whenever and wherever I shall meet you, it will be only to eat you!"

So, leopards are always enemies to all other animals, and they kill them whenever they are able.

IS THE BAT A BIRD OR A BEAST?

Persons

Ndemi (Bat) and his Mother   Hako (Ants)

Joba (The Sun)   Other Animals and Birds

Vyâdu (Antelope)

NOTE

In Tropical Africa, it is not usual to retain a corpse unburied as long as 24 hours. Bat retained his mother's corpse too long. The "Driver" Ants of that country are natural scavengers.

A reason why bats are not seen in the day time:—Also, why they make their plaintive cry at night, as if they were calling for their mother.

Bat lived at a place by itself, with only its mother. Shortly after their settling there, the mother became sick, very near to death. Bat called for Antelope, and said to him, "Make medicine for my mother." Antelope looked steadily at her to discern her disease. Then he told Bat, "There is no one who can make the medicine that will cure your mother, except Joba." Having given this information, Antelope returned to his own place.

On another day, early in the morning, Bat arose to go to call Sun. He did not start until about seven o'clock. He met Sun on the road about eleven o'clock. And he said to Sun, "My journey was on the way to see you." Sun told him, "If you have a word to say, speak!" So Bat requested, "Come! make Medicine for my mother. She is sick." But Sun replied, "I can't go to make medicine unless you meet me in my house; not here on the road. Go back; and come to me at my house tomorrow." So, Bat went back to his town.

And the day darkened. And they all slept their sleep.

And the next day broke. At six o'clock, Bat started to go to call Sun. About nine o'clock, he met Sun on the path; and he told Sun what he was come for. But Sun said to him, "Whenever I emerge from my house, I do not go back, but I keep on to the end of my journey. Go back, for another day." Bat returned to his town.

He made other journeys in order to see Sun at his house, five successive days; and every day he was late, and met Sun already on the way of his own journey for his own business.

Finally, on the seventh day, Bat's mother died. Then Bat, in his grief, said, "It is Joba who has killed my mother! Had he made medicine for me, she would have recovered."

Very many people came together that day in a crowd, at the Kwedi (mourning) for the dead. The wailing was held from six o'clock in the morning until eleven o'clock of the next day. At that hour, Bat announced, "Let her be taken to the grave." He called other Beasts to go into the house together with him, in order to carry the corpse. They took up the body, and carried it on the way to the grave.

On their arrival at the grave, these Beasts said to Bat, "We have a rule that, before we bury a person, we must first look upon the face." (To identify it). So, they opened the coffin. When they had looked on the face, they said, "No! we can't bury this person; for, it is not our relative, it does not belong to us Beasts. This person indeed resembles us in having teeth like us. And it also has a head like us. But, that it has wings, makes it look like a bird. It is a bird. Call for the Birds! We will disperse." So, they dispersed.

Then Bat called the Birds to come. They came, big and little; Pelicans, Eagles, Herons and all the others. When they all had come together, they said to Bat, "Show us the dead body." He told them, "Here it is! Come! look upon it!" They looked and examined carefully. Then they said, "Yes! it resembles us; for, it has wings as we. But, about the teeth, No! We birds, none of us, have any teeth. This person does not resemble us with those teeth. It does not belong to us." And all the Birds stepped aside.

During the while that the talking had been going on, Ants had come and laid hold of the body, and could not be driven away. Then one of the Birds said to Bat, "I told you, you ought not to delay the burial, for, many things might happen." The Ants had eaten the body and there was no burial. And all the birds and beasts went away.

Bat, left alone, said to himself, "All the fault of all this trouble is because of Joba. If he had made medicine, my mother would not be dead. So, I, Ndemi, and Joba shall not look on each other. We shall have no friendship. If he emerges, I shall hide myself. I won't meet him or look at him." And he added, "I shall mourn for my mother always. I will make no visits. I will walk about only at night, not in the daytime, lest I meet Joba or other people."

DOG, AND HIS HUMAN SPEECH (1ST VERSION)

Persons

Mbwa (Dog), and His   A Man Njambo, and Daughter
Mother   Eyâle

NOTE

In the pre-historic times, from which these tales come, all animals, both human and (what we now call) the lower animals, were supposed to associate together, even in marriage. This son Mbwa, in form (and speaking also) like what we now call a "Dog," spoke also with human speech. The reason is here given why this ancestor of Dogs left the country of the Beasts. But, though Dogs now live with Mankind, they cannot use human speech as their ancestor did. They can only say "Ow! Ow!"

———

Dog and his mother were the only inhabitants of their hamlet. He had the power to speak both as a beast and as a human being.

One day the mother said to the son, "You are now a strong man; go, and seek a marriage. Go, and marry Eyâle, the daughter of Njambo." And he said to his mother, "I will go tomorrow."

That day darkened. And they both went to lie down in their places for sleep.

Then soon, another day began to break.

Dog said to his mother, "This is the time of my journey." It was about sun-rise in the morning. And he began his journey. He went the distance of about eight miles; and arrived at the journey's end before the middle of the morning.

He entered the house of Njambo, the father of Eyâle. Njambo and his wife saluted him, "Mbolo!" and he responded, "Ai! mbolo!" Njambo asked him, "My friend! what is the cause of your journey?" Dog, with his animal language, answered, "I have come to marry your daughter Eyâle." Njambo consented; and the mother of the girl also agreed. They called their daughter, and asked her; and she also replied, "Yes! with all my heart." This young woman was of very fine appearance in face and body. So, all the parties agreed to the marriage.

After that, about sun-set in the evening, when they sat down at supper, the son-in-law, Dog, was not able to eat for some unknown reason.

That day darkened; and they went to their sleep.

And, then, the next daylight broke. But, by an hour after sunrise in the morning, Dog had not risen; he was still asleep.

The mother of the woman said to her, "Get some water ready for the washing of your husband's face, whenever he shall awake." She also said to her daughter, "I am going to go into the forest to the plantation to get food for your husband; for, since his coming, he has not eaten. Also, here is a chicken; the lads may kill and prepare it. But, you yourself must split ngândâ (gourd-seeds, whose oily kernels are mashed into a pudding)." She handed Eyâle the dish of gourd-seeds, and went off into the forest. Njambo also went away on an errand with his wife. The daughter took the dish of seeds, and, sitting down, began to shell them. As she shelled, she threw the kernels on the ground, but the shells she put on a plate.

Shortly after the mother had gone, Dog woke from sleep. He rose from his bed, and came out to the room where his wife was, and stood near her, watching her working at the seeds. He stood silent, looking closely, and observed that she was still throwing away the kernels, the good part, and saving the shells on the plate. He spoke to her with his human voice, "No! woman! not so! Do you throw the good parts, to the ground, and the worthless husks onto the plate?"

While he was thus speaking to his wife, she suddenly fell to the ground. And at once she died. He laid hold of her to lift her up. But, behold! she was a corpse.

Soon afterwards, the father and the mother came, having returned from their errands. They found their child a corpse; and they said to Dog, "Mbwa! What is this?" He, with his own language replied, "I cannot tell." But, they insisted, "Tell us the reason!"

So Dog spoke with his human voice, "You, Woman, went to the forest while I was asleep. You, Man, you also went in company of your wife, while I was asleep. When I rose from sleep, I found my wife was cracking ngândâ. She was taking the good kernels to throw on the ground, and was keeping the shells for the plate. And I spoke and told her, 'The good kernels which you are throwing on the ground are to be eaten, not the husks.'"

While he was telling them this, they too, also fell to the ground, and died, apparently without cause.

When the people of the town heard about all this, they said,

"This person carries an evil Medicine for killing people. Let him be seized and killed!"

So Dog fled away rapidly into the forest; and he finally reached the hamlet of his mother. His body was scratched and torn by the branches and thorns of the bushes of the forest, in his hasty flight. His mother exclaimed, "Mbwa! What's the matter? Such haste! and your body so disordered!" He replied, using their own language, "No! I won't tell you. I won't speak." But, his mother begged him, "Please! my child! tell me!" So, finally, he spoke, using his strange voice, and said, "My mother! I tell you! Njambo and his wife liked me for the marriage; and the woman consented entirely. I was at that time asleep, when the Man and his wife went to the forest. When I rose from my sleep, I found the woman Eyâle cracking ngândâ, and throwing away the kernels, and keeping the husks. And I told her, 'The good ones which you are throwing away are the ones to be eaten.' And, at once she died."

While he was speaking thus to his mother, she also fell dead on the ground. The news was carried to the town of Dog's mother's brother, and very many people came to the Mourning. His Uncle came to Dog, and said, "Mbwa! what is the reason of all this?" But Dog would not answer. He only said, "No! I won't speak." Then they all begged him, "Tell us the reason." But he replied only, "No! I won't speak."

Finally, as they urged him, he chose two of them, and said to the company, "The rest of you remain here, and watch while I go and speak to these two." Then Dog spoke to those two men with the same voice as he had to his mother. And, at once they died, as she had died. Then he exclaimed, "Ah! No! If I speak so, people will come to an end!" And all the people agreed,

"Yes, Mbwa! it is so. Your human speech kills us people. Don't speak any more."

And he went away to live with Mankind.

DOG, AND HIS HUMAN SPEECH (2ND VERSION)

Persons

Njambo, His Wife Nyang-
wa-Mbwa, and His Son Mbwa   His Three Other Wives,
(Dog)   Majanga,
The Prophet, Totode, and a   Inyanji,
Sorcerer, Nja-Ya-Melema-Mya- MamⓍndi; and Her Two Twins.
Bato

NOTE

Some African ant-hills are built in upright pillars, varying in diameter from 3 to 10 inches, and in height from 1 ft. to 3 ft.

The bearing of a monstrosity formerly was punished (and in some tribes still) by driving the mother into seclusion in the forest, and generally with killing of the child. In some tribes, twins were considered monstrosities.

The "Heart-beat" of Nyangwa-Mbwa was the commonly believed premonition of coming evil.

There are many kinds of food, of which women are not allowed to partake.

Though the three sisters were daughters of the same mother, the jealousy of two of them for the other one led them to hatred, and an attempt at murder. Their curse laid on Mbwa caused him to be a speechless beast; for, previous to that, he was talking as a human being. "Heart-life" is an entity distinct from both Body and Soul.

Njambu married a woman named Nyangwa-Mbwa. She bore a creature that looked like no animal that existed at that time. But, because he spoke as a human being, he was not considered a Beast. He was given part of his mother's name, Mbwa.

Njambu added other marriages. Among them he obtained three women, each one of whom had a special office. That of Majanga was to keep things clean. That of Inyanji for planting. Mam▨ndi said that her work should be to bear twins. Now, these three women were sisters. The other two were jealous of Mam▨ndi, because her work was greater and more honorable than theirs.

In the course of time, Mam▨ndi conceived; her pregnancy went regularly on. And the time for her confinement came. Majanga and Inyanji went to deliver her. But they tied a napkin over her face, and covered her eyes lest she should see what they would do to her. When the time of the birth was at hand, she bore twins.

Then Inyanji and Majanga threw the twins into the pig-pen. And they took two ant-hills (slender conical structures). They smeared them with blood. And they went and showed them to Njambu as the things which Mam▨ndi had borne. Njambu said, "Go! and throw those things into the forest."

But Mbwa was going about; and as he went, he was scenting, till he came to the pig-pen; and he saw the twins. He took them, and carried them to his mother in their hut, which was isolated from the town. When the two women had left the twins in the pig-pen, their intention was that the pigs might kill them; and the women did not know that Mbwa had removed them. The twins stayed with Nyangwa-Mbwa, and she fed them and nursed them.

But, when Majanga and Inyanji heard that those children were in the hamlet of Mbwa's mother, they said, "We will go there tomorrow."

Early in the morning, Nyangwa-Mbwa had gone to the forest to her garden. When the two women came, they found the twins lying down. So, they struck them a blow; and they died.

The while that Nyangwa-Mbwa was in the forest, her heart beat with anxiety. She at once picked up her basket, and came to her village, and found the corpses of both the twins. Then she began to cry.

Mbwa also came, and found the dead bodies stretched out. Right away, he knew what had happened. So he went to the Prophet Totode, and inquired what he should do. Totode asked him, "Are you able to go to the town of Doctor Nja-ya-melema-mya-bato? (Hunger-for-the-hearts-of-people)." He agreed "Yes, I will go there." Then he went to the town of the Doctor.

A child of the Doctor spoke to Mbwa, and asked, "What have you come to do?" He answered, "I have come to seek heart-life; because my father's wives have killed from me two children."

Already Nja-ya-melema-mya-bato had gone to kill people for himself. In a little while he returned and suddenly, pieces of meat (from the dead bodies) began to fall, kidi! kidi! being thrown out on the ground in the street. Mbwa, awaiting a chance, hid himself under a bed.

Then came the Doctor bringing in the heart-lives of the men

he had killed. Mbwa, without permission, seized two of the hearts, and ran out quickly. Nja-ya-melema-mya-bato followed after him, running rapidly, da! da! da! But he did not overtake Mbwa.

Mbwa ran in haste with the hearts, on to his village. There he thrust the new lives into the children. The twins arose again to life and stood, to show themselves, and then they sat down.

Those twins went on growing, and became stout young men.

One day they said to Mbwa, "We want guns." He went to his father, in the town, and said, "I want two guns." His father produced two guns for him. He took them, went to his home, and handed them to the twins. Then they tried the guns, and loaded them.

Next day, in the morning, they went out early to hunt; they killed two gazelles; and they took them to their village. Mbwa cut up one of the beasts; and he said to his mother, "Cook it." Then he took the other one to his father. His father cut it up; and he called Majanga and Inyanji; and, dividing the meat, he said to them, "Go ye, and cook these in the pot, and those in a jomba." (Mbwa himself was still in the house watching them.) They boiled, and cooked; they put in the salt and pepper; and were about to taste the soup when Mbwa said, "Not so! This meat is not to be eaten by women."

They took the food to the Reception-house, where their husband Njambu ate; and he laid aside some for them. But, what he laid aside for those women, Mbwa drew away and ate. Then he returned to his home. His mother made food; and they ate, all four of them.

Next morning, the twins returned to their hunting. They killed also three antelopes, and they carried them to take them to their home, and left them in the path on the way outside of the village. In the village, they said to Mbwa, "Go, and bring the beasts from the forest."

Mbwa started, and brought them to the village. He carried two to his father. His brothers exclaimed, "Where does Mbwa kill all those animals?" His father cut up the animals, and divided one with his children. He cut up the other, saying, "This belongs to myself." Then he prepared some to be cooked in momba (bundles tied in plantain leaves), and some to be dried, and some to be boiled.

The women boiled the food (Mbwa still watching them). When it was cooked, they lifted up the pot from the fire, and they were about to taste it, when Mbwa said, "No! you must not taste it!" They put it in bowls, and set the food before their husband; and he ate. When he was about to give some to his wives, Mbwa said, "Not so!"

The twins continued with their hunting just the same as at the first. Almost every day they were killing some animal. And Mbwa continued also with carrying meat to the town of his father.

Finally, the twins became full-grown men. Then Mbwa said to himself, "Now, I'm ready to bring this matter to the ears of the people." When another day came, he said to his father, "Tomorrow, call all the people of the town together, in the afternoon."

On the next day, his father did so. Mbwa dressed the twins very finely; and brought out three chairs, two for the twins, and one for his mother. All the people collected together. Thereupon, he brought forward his mother, and the twins. The people fixed their eyes on them; for they had not seen them in their little hamlet in the forest. The people exclaimed, "What fine-looking persons!"

Then Mbwa stood up. He said, "Ye people! I have called you all that ye may recognize these two young men." The people said that they did not know them. He continued, "These are my father's children. For, my father had married these three women. Also, they had three duties; Majanga, her duty of keeping the house clean; Inyanji, her duty of planting; and Mamᴗndi's was the bearing of twins. Mamᴗndi became a mother. On the day of her confinement, her two sisters went to deliver her. They took a napkin and covered her eyes. And she bore these two twins. They threw them inside the pig-pen. And they took two small earthen pillars instead, and they went and showed them to their husband. Then, I entered the pig-pen; and I took these children out; and brought them to my mother. So, these children grew up. And they began hunting. You, my father, you remember when I brought you the wild meat, and you were about to give to these women; but, I went and took away the food. The reason is, because they are the ones who tried to kill the children. I brought them up from childhood to be men as now. So, this caused me to bring this case before the presence of all people; for, I say that those two women were murderesses. So, then, my father, these are your children; but, if you retain those women, these two twins shall not be your sons."

Upon this, the father of Mbwa said, "Catch ye both of the women!" And they were bound in that self-same hour. (They had supposed that the twins had died when they had struck them in the hamlet of Mbwa's mother.) They could not deny. In their anger, as they were led away, they called out to Mbwa, "Mbwa-O!" He assented, "Eh? What is it?" They replied in anger, for having informed on them. And they laid a curse on him, saying, "You will never speak again with the voice of a human being. You shall be a dumb beast."

But, the people took them, to be thrown into the depth of the sea.

TALE 23
THE SAVIOR OF THE ANIMALS

Persons

Njambo and Wife and Son Utigebodi	Nyati (Ox)
Ngwayi (Partridge)	Kudu (Tortoise)
The Prophet Njambi	Njâ (Leopard)
Yungu (Eagle)	Ngomba (Porcupine)
Etoli (Rat)	Inâni (Bird)
Njâku (Elephant)	

NOTE

This story plays on the meaning of the name U-tige-bode. It is an ancient word, not now used, meaning, "He-Who-Saves-People." In the Son's given name; his saving of the unworthy, in response to their appeals for mercy; his bearing of his father's wrath; his punishment on a tree; the derision of the very passers by, for whom he was to die, I think the legend echoes, even though faintly, the story of the Christ.

Njambo married two women. He begot twenty-three children. And they all died. Also one of the wives died. There were left only himself, and one wife.

The woman was old, and the man also was old. But, the woman was again to become a mother; and, at the proper time, she bore a child. The child was a male. The woman called the

245

husband, saying, "Come! and give your boy a name." The husband said, "The name of the child is Utigebode."

After this, the child grew to be a large man. One day, he said to his father, "Paia! I'm going to set snares in the forest." The father replied, "Yes! go! and catch me food!" He went. And he returned that morning. In the afternoon, he went back to examine the snares. And he found that two Partridges were caught. He exclaimed, "I'm very glad! My father shall eat one today, and the other shall be kept for tomorrow." Then the Partridges asked him, "What is your name?" He answered, "One-Who-Saves-People." Then the Partridges said, "If that is so, why are you about to kill us?"

On another day, in the morning, he went again to examine his snares. And he found two Antelope (Tragelephas). He was glad; and he said, "I feel very good! My father shall eat one; and the other can be cooked for another day." The Antelopes asked him, "What's your name?" He answered, "One-Who-Saves-People." Again, they asked, "Why then are you about to kill us?" He replied, "That's so! Well! go!" And he returned to town.

That afternoon he went out again, and found two Gazelles. And he said, "I'll take these two to town at once; and my father shall eat one today, and the other tomorrow." But the Gazelles said, "No!—you are the One-Who-Saves-People! Why then should you kill us?" So he loosed them, and let them go.

He did the same way to two Elephants. And with two Oxen. At another time he found two Tortoises. And the Tortoises spoke to him as had done the others. And on another day, he found two Leopards. And, he released the Leopards, in the same way. At another time, two Porcupines, in the same way.

One after another, almost all the Beasts were thus trapped and released. There was not one beast brought by Utigebode to his village; he freed them all.

So, his father said to him, "My child! since you have set your snares, I have not seen you bring in a single beast, even an Etoli. What are you doing? I shall change your name. For, now that I am old, it is right for you to save me, and help me with food."

Utigebode replied evasively, "Since I set the snares, I have not caught even a Inâni." The father said, "Well! if it is true that you have not killed any Beast or Bird, I will know tomorrow."

The next day broke; and the father went to the village of Prophet Njambi. The Prophet saluted him, "What have you come for?" Njambo replied, "I come to you for you to tell me about my son, whether in his hunting he kills beasts, or whether he does not." Njambi answered, "He snares them constantly; but, because of the name you gave him, he saves the lives of the people of the tribes of Beasts."

The prophet added, "If there be a doubt, I will show you a way to prove my words. When you go back to town you will meet Ih⬚li at the end of the village. When you meet with him, call for the people to set nets to catch him. But, yourself shall stand and watch what the Beast does before your eyes."

Njambo arose to go, and bade goodbye, saying, "This is my return journey to my village."

And it was so that, on nearing the end of the village, he met with Gazelle. Njambo shouted, "Men! spread your nets! Here is a Beast! Let us catch it!" His men brought their nets, and began to surround Gazelle. And the son Utigebode came to assist. The men were shouting, "Hâ-hâ! Hâ-hâ!" to frighten the animal towards the nets. Gazelle looked forward, watching Utigebode closely; and it said to itself, "If I go toward the nets, I shall be caught; but, I will go toward Utigebode and shall be saved."

So, Gazelle ran toward Utigebode, and he caught it as if to kill it. But Gazelle cried out, "Eh! Utigebode! *you*, the savior, will you be the one to kill me?" So, Utigebode said, "Pass on! for, it is true that I am The-One-Who-Saves." And Gazelle fled to the forest.

Then Njambo was very angry, and said to Utigebode, "Ah! my child! I have found you in your falsehood! Was it not you who said you caught no Beast? So! you have been releasing them!"

Then the company all went back to their village with their nets. They arrived there during the daytime. And the father ordered his son, "Go! climb that coco tree, and bring me a nut." The son began to climb the tree. But, as he climbed, the father, by Magic-Power, caused the tree to grow rapidly upward. When, finally, Utigebode reached the top, he was unable to come down the excessively long tree-trunk. He began to call to his father for help, "My father!" But the father was still very angry, and replied, "Call your friends, the Beasts and Birds, to save you. I will not help you." And Njambo went to sit down in his village, leaving his son in the treetop.

The son saw Eagle passing, and he called to it, "Yungu! Help me!" Eagle replied, "I am not able to carry a Man; you are heavy;" so, Eagle passed on. Utigebode saw many Beasts one after another passing below, and he called to them, "Save me!" But, they said, "We have no wings with which to go up to you. How can we get you down? We are not Birds that could let you down. We Beasts are unable to help you. Do not expect us."

He was left there in the tree-top a period of two weeks, living only on the coconuts; and then he died, and his body fell to the earth. Njambo came out to see the corpse, and he said to it, "You have died through lack of obedience. You disobeyed me; and your beasts did not help you."

The father and the mother lived another year in their village; and then they died, because they had no children to help them with food or clothes. And the people came from other villages to bury them.

TALE 24

ORIGINS OF THE IVORY TRADE (1ST VERSION)

Persons

King Ukanakâdi, and His Son   Njâku (Elephant); An Ox
Lombolokindi, and His Mother,   (A Metamorphosed Man)
With Birds and Other Animals   A Foreign Vessel, and
Tombeseki (A Magic-Spear); An   Traders
Old Woman

Ukanakâdi lived in his great house, having with him his many wives. One of them bore him a son whom he named Lombolo-kindi.

As time passed on, the child grew in size, and strength, and skill. Because of this, his mother was treated by Ukanakâdi with special favor. This aroused the jealousy of one of the other wives. She took the child one day, and secretly gave him a certain evil medicine, which caused him to be constantly hungry, hungry, hungry. Even when he ate enormously, no amount of food could fill his stomach or satisfy his appetite.

Ukanakâdi finally was angry at the child, and said to the mother, "All the food of my plantations is finished, eaten up by your child. We have no more plantains, no more cassava, no more eddoes, nor anything else in our plantations or in our kitchen-gardens. You have brought a curse upon us! Go away to your father's house!" (He said this, not knowing that a Fetish-Medicine had caused all the trouble.)

So the mother went away with her child to her father's house. But there too, the boy ate up all the food of the gardens, until there was none left. Then her father said to her, "All my food is done here; go with your child to your grandfather, and find food there."

So, she went to her grandfather's. But there the same trouble followed.

After she had been there some time, and the child was now a stout lad, and she saw that they were no longer welcome, she said to herself, "Alas! it is so! All my people are weary of me! I will not longer stay at grandfather's. I will go wandering into the forest, and, with the child, will see what I can get."

Taking with her only two ears of corn, she went far off with the lad into the forest. After much wandering, and eating only wild fruits, she selected a spot without having any idea of the locality, and built a shed for a camp in which to stay. At this place, she planted the corn. It quickly sprang up, and bore abundantly. And she planted other gardens. After a time came very many birds; and they began to eat up the corn. She exclaimed, "My son and I alone have come here, and have planted our corn. How is this that all the birds have come so soon to destroy it?" And the son, who by this time had grown to be almost a young man, said to her, "Mother, why do you allow the birds to eat? Why don't you do something?" She replied, "Why do the birds thus destroy the corn? What can I do?" So he came out of the shed into the yard in front of their house and shouted at the birds, "You birds! who have come here to spoil my corn, with this stick I will kill you all!" But the birds jeered at him, saying, "No! not all! Only one shall die!"

The young man went into the house, took up a magic spear-head he owned, fitted it onto a stick as a shaft; and going out again, he hurled it at the birds. The spear flew at them, pursuing each one, and piercing every one of them in succession. Then it flew on and on, away out into the forest.

The young man took up another medicine-charm that he had with him, and, calling to his spear by name, shouted after it, "Tombeseki-o-o! Come back, back, back, Here! again, again, again, Return!" The spear heard him, and obeyed, and came back. He laid hold of it, and put it again in the shed. So, he and his mother lived there. She planted a very large garden of plantains, cassava, and many other vegetables, a very large quantity. And her gardens grew, and bore fruit in plenty.

Then there came all kinds of small Animals, hogs, and antelopes, and gazelles, very many; and they spoiled the gardens, eating the fruit, and breaking down the stalks. The mother exclaimed, "My son! the animals have finished all my food of the gardens; everything is lost! Why is this?" He replied, "Yes, it is so! And when they come again tomorrow, I know what I will do to them!"

When they came the next day, he went into the house, took the spear, flung it; and it flew from beast to beast, piercing all of them in succession. Then it went off, flying into the forest, as before. He called after it to return. The Spear heard, and obeyed, and came back to the house.

Then he and his mother sat down in the house, complaining of their hunger, and how the animals had spoiled their gardens. So the mother went out, and gathered up what little remained, brought it into the house, and cooked it, leaves and all.

When the mother had planted a third garden, and it had grown, a herd of elephants came to destroy it. She cried out, "Ah!

Njâku! what shall I do? You have come to destroy all my gardens! Shall I die with hunger?" The son brought out his Spear, and shouting at the elephants, threatened to kill them all. But the herd laughed and said, "When you throw that spear, only one of us shall fall." He threw the spear at the one that spoke. It struck him and all the elephants in succession; and they all died. The Spear kept on in its flight into the forest. The young man cried after it, "Spear! Spear! come back, come back!" And it came to him again.

Each time that the Spear had thus gone through the forest, it had mowed down the trees in its path; and thus was made the clearing which the mother had at once utilized for the planting of her successive gardens.

After the elephants, mother and son sat down again in their hunger; they had nothing to eat but leaves. These she cooked; and they ate them all at once.

Then she planted another garden, thinking that now there were no more beasts who would come to ravage. But she did not know that there was still left in the forest one very, very large Elephant that had not been in the company of the herd that the son had killed.

There was also, in that forest, one very, very large Ox. When the gardens had grown, that Ox came, and began to destroy. The young man hurled his Spear at the Ox. It was wounded, but did not fall; and it went away into the forest with the spear sticking in its side. The young man pursued the Ox, following, following, following far away. But he did not overtake it.

On his way, he reached unexpectedly a small, lonely hut, where an Old Woman was living by herself. When she saw him, she said to him, "Do not follow any longer. That Ox was a person like yourself. He is dead; and his people have hung up that Spear in their house."

The young man told the old woman that he was very hungry. So she cut down for him an entire bunch of plantains. He was so exceedingly hungry that he could not wait; and before the plantains were entirely cooked, he began to eat of them, and ate them all. The old woman exclaimed, "What sort of a person is this who eats in this way?" In her wisdom, thinking over the matter, she felt sure it was some disease that caused his voracity.

The man, being tired with his journey, fell asleep; and she, by her magic power, caused him to hear or feel nothing. While he was in this state, she cut him open. As she did so, his disease rushed out with a whizzing sound; and she cut away, and removed a tumor, that looked like a stone of glass. That was the thing that had caused his excessive hunger all his life. By her Power, she closed the wound.

When he awoke, she cooked food for him, of which he ate, and was satisfied with an ordinary amount like any other person. She then told him what she had done, and said, "As you are now cured, you may pursue that Ox. You will reach his town, and you will obtain your Spear. But, as you go there, you must make a pretense. You must pretend that you are mourning for the dead. You must cry out in wailing, 'Who killed my Uncle-o-o! who killed my Uncle-o-o!'" Thus he went on his way; and finally came to a town where was a crowd of people gathered in and about a house of mourning. Beginning to wail, he went among the mourners. They received him, with the idea that he was some distant relative who had come to attend the funeral. He walked up the street of this town of the Ox-Man, and entering into the house of mourning, said, "Had not the way been so long, my mother also would have come; but, I have come to look at that Thing that killed my Uncle." They welcomed him, commended his devotion, and said, "You will not go today. Stay with us. Sleep here tonight; and tomorrow you shall see and take away with you, to show to your mother, that Thing."

So, the next day, they gave him the Spear, and said, "Go, but do not delay. Return for the closing ceremony (the "Washing") of the mourning." He went away, and came again to the Old Woman. She said to him, when he showed her the Spear, "I told you truly that you would obtain it. But, go with it and this bundle I have made of the tumor of your disease, and show them to your mother."

So he came back to his mother. She rejoiced; and, not knowing that he was cured, she cooked a very large and unusually varied quantity of food, for his unusual hunger, two whole bunches of plantains, and eddoes, and potatoes, and yams, etc. Of this he ate only a little, sufficient for an ordinary hunger. As he had not yet told her of his being cured, she cried out in surprise, "What is this? My son will die, for not eating!" And she asked him, "What is the matter?" He replied, "No, I have eaten, and am satisfied. And, mother, this bundle is what I was cured of." Then he told her of what that old woman had done.

On another day, that great Elephant that had remained in the forest, came and began to eat in the garden. The son said, "Mother! what shall I do? I thought I had killed all the elephants. I did not know there was this great big one left!" (Nor did he just then know there were left a very great many more.)

Taking his Spear, he hurled it, and wounded the elephant. It did not fall, but went away with the Spear in its side. The man followed, followed, followed, pursuing the elephant, not, as the other animals had gone, into the forest, but away toward the sea; and it died on the sea beach. There the man found it and his Spear.

The Sea was new to him; he had not seen it since his childhood. He climbed up on the elephant's body, in order to see all around. As he turned his eyes seaward, he saw a ship coming on the horizon. Also, the people on this ship were looking landward, and they said, "There is something standing on the shore like a person. Let the vessel go there, and see what is ashore."

So, the ship anchored, and a surf-boat was launched into the water to go ashore. When the crew landed, they saw the carcass of the elephant, and a person standing with a spear who warned them, "Do not approach near to me!" But they replied, "We do not want you, nor will we hurt you. But we want these tusks of ivory of this elephant. We want elephants." Wondering at this wish, he cut out the tusks, and gave them to the strangers, adding, "Off in the Forest are very, very many more tusks, more than I can number. You seem to like them; but they are of no use to me." They earnestly said, "But, bring them, bring them! We will buy them of you with abundance of goods." He agreed, and promised, "I am going now; but, let your ship wait, and I will bring all of those things as many as it is possible for me to carry."

So, he went back to his mother; and he and she carried many, many tusks. They filled the ship full; and the crew of the ship sent ashore an immense quantity of goods. When the vessel went away, it left ashore two carpenters, with direction to build a fine house, and have it completed before the vessel should come again.

The man remained there awhile with the carpenters, after the ship had gone.

One day, looking, on a journey down the coast, at a point of land, he was surprised to recognize his father's town, where he and his mother had lived in his childhood. He said to himself, "That's my father's town! I want them to come to me, and live at my town!" He sent word to them; they removed, and all of them came to live with him. And he married one of their young women. (In the meanwhile, he had brought his mother from the forest.)

While he was living at his new home, one day looking seaward, he saw the promised ship coming to get more ivory, and to give more goods. And he went off to the vessel.

Among the women who were still living of his father's people who had known him as a child, was the one who had given him the evil "medicine" long ago; her object in giving it having been to kill him. After he had gone off to the vessel, this woman came to his wife's home, and, seeing the Spear hanging tied from the roof, said, "What is that Thing tied there?" His wife replied, "It is a kind of "medicine" of my husband's. It must not be touched." But the woman said, "I know that Thing; and what it does." Then she seized it, and put into it its handle the man had removed. She hurled the Spear out to sea, and it went on and on, passing over the ship. The man sitting in the saloon, said to the crew, as he recognized the Spear in its flight, "I saw something pass over the ship!" He went up on deck, and called after it, "My Spear! come back! come! come! come back!" And he told all the people of the vessel to go below lest they should be injured. The Spear turned and came back to him; and he took possession of it. Then said he to the crew, "Come! escort me ashore!" They landed him ashore, and waited to see what he intended doing.

He called all his father's family, and asked, "Why is it that you have tried to kill me today with this Spear! For this, I will this day kill all of you." He summoned all the people to come together. When they had come, he had his mother bring out that tumor bundle, and said, "This is the thing of long ago with which that woman (pointing to the one who in childhood had given him the evil disease) tried to injure me. And, for the same reason, she threw the Spear today; thus trying a second time to kill me. None of you have rebuked her. So, I shall kill you all as her associates."

Though they were of his father's family, he attacked and killed them all. The whole town died that day, excepting himself, his wife, his mother, and his sister. These four, not liking to remain at that evil place, went off and took passage on the ship.

So, he journeyed, and came to the country of the white people at Manga-Manↄne; and never returned to Africa. But, he kept up a trade in Ivory with his native country. But for him, that trade would not have been begun. For, besides his having brought the first elephant to the sea coast, he told the people of Manga-Manↄne beyond the Great Sea, about the tribes of people, and about the elephants that were so abundant, in Africa. And that is all.

ORIGIN OF THE IVORY TRADE (2ND VERSION)

Persons

King Njambu, and His Four Wives

Ngwe-Konde (Mother-of-Queens)

Ngwᴇ-Legᴇ (Mother-of-Poverty)

Ivenga (Watching); Ngwe-Sape (Mother of a Lock)

Njambu's Son, Savulaka (Gluttony)

The Spirit of an Uncle; Mekuku (Spirits of the Dead)

A Magic Spear; A Great Elephant (A Metamorphosed Man)

Birds, and Other Beasts

Njambu built a town; and married four women. This one, Ngwe-Konde, that one Ngwᴇ-Legᴇ, another one Ivenga, another Ngwe-Sape.

After Njambu had lived there a short time all his wives were about to become mothers. Then Ngwe-konde took a net, and (by Magic Art) threw it into the womb of Ngwe-lᴇge. The net entered the belly of her child.

At the time of their confinement, they all gave birth. The infants were washed. They were dressed also, and were given suck. Also, they were assigned their names. That of Ngwe-lᴇgᴇ's was Savulaka. When he was given the breast, he was not satisfied, he was only crying and crying; for, whoever held him, there were only cries and cries. When his mother would nurse him, there was only crying. His father said, "If it is like this, then, lest he die, feed him the food of adults."

His mother cut down a plantain bunch; she boiled it; it was cooked. The child ate, and finished the plantains; and yet it was crying and crying. They cut down another bunch; it was boiled, it was cooked. At only one eating, he finished the food, with cries in his mouth. Two more bunches were boiled; he ate. All at once, though born only that day, he spoke, "My mother! Hunger!" Four bunches were cut down; they were cooked; he ate, and finished them, but with crying.

Then he was cooked for ten times; he ate; and at once finished. The people cooked, and he ate. The plantains of his father's town were all cleared off, the entire town was left like a prairie. The father spoke to the mother, and said, "No! go away with him to your father's town."

Ngwe-l⊠g⊠ picked up her child, carrying him away. She with the child went on, to the town of her father.

Her father asked her, "My child! wherefore the crying, and your carrying the infant?" She replied, "My father! I know not! This one whom you see, since he was born, is not filled. He has made an end to all the plantains of his father's town, leaving the town a prairie. And his father said to me, 'Just go and take him to your father's.' So, I have brought him."

The towns-people all were laughing, "Ky⊠! ky⊠! ky⊠!" They said, "What? Really, food? No! it's something else, not food. But, enter into the house." She says, "You are talking foolishly." The child began to cry. They said, "Let us see!"

Then, at once, they began to cook; the food is ready; he eats; and finishes it. Other food was placed; he ate it at once. Food was cooked again. At once, all of it, and the dishes, and the jars, and the plates, were swallowed up by him. Food is cooked again, and he ate; and then said, "My mother! Hunger!" Food is cooked again; he ate until he finished all the pots. All the food of the town, and all the gardens were done.

Her father spoke to her saying, "My child! Just carry him to the town of your grandfather."

She then carried the child, still crying with hunger, and made her journey, and came to her grandfather's town.

The people there said, "What is it; for the crying?" She told all the whole affair to them. They inquired, "Food?" She replied, "Yes." They cooked, and he ate, and finished. They cooked again; and he finished all, even to the leaves in which the food was wrapped. They said, "Such a kind of child has never been born before!"

Suddenly, the child Savulaka ceased to be a child; and, as a man, said to his mother, "My mother! Wash me some mekima (rolls of mashed boiled plantains)." So, his mother made the mekima.

In the morning, very early, Savulaka starts on a journey. He went stepping very quickly, on, still with his journey; and, as he went, he talked to himself. He said, "This thing which has been done to me, now, what is it?" He still went on with the journey, until, at night, he lay down in the forest. Early in the morning, he starts again for his journey. As he was going in the forest he met with a Person (a brother of his mother, who belonged to a town of the Mekuku). This Person inquired, "Where are you going to?" (Savulaka was still eating the mekima, even its leaves going into his mouth.) This Person also said to him, "Stop at once!" Then he stood still.

The Person said, "I, your Uncle, the brother of your mother, am the one who is inquiring of you." Savulaka answered him, saying, "I'm not able to tell you." But presently he did tell all the matter to him. So, the Uncle said to him, "Come, to my town."

Then both of them returned on the path. In a moment, in the twinkling of an eye, they are at the town. The Uncle said, "My child, you are cured!" He put for him a medicine in a syringe, and gave him an injection. When he withdrew the syringe, here, at once, a net began to come out quick as ever it could move from the bowels! Then his Uncle spoke and told him, "It is thy father's wife who put the net into your bowels."

Food was cooked for him; he began to eat a little as people usually eat. His Uncle said unto him, "You shall go tomorrow."

On the morrow, early in the morning, his Uncle took all kinds and sorts of vegetables; and he took also a Spear; and malagetta pepper ("Guinea-grains," a species of cardomom), and handed them to him; and told him, "When you reach home, you must plant a garden."

The Uncle said to him, "Close your eyes!" He closed his eyes tight. On opening his eyes, he at once found himself near his home, and his mother on the path, her form bent stooping down seeking for him. He then entered their house, and sat down, and his mother greeted him to her satisfaction.

The mother took food, and boiled it; it was cooked; she removed it from the fire; she sat the food before Savulaka. And he ate only two fingers of plantains. His mother began to wonder.

Then he said to himself, "Now, let me try to do as my Uncle

has told me." He said, "Ngalo! (a fetish charm) I want this forest here to be cleared, all of it." (As quickly as I speak here, at once the garden was finished, like the passing of yesterday.) He said to his mother, "Take a list of all the plants I have brought; then let us go and plant them." So, he and his mother went to plant; that very day the garden was completely finished.

Previously to that, his Uncle had warned him, "When the plants are sprung up, you will see Kⵝnⵝnⵝ (a kind of small bird) coming to eat them. When they shall arrive, they will be many. Then you take the Spear; fail not to use the cardomoms with it."

The food increased; and the small birds came in countless numbers. Savulaka took up the Spear, and threw it at them; and all, even to the young birds, perished. Then he returned to his mother, and said, "My mother! go and pick up the sⵝⵝ" (another name of kⵝnⵝnⵝ). She gathered them; leaving many remaining abandoned in the forest. The village was filled with the sⵝⵝ.

The same thing happened with all other kinds of birds. The same with every Beast.

Then Elephants came to the garden. The man picked up the Spear and the cardomoms. When he came to the garden, he lifted up the Spear, and threw it, and wounded the Elephants. Numbers of Elephants that were eating in the garden, were killed. They were gathered, and the whole village was filled with the smell of the rotting meat; so that hardly any one would come to the village. I am not able to tell you the abundance of tusks; the mendanda (long ones), and the makubu (short thick ones), and the begⵝgⵝ ("scrivillers," the small ones), that cannot be counted.

The next morning, other elephants came again. The man took up the Spear, but he forgot the cardomom-pepper. When he arrived where they were, he did not wait, but hastily threw the

Spear after an elephant, the leader of the herd, who turned aside, and ran away with the Spear in its body. The man followed him, but he did not reach him. Then he returned to his mother; and said to her, "My mother! mash me some mekima." (Food for a journey.)

In the next morning, the man started on the journey, stepping quickly as ever, until he came to his Uncle's town. He was about to pass his Uncle by, not seeing him (a Spirit). The Uncle said to him, "Stand there!" So he stood. The Uncle directed, "Enter the house!" He entered, and sat down; and his Uncle said to him, "Did I not tell you that when you are going to kill an animal, you must not omit the pepper-grains? Sit down there; wait. Don't you go out. I must go and take for you your Spear."

But, lo! it was the Chief of that very town, whom he had wounded, and who had come back to the town, and died. (That chief had metamorphosed himself into the form of an elephant.) The uncle passed out, and went to the other end of the town; and there he found the Spear. He took it, and gave it to Savulaka, and said, "Go!" Savulaka went; and met his mother on the way, waiting for him. Then they went home to their village.

Next morning, he fastened the Spear handle. Elephants in the plantation shouted, "We have come!" The man stood up, and snatched his Spear. The Elephants stood waiting. The man said, "Here it is!" and flung it at them. And the carcasses of all fell in a heap. He said to the people of the village, "Go ye!" They went, and found dead bodies without number; the tusks the same, without number.

After that, White-Man came with a quantity of goods. The Town of Savulaka was crowded with goods in abundance; every kind of foreign article. White men came to see Ivory. The sailing-vessels and steamers came any day (not only on scheduled dates).

Thus it was that Ivory was exported, and goods imported. Business of Trading was made. Savulaka had a great many traders. All his father's brothers, and mother's brothers, all their dwelling was in the town of Savulaka. Rum was drunk constantly, and they were constantly intoxicated. Ivory went to White Man's Land. White men's things came, and were sent up to the Interior.

This Trade is going on to the present days. It was a man who commenced with the thought of Trading; it was commenced by that one man. All the African tribes are now changed from what they were originally.

At first we negroes had no (proper) knowledge. They spoke with wonder over the things that are made in Europe by white men. They said, "These are made by the Spirits of the dead; they are not made by the living." Because our people believed that the departed spirits have their home beyond the Sea. Why? Because Savulaka brought his wonderful Spear (by which so much ivory was obtained) from the Spirit-Town.

TALE 25
DOG AND HIS FALSE FRIEND LEOPARD

Persons

Mbwa (Dog)   Njâ (Leopard)

Ngiya (Gorilla)

NOTE

The origin of the hatred between dogs and leopards. Friends should not have arguments. An argument separates a company.

Dog and Leopard built a town. Dog then begot very many children. Leopard begot his many also. They had one table together. They conversed, they hunted, they ate, they drank.

One day, they were arguing: Leopard said, "If I hide myself, you are not able to see me." Dog replied, "There is no place in which you can hide where I cannot see you."

The next day, at the break of the day, Leopard emerged from his house at Batanga, and he went north as far as from there to Bahabane near Plantation. Dog, in the next morning, emerged. He asked, "Where is chum Njâ?" The women and children answered, "We do not know." Dog also started, and went: and as he went, smelling, until he arrived at Plantation (about 15 miles). He came and stood under the tree up which Leopard was hidden; and he said, "Is not this you?"

Both of them returned, and came to their town. Food had been prepared; and they ate. Leopard said, "Chum! you will not see me here tomorrow." When the next day began to break, Leopard started southward, as far as to Lolabe (about 15 miles). Next day, in the morning, Dog stood out in the street, lifted up his nose, and smelled. He also went down southward, clear on till he came to Lolabe; and standing at the foot of a tree, he said, "Is not this you?"

Leopard came down from the top of the tree; they stood; and then they returned to their town. Food was cooked for them; they ate, and finished.

Leopard said, "Chum! you will not see me tomorrow again, no matter what may take place." Dog asked, "True?" Leopard replied, "Yes!"

In the morning, Leopard started southward, for a distance like from Batanga to Campo River (about 40 miles).

At the opening of the next day, Dog emerged, and, standing and smelling, he said, looking toward the south, "He went this way." Dog also went to Campo. He reached Leopard, and said, "Is not this you?"

They came back to their town; they were made food; and they ate.

The next day, Leopard emerged early. He went northward, as far as from Batanga to Lokonje (about 40 miles). Dog sniffed the air, and followed north also. In a steady race, he was soon there; and he reached Leopard. So, Leopard said, "It is useless, I will not attempt to hide myself again from Mbwa."

Thereupon, Dog spoke to Leopard and said, "It is I, whom, if I hide myself from you, you will not see." Leopard replied, "What! even if you were able to find me, how much more should I be able to find you!" So, Dog said to him, "Wait, till daybreak."

When the next day broke, Dog passed from his house like a flash unseen, vyu! to Leopard's. And, underneath the bed of Leopard in his public Reception-house, he lay down. Then Leopard (who had not seen him) came to the house of Dog; he asked the women, "Where is Mbwa?" They said, "Thy friend, long ago, has gone out hence, very early." Leopard returned to his house, and he said to his children, "That fellow! if I catch him! I do not know what I shall do to him!"

He started southward on the journey, as far as Lolabe; and did not see Dog. So he returned northward a few miles, as far as Boje, and did not see him. Down again south to Campo; and he did not see him. That first day, he did not find him at all. Then he returned toward Batanga, and went eastward to Nkâmakâk (about 60 miles); and he did not see him. He went on northward to Ebaluwa (about 60 miles); did not see him. Up north-west to Lokonje; he did not see him. And Leopard, wearied, went back to his town.

Coming to the bed (not knowing Dog was there) he lay down very tired. He said to his people, "If I had met him today, then you would be eating a good meat now." All these words were said in the ears of Dog, the while that Dog was underneath the bed.

Then Dog leaped out, pwa! Leopard asked, "Where have you been?" Dog answered, "I saw you when you first passed out." Leopard said, "True?" And Dog says, "Yes!"

Then Dog went out far to his end of the town. And, knowing that Leopard intended evil toward him, he said to his children,

"Let us go and dig a pit." So they went and dug a pit in the middle of the road.

Then Dog told his wives and children, "Go ye before, at once!" He also said, "I and this little Mbwa, which can run so fast, we shall remain behind." Then the others went on in advance.

(Before that, Leopard, observing some movements of the Mbwa family, had been speaking to himself, "I do not know the place where Mbwa and his children will go today.")

Dog warned this young one, "When you are pursued, you must jump clear across that pit."

Then Dog, to cover the retreat of his family, came alone to Leopard's end of the town. He and his children chased after him. Dog ran away rapidly, and escaped.

When Leopard's company arrived at the house of Dog, they found there only that little dog. So they said, "Come ye! for there is no other choice than that we catch and eat this little thing."

Thereupon, Leopard chased after the little dog; but it leaped away rapidly, and Leopard after him. When the little Dog was near the pit, it made a jump. (Leopard did not know of the pit, nor why the Dog jumped.) When Leopard was come to the pit, he fell inside, tumbling, volom!

His enemy Gorilla was following after Leopard, also in pursuit of Dog. He also fell into the pit, headlong, volom! Finding Leopard there, Gorilla said, "What is this?" Leopard stood at one side, and Gorilla at the other. When the one would be about to go near the other, if the other attempted to go near him, he would begin to growl, saying, "You must not approach here!"

Dog, standing at the edge above, was laughing at them, saying, "Fight ye your own fight! Did you want only me?"

But Leopard and Gorilla were not fighting in the pit. If the one approached, the other retreated.

Dog spoke to them and said in derision. "I have no strength; but as to your fight, was it seeking only me?"

A TRICK FOR VENGEANCE

Persons
Kudu (Tortoise)   Njâ (Leopard)
Ko (Wild-Rat)

NOTE

Because of deaths and sicknesses, African natives are constantly changing the location of their villages, believing the old sites infested by malevolent Spirits.

The whole mass of Beasts were living in one place. They built houses; they cleared the forest for plantations.

After this, Tortoise said, "I'm going to find my own place." So, he went and built in a place which he called Mal⊠nd⊠-ma-Kudu. The fame of it was spread abroad, people talking about "Mal⊠nd⊠-ma-Kudu." Leopard arose, came to the town of Tortoise, and said, "I have come to build here." Tortoise consented, "You may build." Leopard said, "I'm going to build at the end of the path, and by the spring." And he built there.

One day, a child of Tortoise was passing by near the spring; and Leopard seized him, ku!

Another day, another one was passing; Leopard seized him, also, ku!

Then Tortoise said, "This is an evil place, I'm going to move from here." So he went and built another town called Jamba. Leopard came also, saying, "Kudu! I'm coming to build!" Then Tortoise said, "Really! what have your affairs to do with me? Nevertheless, come and build." And Leopard built at the end, by the spring.

When the children of Tortoise were passing by the spring, Leopard constantly killed them.

Tortoise wondered, "This thing which is destroying my children, what is it?"

Thus day by day, Leopard was killing the children of Tortoise.

Tortoise prepared again to remove, saying that he would go away and build another town to be called Dang. He went there. And the fame of it was spread around, people saying, "Dang, the town of Kudu!" Everybody was saying, "We are going to the town of Kudu; Dang, the town of Kudu!"

Leopard comes again, and says, "I also have come to build here." Tortoise said to him, "Wait! really; why did you leave the other people?" However, Tortoise said to him, "Build." And Leopard built as usual. Also, when the children of Tortoise were passing to the spring, they were missing. And Tortoise felt sure that Leopard had seized them.

Thereupon Tortoise made a plan for himself. He called Wild-Rat privately, saying, "I have heard that you know how to dig holes." Wild-Rat replied, "It is my work." Tortoise said, "But, I want you to dig me a tunnel from this room here, out to, and up towards the street, by measure." So, Wild-Rat dug a big hole, in size sufficient for Tortoise and his traveling-bag and his spears.

Then Tortoise went and gathered together his spears and his

traveling-bag. He went out the next day, early in the morning, and stood and announced in the street, "All the Tribes must come! I want to tell them the news of what I have seen."

Then all the Beasts came to meet in the town of Tortoise. It was full of every kind of beast. Tortoise spoke, and said, "I have called you to say, that really we are not worth anything at all. Actually, the only dwelling we have is in the grave. All those my children who have died here, is it possible that it is my Father (of Spirits) who takes them? I met them sitting down in the Reception-House of that father, playing." The people said to him, "This is a Dream." He replied, "No! it is open to sight." Some said, "It is a lie." But Tortoise said, "You have doubted me? Well, tomorrow you must dig me a grave; and you shall see how I am going." They said, "Yes! let us see!"

On the next day, in the morning, they were called together. He said, "Dig me a pit here." (He pointed to the privately measured spot over the tunnel which Wild-Rat had already made for him.) They dug it wide and deeply. Then, this Tortoise took his spears and his bag; and with these under his arm, he descended into the pit, and bade the people fill in the earth. He went to one side, until he reached and entered that tunnel of his which Wild-Rat had dug for him. And unseen he passed up to his room in his house, and lay down. Before that, he had promised the people, saying, "I shall lie there (in the pit) for six days."

Before Tortoise had disappeared, the people (following his orders) began to throw back the earth into the pit, filling it solidly.

After Tortoise had laid in his house for six days, he suddenly appeared in the street; and he called all the mass of the Beasts, and he told them the news. He said, "Over there is so beautiful! I will not stay in this town any more for as long as ten days. But, as I am here, I shall lie here only for three days, and two days over there." At once Tortoise was regarded as a person of great importance, and his fame was spread abroad.

Thereupon, Leopard, (feeling jealous of the wonderful experience of Tortoise) said to his children, "Even Kudu! How much rather that I should get to that beautiful place! Dig me mine own pit. I also am going to see my forefathers. I and they, we have not seen each other for a long time." So, they dug a big pit. He announced, "I will lie there for seven days; on the eighth, then I shall come."

Then he descended into the pit. And they rapidly filled it up with earth. Leopard, below, sought a cavity by which to pass on (as he thought) to the Land of Spirits; but, there was none. And he died.

His children waited eight days; but they saw not their father. Then they asked Tortoise, "As to our father, up to this day, what has happened to him?" Tortoise answered them, "Why are you asking me this? When I went, what did my family ask of you? Maybe, your father remained to follow the pleasures of over there!"

The women of Leopard had kept him some food, making it ready for him for the eighth day. But (giving up hope of him) they ate it. While they were still waiting, actually Leopard had begun to rot there (in the pit).

Tortoise, fearing possible difficulty, gathered together his wives and remaining children, and fled with them into the forest afar off.

TALE 27
NOT MY FAULT!

Persons

Yongolokodi (Chameleon)   Men, Hunters

Ko (Wild Rat)

Chameleon and all the other Beasts built their villages near together, making a large town. And there was a time of great hunger. After that, there came a harvest time of large fruitage. The great produce could not be gathered for abundance.

Then came Chameleon to the village of Wild-Rat, and he said to him, "Chum, Ko! this harvest is a great thing!" Rat said, "Don't speak about it!"

Not long afterward, Mankind laid their snares, and the hunters prepared their bows. For, beasts and birds had come in crowds to eat of the abundance; and Man had overhead them speaking of it. Gunners came; the shots resounded; bows were twanged; the snares caught.

Rat fell into one of the traps. Chameleon seeing him, and desiring to justify himself, reminded Rat that Rat himself had told him not to let others know of the great abundance, and that he himself had obeyed; that therefore he was not the cause of Rat's misfortune. So, Chameleon said, "*I* did not speak of it."

DO NOT IMPOSE ON THE WEAK

Persons
Yongolokodi (Chameleon)   Njâ (Leopard)

NOTE

Chameleons move very slowly. This story is given as a reason why, even if one is small in body, he should not be despised, as though he had no strength, or as though he could with impunity be deprived of his rights, *e.g.*, in a race or in wrestling, or in any other circumstances.

Leopard and Chameleon lived apart. This one had his village, and that one his. This one did his own business; that one his. And they were resting quietly in their abodes.

Chameleon had a herd of sheep and of goats.

Leopard came to the village of Chameleon on an excursion; and he saw the herd of sheep and of goats. He said to Chameleon, "Chum! give me a loan of sheep to raise on shares." Chameleon made food for him; and, when they had eaten, he said to Leopard, "You can send children tomorrow, to come and take the loan of sheep on shares." They had their conversation, talking, and talking. When they had ended, Leopard said, "My Fellow! I'm going back." His friend said to him, "Very good."

Leopard went on to his village. He said, "My wife! I came on an excursion, to the town of Yongolokodi. He treated me with hospitality to the very greatest degree. Also he has given me sheep on shares."

The next day, in the morning, he sent his children to the town of Chameleon to take the herd of sheep. They went; and they brought them; and goats also. (A "day" in an Ekano Tale is without limit as to length or shortness.)

The goats and sheep increased, until the village of Leopard was positively full of them crowded in abundance.

About three years passed, and Chameleon said to himself, "Our herd with Chum must be about sufficient for division." Thereupon he started on his journey crawling, naka, naka, naka, until he came to the house of his friend Leopard. Leopard said to his wife, "Make food!" It was cooked, they ate, and rested.

Chameleon said to Leopard, "Chum! I have come, that we should divide the shares of the herd." Leopard replied, "Good! but, first go back today. Who can catch goats and sheep on a hot day like this? Come tomorrow morning." Chameleon said, "Very good." And he went back to his village.

The next day, in the morning, he rose to go to the village of Leopard. (Actually, after midnight, Leopard had already opened the pens, and all the animals were scattered outside.) He protested regret to Chameleon, and said, "Chum! go back! I don't know how those fellows have opened their pens. I was expecting you, for this day; I had let my herdman know that a person was coming on the morrow. So, go back. And, as I am going tomorrow to the swamp for bamboo, you must come only on the second day." Chameleon submissively replied, "Very good."

Chameleon continued coming; and his treatment was just so every time, with excuses.

Leopard, hoping, said to himself, "Perhaps he will die on the way," because he saw him walking so slowly, naka, naka. And Chameleon kept on patiently going back and forth, back and forth.

One night, Leopard and his wife were lying down; whereupon his wife asked him, "What is the reason that you and Yongolokodi have not divided the shares of the herd? Do you think he will die of this weakness?" Leopard answered, "No! it is not weakness, Njambe is the one who created him so; it is his own way of walking."

Finally, Chameleon said to himself, "I must see what Njâ intends to do to me; whether he thinks that he shall eat my share." He went by night and waited outside of Leopard's. Next day, in the morning, as Leopard rose to go out, he found, unexpectedly, as he emerged from the house, Chameleon sitting on the threshold. There was no other deception that Leopard could seek; for, the animals were still in their pens. So, he called his children, and said, "Tie the goats and sheep with cords." So they tied them all. And he and Chameleon divided them. Then this one returned to his place; and that one to his.

BORROWED CLOTHES

Persons
Koho (Parrot) Kuba (Chicken)

NOTE

A story of the cause of the enmity between chickens and parrots. When a chicken comes near to a parrot, the latter turns to one side, saying, "wâ!"; for fear that the chicken will take his fine feathers from him.

Parrot and Chicken were fowls living in a village of Mankind near a town; which they had built together. They were living there in great friendship.

Then Parrot said to Chicken, "Chum! I'm going to make an engagement for marriage." So, he prepared his journey. And he asked Chicken, "Chum! give me now thy fine dress!" (For the occasion.) Chicken, said, "Very good!" and he handed his tail feathers to him. Thereupon, Parrot went on his marriage journey.

When he came home again, he said to himself, "These feathers become me. I will not return them to Kuba."

So, when Chicken said to him, "Return me my clothes," he replied, "I will not return them!" Chicken, seeing that Parrot was retaining the feathers, said sarcastically, "Accept your clothing!" Thereupon, Parrot, pretending to be wronged, said, "Fellow! why do you put me to shame? I did not say that I would take your clothing altogether, only that we should exchange clothes."

At night, then, Parrot took all his family, and they flew up in the air away. At once, he decided to stay there, and did not come to live on the ground again. Chicken was left remaining with Mankind in the town.

Whenever Chicken began to call to Parrot up in the treetops, asking for his clothes, Parrot only screamed back "wâ! wâ!" That was a mode of speech by which to mock at Chicken.

THE STORY OF A PANIC

Persons

Edubu (Adder)	Ngubu (Hippopotamus)
Ikingi (Fly)	Nyati (Ox)
Ko (Wild-Rat)	Bejaka (Fishes)
Ngomba (Porcupine)	Ngando (Crocodile)
Njâku (Elephant)	

NOTE

Native Africans after bathing, rub more or less of some oil, either native palm, or foreign pomade, on their bodies.

In the Dry Seasons, when the rivers are low, fish are caught by building dams across the streams, and then bailing out the water from the enclosed spaces. Observe flies, as carriers of disease.

Adder went to bathe. He returned, and anointed himself with nyimba oil (oil of bamboo-palm nuts), and then climbed out on to a branch of a cayenne-pepper bush.

Fly came and settled upon Adder's back. Adder, being annoyed, drove Fly away. Then Fly said to Adder, in anger, "Know you not that it is I who cause even Njâku, with his big tusks, to rot? And that I can cause Nyati and Ngubu to rot? And I can cause Mankind to rot! Then how much more you, this Thing who has only ribs and ribs!"

When Adder heard this, he was alarmed, and he entered into the hole of Wild-Rat. Wild-Rat asked him, "Chum Adder! where do you come from in such haste?" He answered, "I have seen a Being which does not hesitate to cause Beasts and even Mankind to rot. Therefore, I am fled, by reason of fear of Ikingi."

Whereupon Wild-Rat, frightened, arose, and entered hastily into the town of Porcupine. Porcupine, alarmed, asked Wild-Rat, "What is it?" He answered, "I'm afraid of Ikingi; Edubu says that it is he who causes both Mankind and Beasts to rot."

Then Porcupine, in fear went out, running, going to the town of Hog. Whereupon Hog, being startled, asked him, "Chum! what is it?" He answered him, "I'm afraid of Ikingi. Ngomba says that he is the one who causes both Beasts and Mankind to rot."

Hog at once ran out in terror, and went to a river with all his family. And the water of the river was promptly crowded out, leaving its channel dry.

Then the Fishes (mistaking this motion of the water) arose in haste, saying, "The people who bail the river have come!" And they fled.

Then Crocodile opened his mouth wide; and the fishes in their flight began to enter into his stomach. Among them was ingongo-Kenda (a young kenda; a fish with spines like a catfish). When Crocodile was about to swallow, the spines caught fast in his throat. And Crocodile died at once.

Then the Fishes sang a song of rejoicing.

> "Ngando, with stealing,
> Ngando died by a sting in his throat."

Such was the death that Crocodile died, on account of his

attempt to swallow Fishes, who had rushed into his open mouth, as they fled, alarmed by the confusion raised by the panic of the other animals.

A FAMILY QUARREL

Persons
Ih␣li (Gazelle)   Njâ (Leopard)

NOTE

Among native Africans, in the case of a man and his wife, even if they fight together, her father or her brother usually do not interfere. For, every man who is married knows that his own wife will some day offend himself.

Gazelle and Leopard built a town; living this one at his end of it; that one at the other end. After they had built; they cleared the forest for plantations; they married wives; and they sat down, resting in their seats.

Gazelle had married the sister of Leopard who was of a proud disposition. And Leopard had publicly threatened, "The person who makes trouble for my sister, I will show him a thing."

One day, the sister of Leopard began to give Gazelle some impertinence. Gazelle said to her, "Shut your mouth!" She replied, "I won't shut it!" Gazelle threatened, "Lest I beat you!" She dared him, "Come and beat me! You will see my brother coming to chew you!" Gazelle ran after her, struck her, ndo! and knocked her to the ground, ndi! As she lay there, he kept on beating her, and beating her, and shouting, "Who has married! Who has not married?"

Leopard bristled up his whole mane, full of anger, and was about to go to Gazelle's end of the town to fight. But the older people said to him, "You hear what Ih◻li says, 'Who has not married'?"

Leopard was at once disheartened. He saw there was no place for his bravery in a matter of marriage.

THE GIANT GOAT

Persons

Kudu (Tortoise)	Ngweya (Hog)
Njâ (Leopard)	Betoli (Rats)
A Giant Goat (Mbodi)	Ngwai (Partridge)

NOTE

Tortoise and Leopard had lived in peace in the same town, until their mutual use and abuse of the great Goat, the gift of Njambe, the Creator. A leopard is not satisfied unless he first takes the heart of the animal he has killed.

Tortoise and Leopard built a town together. There they stayed. After they had built, they cleared plantations. Their food was only vegetables; for, they had no meat. Their hunger for meat became great. Their hunters killed nothing.

One day, Tortoise, as he went in search of food, going and penetrating in the forest, came upon the Goat of Njambe (a mythical, enormous animal) in the forest by itself, and tied. It told Tortoise who and what it was, and invited him to enter. He said to It, "Mbodi, Friend-of-Njambe! open for me your house!" The Goat opened an aperture of its body; Tortoise entered in; and It closed the aperture. Inside of the Goat, Tortoise cut pieces of fine fat, and tied them into two bundles. Then he said, "Mbodi, friend of Njambe! open for me the house!" It opened the aperture; Tortoise at once went out; and It shut it.

Tortoise returned to his town, and cut up the meat. He said to his women, "Make ready leaves for momba!" (bundles of green plantain leaves in which meats are cooked over hot coals). They at once plucked the leaves, tied up the momba, and put them over the fireplace. They set soup also on the fireplace. When it was boiled, they spread the table, sat down together, and ate.

The children of Leopard, smelling a tempting odor, came to Tortoise's end of the town. The children of Tortoise showed their food to them, saying, exultingly, "Ye! do you eat such as that?" A child of Leopard said, "Chum! let me taste it!" And he allowed him to taste it.

The children of Leopard went off hurriedly to their father, saying, "Father! such an animal as your friend has killed! Perhaps it is Ngweya; we do not know."

Then Leopard went to where Tortoise was, and he asked him, "Chum! as to this meat-hunger, what shall we do? Let us arrange for the town." Tortoise responded. "Yes, I am willing." So, in the evening, he invited his friend Leopard that he should come and eat food. Leopard came; they sat down together; and they ate. When Leopard had tasted, he exclaimed, "Man! what animal is this?" But Tortoise would not tell him. When they had finished eating, Leopard said to himself, "I must know where Tortoise goes!"

On the next day, before the Ngwai (a Bird, that announces the first coming of daylight) had sounded, Tortoise went out clear on to where was that giant Goat. He spoke, as on his previous journey, "O! Mbodi! Friend of the Creator! open for me the house!" It at once opened the aperture; he entered in; and began to slice pieces of meat from the Goat's inside. When he had finished, he said, "Open for me the house!" It opened the aperture; and he emerged and went back to his town. There he spoke to his women, saying, "Cook ye!" They boiled the meat; it was cooked; he invited Leopard; they ate; and finished. And Leopard went back to his house.

But, when night came, Leopard took ashes, and, going to the house of Tortoise, thrust the ashes into Tortoise's traveling-bag, and stabbed holes in it. Said he to himself, "When Tortoise carries it, then the ashes will fall down." This he did, so that he might follow to the place where Tortoise would go.

Next day, Tortoise was up at the same time with the first Ngwai. And at daybreak, Leopard followed, observing the ground closely with his eyes; and he saw the ashes. The fellow, at once, went on his journey, striding quickly, quickly, until he reached to where the great Goat was standing. It explained to him, as it had to Tortoise, its use, and invited him to enter. Said he, "O! Mbodi of my father Njambe! open to me the house!" And It opened the hole. He entered; and he discovered Tortoise cutting meat. Tortoise was displeased, and said to him, "Chum! is that the way you do?" They cut pieces of meat, they got ready, and they went back to town.

The next day, although Tortoise was vexed at Leopard, they started together on their journey; and they arrived at the Goat. They said as before, "O! Mbodi! Friend! open to us the house!" It opened the aperture; and they entered. Tortoise warned Leopard, "Chum! Njâ! don't touch the heart!" They cut meat. Then Leopard said that he was going to lay hold of the heart. But Tortoise said, "No!" Leopard cut and cut, and was going on to the heart. Tortoise again said to him, "Not so!" They went on cutting. Finally Leopard laid hold of the heart! The Goat at once made a great outcry, "Ma-a! Mba-a!" and died instantly.

The people of the town that was near by, heard, and they said, "The Mbodi! what has happened to it? Young men! go ye! Hasten ye! for, that Mbodi is crying!" They went, and discovered the body of the Goat stretched out. They went back to the town and told the people that, "The Mbodi is dead!"

While this was going on, as soon as Tortoise inside the body knew that the Goat was dying, he began to seek for a hiding-place. He said, "I am for the stomach!" Leopard said, "No! that is the hiding-place of the elder one" (himself). Then Tortoise said, "I will go and hide in the bowels." Leopard said, "That also is the hiding place of the elder." Then Tortoise said, "Well! I'm going to hide in the fountain of the water of the belly" (the urinary bladder). Leopard said, "Yes! that is the share of the younger." Tortoise thrust himself in there. Leopard jumped into the stomach.

When the people came, they discovered the Goat lying flat, and they said, "Tie ye it!" (to carry it away). Others said, "No! let it be butchered here." They all said, "Yes!" And they cut it in pieces. They took out the entire stomach, and laid it aside. They took that fountain, and flung it out in the bushes.

Concealed by the bushes, Tortoise crawled out of the sac, and, pretending to be displeased, called out, "Who dashed that dirty water in my face, as I was coming here, seeking for my fungi here in the forest?" They apologized, saying. "Chum! we did not know you were in those bushes. But, come, and join us." So, he went there; and he, in pretence, exclaimed, "What thing can so suddenly have killed Friend-Creator his Mbodi there? Alas! But, Imã! what a large stomach that is! Would you say that it was not it that killed Mbodi? Let us send some children to pierce that stomach. But ye! when ye shall go to pierce it, first bring spears, then jab the spears through it. I have not seen such a stomach as that!"

They finished the cutting in pieces; and they gave Tortoise his share of the animal. He left, bidding them await his return. He went hastily with the meat to his town, and sat down to rest for only a little while. Then he rapidly went back again to see what would happen to Leopard.

The family of Njambe had taken that stomach and laid it in the water of a stream. Then they took spears, and they stabbed it. Leopard, being wounded, struggled up and down as he tried to emerge from inside the stomach. The people, when they saw this, shouted, "Aw! lâ! lâ! lâ!" And there was Leopard lying dead! For, in stabbing that stomach, the spears had reached Leopard.

Tortoise said to them, "Give me the skin of Leopard!" So they handed it to him. He went off with it to his house. When it was dried, he took it into his inner room, and hung it up. He said to his children, "Let no person bring any of the children of Njâ into this room."

Before that time, the children of Tortoise and of Leopard always hunted small animals; and they were accustomed daily to kill rats in their houses.

On another day, the children of Leopard having no meat, and not knowing that their father was dead said, "A hunt for Betoli tomorrow!" The children of Tortoise replied, "Yes!"

Early in the next day then, the children of Leopard made ready and called for those of Tortoise; and they all started together.

They began at first at Leopard's end of the town; and, going from house to house, opened the houses and killed rats. They passed on toward Tortoise's end of the town, opening houses, and killing rats. When they came to the room of Tortoise himself, his children said to the others, "No!" The children of Leopard asked them, "Why?" As they arrived at the door, the children of Tortoise said, "Our father said that, even for catching rats, we should not enter that room." But the children of Leopard broke down the door, and entered into the room. There they lifted their eyes, and discovered the skin of their father Leopard hanging! At once, they all hasted out of the house. But, suppressing their sorrow and indignation, shortly after this, they all said, "To go to throw wheels on the beach!" (a game; solid wheels, about eight or ten inches in diameter, and some three inches thick, chopped out of an enormous tuber). They made ready their little spears, and they all went in a company. Their challenge was, "To the beach!" These arranged themselves on one side, and those on the other.

The children of Tortoise began the game, rolling the wheel to the children of Leopard. These latter, as the wheel rolled by, pierced its center with all their spears; none failed. The Leopard company shouted in victory. "Boho, eh?" And the Tortoise company dared them with, "Iwâ!" Then the Leopard company insultingly retorted, "We are the ones who are accustomed to sleep with people's sisters, and continue to eat with them!" (*i.e.*, that they could commit crimes with impunity, and still be allowed the intimate friendship of eating together, without the others daring to punish them).

Then the Leopard company bowled the wheel toward the side of the Tortoise company. These latter pierced the wheel with all their spears; none missed. The Tortoise company shouted for victory, "Boho! eh?" And the Leopard company dared them with, "Iwâ!" Then the Tortoise children shouted boastfully, "We are those who are accustomed to kill people's fathers, and hang up their skins, eh?"

At this, the Leopard children began to rage, and joined a fight with the children of Tortoise.

The children of Tortoise, and himself, and their wives and their children, fled and scattered over the logs into the stream of water, and hid themselves in holes, and never came back to town.

TALE 33
THE FIGHTS OF MBUMA-TYĔTYĔ AND AN ORIGIN OF THE LEOPARD

Persons

Mekuku, and Two of His Sons Mbu-ma-Tyⵣtyⵣ and Njâ

King Njambu

Betoli (Rats)

Mwamba (Snakes)

Ngângâlâ (Millepedes)

Kedi (Stinging Ants)

Njambu Ya Mekuku (Spirits), and His Town

Women Hidden in Chests

Ngwaye (Partridge)

Kâ (Snails)

Ihonga-Honga (A Giant Tooth)

Hova (A Magic Gourd)

Tângâ (Horn)

Ibumbu (Bundle of Medicine)

Kanja (A Bowl)

Ikanga (Spear)

Ngalo (A Magic Amulet)

NOTE

Ngalo is a powerful fetish-charm. Sitting in a visitor's lap for a few moments, is a mode of welcome.

"Njambu" is one of their forms of spelling the name of the Creator; very commonly used also for human beings. The account of the wrestling-match is suggestive of the surroundings of a modern athletic field.

Njambu built a Town. He continued there a long time. After he had finished the town, he married very many wives. After a short time they all of them bore children. Those births were of many sons. He gave them names: Among them were, Upuma-mwa-penda (Year-of-doubt), and Njâ (Leopard).

And again, his wives, after a short time, all of them became mothers. This time, they gave birth to a large number of daughters. He gave them also names.

His town was full with men and women; they were crowded. And all busy. They that worked at stakes, went to cut saplings; those that made rattan-ropes, went to cut the rattan-vine; they that shaped the bamboo for building, went to cut the bamboo-palms; they that made thatch went to gather the palm-leaves; they that set up the stakes of the house-frame went to thrust them into the ground; they who fastened the walls, fastened them; they who tied thatch on the roof, tied it; they who split the rattan vines for tying, split them.

The town was full of noise. The children of Njambu kept their father's town in motion. They rejoiced in the abundance of people and their force. They took dowries also for their sisters, and gave them in marriage to young men of other towns.

Arguments were discussed; stories about White Men were told; amusements were played; food was eaten; and the sons of Njambu married wives.

One of Njambu's sons, Upuma-mwa-penda, said to his mother, "Make me mekima," (mashed plantain). His mother asked him, "Where are you going with the mekima?" He answered, "I'm going to seek a marriage." And she said "Good!"

In the morning, he took his rolls of mashed plantains, and

started to go on his journey. He said to his mother, "You must keep my house." She replied, "It is well."

He went on, on, on, until, on the road ahead, he met with two Rats, who were fighting. He took an ukima-roll, divided it, and gave to them, saying, "Take ye and eat." They accepted, and told him, "You shall arrive at the end."

He goes on stepping quickly, quickly; and meets two Snakes fighting. He parted them. He took an ukima-roll and gave to them; they ate. They said to him, "You shall reach the end."

He goes on with his journey, until ahead were two Millepedes fighting. He said to them, "For what are you killing each other?" He parted them, and gave them an ukima-roll. They took it and said, "You shall reach the end!"

He lay down in the forest at night. At midnight, his mother saw, in her sleep, something that said, "Go with thy two daughters in the morning, and take food for Mbuma-Tyȇtyȇ (another name for Upuma-mwa-penda)."

Early in the morning, she awoke her two daughters, and said, "Come! let us go to follow after your brother; he is still on his way."

They started, on, on, on, until they found him sitting down in the path. They brought out the food from their traveling-bag, and they said, "We have come to give you food." They prepared the meal, and they ate. And they slept that night in the forest.

Next morning, they started again, and they walked on, on, on, with their journey. As they came on their way, they listened ahead, and they heard something, saying, "Eh! fellows, eh! eh! fellows eh! Nobody shall pass! Nobody shall pass here!"

When they drew near, they met an immense quantity of Red stinging Ants spread from the ground up to the tree-tops, entirely closing the way. Mbuma-ty⊠ty⊠ and his company said, "Ah! these are they who were shouting here!" He advanced to the fight, and called to his younger sister, "Come on!"

She lifted her foot just to tread upon the Ants; and they instantly entirely covered her. He and his company tried in vain to draw her back. The Ants shouted, to strengthen themselves. "Eh! fellows, eh!"

He, still fighting, called to the elder sister, "On ahead!" Just as she lifted her foot, there came all the Tribe of Red Ants, and would have covered her up. The woman jumped to one side vigorously, and stood there in that spot, fanning away the sweat of her exertions, p⊠, p⊠, p⊠. She returned again to the Ants; and they met. She called out, "Ngalo! hot water!" and it appeared. She took it, and dashed it at the Red Ants. But they all went into their holes; and came out at another opening, again closing the path. She still stood there ready to fight; but they covered her, and dragged her behind them.

The Ants shouted over their victory, "Eh! fellows, eh! Today no person passes here!"

The son called to his mother, "Mother! come on!" His mother said, "My child! I am unable." He called, "Ngalo! Fire!" Fire at once appeared. Having drawn back the corpses of his sisters, he seized the fire, and thrust it into the nests of the Ants. He thrust it also among the trees. The flame ignited them; and the surrounding forest burned to ashes with all the trees. And the Ants were all burned too.

Then he brought his sisters to life, by taking that ashes, and throwing it over them, and down their throats into their stomachs.

When the day darkened, he said, "Ngalo! a house!" A tent at

once appeared, with a table, and tumblers, and water, and all food. They sat there and ate. When they finished eating, they set tea on the table. They drank; they talked of their experiences. When they ended, they said, "Let us lie down together." So they lay down for the night.

As the next day was coming, a Partridge gave forth its voice, "Rise! tyâtyâ lâ! tyâtyâ lâ!" And the day broke also. They wash their faces; they set tea on the table, and drank it. They folded the tent-house, and swallowed it, (as a mode of carrying it). They started with their journey, and went conversing on the way.

As they came along, Something was heard ahead. They listened, and heard a song. "Gribâmbâ! eh! Gribâmbâ! eh!" Mbuma-ty⊠ty⊠ and his mother and sisters kept on going toward the sound, which continued, "Dingâlâ! eh! A person will not pass! No doubt about it! Dingâlâ! eh! Wherever he comes from, he can pass here only by coming from above."

The man and his company approached the source of the song, and exclaimed, "There it is!" They went on and found the entire tribe of Snails filling the road hither and yonder. He said to his mother, "What shall we do with the Kâ Tribe?" They sat down to consider. They decided, "A fight! this very day!" They sat still, and rested for a while. Then he went ahead and shouted to his younger sister, "Come!" She called out, "Ngalo! a short sword!" It appeared. She called again, "A strong cloth!" It appeared, and she dressed herself with it.

As she approached the Snails, one of them fell on her head with a thud, ndi! She took the sword, and struck it, ko! The Snails shouted, "We're nearing you!" A crowd of them came rapidly, one after another; in a heap, they entirely covered her, vyâ! And she lay a corpse! The Snails swarmed over her, and taking her, threw her behind them. They shouted in victory, "Tâkâ! Dingâlâ! eh!"

Then the elder sister said she was going to help her brother in facing the Snails. Her mother objected, "You? Stay!" But she replied, "Let me go!" She girded her body tightly, and then she entered the fight. The Snails surrounded her. They were about to drag her to their rear, when, she, at the side of the path, attempted to spring from them. But they swarmed over her. And she lay a corpse! The mother was crying out, "O! My child!" when the Snails covered her too.

Mbuma-ty⊠ty⊠ retreated, to rest himself for a short time, and called out, "Ngalo! a helmet!" It appeared. He fitted it to his head. He called again, "Ngalo! a glass of strong drink, and of water too!" It appeared. He asked for tobacco. It appeared. "Matches!" They appeared. He struck a match, and smoked. As he thrust the cigar in his mouth, it stimulated him; it told him things of the future in its clouds of smoke. After he had rested, he stood up, again for the fight.

The Snails tuned their song:

"Iyâ! Dingâlâ! disab⊠te!
Iyâ! Dingâlâ! sâlâlâsâlâ! Disab⊠te!
Iyâ! Dingâlâ! Iyâ! Dingâlâ!
Iyâ! Dingâlâ! Sâlâlâsâlâ!
Iyâ! Dingâlâ! Eh! Bamo-eh!"

The Snails, in their fierce charge, killed him, and were about to take away the corpse; when, his Ngalo returning him to life, he sprang erect, and cried out, "Ah! my Father Njambu! Dibadi-O!"

And he took up his war-song:—

"Tata Njambu ya milole, milole mi we.
Ta' Njambu! milole mi we.
Ta' Njambu! milole mi we.
Milole mi we. Ta' Njambu!"

All that while, the mother and his sisters were lying dead.

The Snails were shouting in their victory, "Tâkâ!"

Mbuma-ty⊠ty⊠ took a short broad knife in his hands, and shouted, "Dibadi!" He girded his body firmly, and stood erect. He called out in challenge, "I've come!" The Snails answered, "You've reached the end!"

They fought. The man took his sword. The Snails fell down on him, ndwa! But the man stood up, and moved forward. He laid hold of a small tree. He cut it, and whirled it about at the Snails. And the Snails fell down on the ground, po! But they rose up again flinging themselves upon the man, ndwa! The man jumped aside crying out, "Ah! My father Njambu! Dibadi-O!"

He took fire, thrust it among the tribe of Snails, and every one fell down on the ground, mbwâ!

Then he shaped a leaf into a funnel, and dropped a medicine into the noses of his mother and sisters. They slowly rose and tried to sit up. He poured the ashes of the Snails over them, po! They breathed it into their stomachs, kii! and they came fully to life.

Then they said, "You are safe! Now! for our return home!" He said, "Good!" And they returned.

Mbuma-ty⊠ty⊠ continued his own journey, on, on, on, until at a cross-roads, he found a giant Tooth, as large as a man. Tooth asked, "Where are you going?" Said he, "I'm going to seek a marriage at a town of Njambu-ya-Mekuku." Then, with his axe in hand, he turned aside from the path; chopped firewood, chop,

chop, chop, chop, mbwâ! Then he kindly carried a lot of it, and presented it to Tooth. He also opened his bag, and taking out an ukima roll, laid it down at the feet of Tooth; also a bundle of gourd-seeds, and laid it down; and then he said, "I'm going." But the giant Tooth, pleased with him, said to him, "Just wait!"

So, he waited; and, while waiting, said, "Ngalo! a fine house!" It appeared there. "A table!" There! "Good food!" There! "Fine drink!" There! They two ate, and drank, and had conversation together.

Tooth said to him, "Where you go, do not fear." It brought out from its hut a water-gourd, and said, "I will not show you more, nor will I tell you anything at all, but this Hova itself will tell you." Then Tooth said to him, "Go well!"

The man took the Gourd and clung to it as if it was a treasure.

He started again on his journey, and had gone but a little way, when he found Kuda-nuts in immense abundance. He took up one, drew his knife, cracked the nut, and threw the kernel into his mouth. He stooped again, and was about to pick up another, when the Gourd warned him, "I! I!" So, he left the nuts.

He came on in his journey, and found in abundance wild Mangoes. He took one, split it, and bit out a piece; and was about to add another, when the warning came, "I! I!" So, he left the Mangoes; yet his belly felt full. Still on his journey, thirst for water seized him at a stream. He took his cup, plunged it into the water, filled it, drank, and was about to take more, when the warning said, "I! I!" And he left the water. Yet his belly felt full.

On his journey still, till he came to a large river. There he stood, and listened, as he heard a boat-song, "Ay⊠h⊠! âh⊠! ây⊠h⊠! ⊠!" There passed by the sound of paddles, wom'! wom'! but he saw no person; nor did he see any canoe. Gourd said to him, "Call!" Then he called out, "Who are these? Bring me a canoe!" A voice replied, "Who are you?" He answered, "I!" The canoe came nearer, its crew singing, singing, until it grounded on the beach. He saw what seemed only a great log! Gourd said to him, "Embark!" He got in. The crew also (apparently) got in again; for, the sound of paddles was again heard, worom'! worom'!

Instead of going straight across the river, they pulled far up stream, and then came all the way down again on the other side. As they came, they were constantly keeping up the song, until they grounded at the landing-place at that other side. Still he saw nothing of the invisible boatmen, when he landed.

Ascending the bank of the stream, he saw a strange new town. He entered its public reception-house, and sat down. As he was looking for some one to come, a Horn came and sat on his lap, and then moved away. A Bundle of Medicine came, sat, and moved away. A Bowl came and sat. A Spear came and sat. All these Things saluted him. Behold! they were the People of that Town (in disguise); but he saw none of them.

Gourd said to him, "Come and escort me into the back-yard." He at once stepped out; and, when in the back-yard, It said. "Put me down." (It had been carried suspended from his shoulder.) He put It down, standing It at the foot of a plantain-stalk. Gourd making a leaf funnel, dropped something into his eyes. His eyes suddenly, kaa! were opened, and he saw everything, and all the people, and the whole street.

Returning to the house, he sat down. Maidens came. Such goodness as you have scarcely known! Forms lovely to see!

The Chief of the town said, "Make ye food!" It was made at once. Then one whom he chose was given him for his wife.

She and this young son-in-law were left sitting in the house. The wife began to weep, saying to herself, "What will be his manner of eating?" (a test to be applied to him as suitor). The Gourd called him with a voice like the stroke of a bell, ng⬛ng! He went out to the Gourd, and It said to him, "When you shall eat, take one piece of plantain, flesh of the fowl, and then dip one spoonful of the udika (wild-mango gravy), put them in your mouth; and thou shalt say unto her, 'Take; you may remove the food.' You shall see what will happen." He did so. His wife laughed in her heart; and she went and told her mother, "He is a person of sense." The towns-people said to her, "What did he do?" She evasively said to them. "Let us see!"

In the evening, the father-in-law said to him, "You have found us here in the midst of a work of garden-making for your mother-in-law." (A man is always expected to do some work for his wife's mother.) He said. "That's good, Father!"

Gourd called to him, and told him, "It is not a garden; it is an entire forest; it is not planted; it is all wild country. But, tomorrow, at daylight, early, you say to your wife that she must go and show you. You must take one young plantain-set, and a machete, and an axe. When you shall arrive there, then you shall say to her, 'Go back!' And she will go back. Then, you will slash with the machete, kwa! and leave it. You take also the axe and cut, ka! and say, 'Ngunga-O! Mekud' O! Makako ma dibak⬛ manjeya-O!' You shall see what will happen. Then you insert the plantain-set in the ground. Then you set up a bellows, and work it. And you shall see what will happen."

(All that Garden-Plan was made by the townspeople in order that he might weary of the task, and they then find excuse for killing him. For they were Cannibals.)

At daybreak, he did so. He called his wife. He and she went on until they came to the chosen spot. Said he, "Go back!" The woman went back. He did just as he had been directed, as to the clearing, and the felling, the incantation, and the planting. The plantains bore, and ripened at once. Every kind of food developed in that very hour.

The man went back to the town, and sat down. They set before him food.

They sent a child to spy the garden. The child returned, excitedly saying, "Men! the entire forest! with all such foods! only ripe ones!" They said to him, "You're telling a falsehood!" And they said, "Let another go and see." He went; and returned thence with a ripe plantain held in his hand.

In the evening, the Chief said to him, "Sir! tomorrow, people will have been filled with hunger for meat. A little pond of your mother-in-law is over there. Tomorrow it is to be bailed out." (In order to get the fish that would be left in the bottom pools.)

Gourd called him, ngᴤng! He went to It, and It said, "That is not a pond, it is a great river, (like the Lobi at Batanga). However, when you shall go, you must take one log up stream and one log down stream (for a pretence of dams). You shall see what will happen. Then you must bail only once, and say, 'Itata-O!' You shall see."

Next morning, he did so. And the whole river was drained; and the fish were left in the middle, alone. He returned to the town, and sat down. The people went to see; and, they were frightened at the abundance of fish. For a whole month, fish were gathered; and fish still were left.

The Chief went to call his townspeople, saying, "We will do

nothing to this fellow. Let him alone; for, you have tried him with every test." They said, "Yes; and he has lingered here," (*i.e.*, was no longer a stranger; and therefore should not be eaten). But, they said, "Tomorrow there will be only wrestling." (This was said deceitfully.)

In the evening, the father-in-law called him, saying, "Mbuma-ty⬚ty⬚, tomorrow there is only wrestling. You have stayed long here. As you are about to go away with my child, there is left only one thing more that she wants to see, that is, the wrestling tomorrow."

Gourd called him, and said to him, "It is not only for wrestling. You know the part of the village where is the Wrestling-Ground. There is a big pit there. You will take care if you are near that pit; and you must push them in."

In the evening, food was made, and soon it was ready. He and his wife ate, and finished. They engaged in conversation. They took pleasure over their love that night.

The next day, in the morning, very early, the drums, both the elimbi and the common, began promptly to tell things in the street. (The Elimbi is a specially made drum used to transmit information by a system of signal strokes. News is thus carried very far and very rapidly.) The Gourd called him, and handed him a leaf of magic-medicine, to hold in his hand, saying, "Go; fear not!"

The townspeople began to shout back and forth a song (to arouse enthusiasm). Two companies ranged on each side of the street, singing. "Engolongolo! hâ! hâ! Engolongolo! hâ! hâ!"

> "Engolongolo! hâ! hâ!
> Engolongolo! hâ! hâ!"

Hearing their song as a challenge, the young man went out of the house into the street. Up to this point, the strongest wrestler of the town, named Ekwamekwa, was not with them; he was out in the forest, felling trees.

When the towns-people saw the young man standing in the street, they advanced as many as a hundred all at once. He laid his hands upon them, and they all went back; he also went back. Soon he advanced again, and his single opponent advanced. They two laid their hands on each other's shoulders. The townspeople began another song, as if in derision. "O! O! A! O! O! A! O! O! A!"

At once, he seized his opponent, and threw him into the pit. Thereupon, his father-in-law shouted in commendation, "Iwâ!"

Another one came forward; Mbuma-ty⊠ty⊠ advanced; and as they met together, he took him, and threw him into the pit. Again the shout, "Iwâ!"

The sisters of the two men in the pit began to cry. The others said to the girls, "What are you doing? He shall die today! It is we who shall eat those entrails today!" (Among cannibals, a choice portion.)

Another one was coming, and, as they met together, again the shout of derision, "O! O! O! A! O! O! O! A! O! O! O! A!" But, at one fling, Mbuma-ty⊠ty⊠ cast him into the pit. "Iwâ" was repeated.

The sister of him who was thrown thus into the pit began to cry. The people rebuked her, "Mbâbâ! mbâbâ! Join in the singing!"

Another one was coming; Mbuma-ty⊠ty⊠ advanced; and as they came together, he lifted him, holding him by the foot. The singers, to encourage their man, said responsively, "Dikubwe! Dikubwe! Fear not an elephant with his tusks! Take off! take off!"

Mbuma-ty⊠ty⊠ lifted him, and promptly pushed him down into the pit, with a thud, 'kodom'!

The people began to call out anxiously, "W⊠-e! w⊠-e! O! They are overcome! They are overcome! O! Some one must go hastily, and call Ekwamekwa, and tell him that people are being destroyed in the town, and he must come quickly."

Some one got up, and ran to call Ekwamekwa, wailing as he went, "Iyâ! Iyâ! Iyâ! Ekwamekwa, iyâ-O! Come! People are exterminated in the town!"

He heard with one ear (*i.e.* at once). He snatched up his machete and axe, saying, "What is it?" The messenger repeated, "Come! a being from above has destroyed many a one in the town!"

The man Ekwamekwa, full of boasting, said, "Is it possible there is no man in the town?" He came, already shaking the muscles of his chest, pwâ! pwâ (a custom with native wrestlers, as a lion his mane). His muscles were quivering with rage, nyâ! nyâ! nyâ!

The drums, both the elimbi-telegraph and the common, were being beaten, and were sounding without intermission. The singers were shouting; the wrestlers' bodies had perspiration flowing from them. The noise of the people, of the telegraph drums and other drums, and sticks (sticks beating time) were rattling kwa! kwa! kwa!

As Ekwamekwa appeared, the women and children raised their shrill voices. The shouters yelled, "A! lâ! lâ! lâ! â!"

Mbuma-ty⊠ty⊠ advanced at once. He and Ekwamekwa laid hold of one another, and alternately pressed each other backward and forward. The one tried tricks to trip the other, and the other tried the same. Ekwamekwa held him, and was about to throw him on the ground. The other jumped to one side, and stood, his muscles quivering, po! po! po! tensely. Ekwamekwa seized him about the waist and loins. The people all were saying, "Let no one shout!" (lest Ekwamekwa be confused). They said, "Make no noise! He is soon going to be eaten!" And it was a woman who said, "Get ready the kettle!"

Ekwamekwa still held him by the loins. So, they called out, "Down with him! Down with him!" But Mbuma-ty⊠ty⊠ shouted, "I'm here!" He put his foot behind Ekwamekwa's leg, and lifted him, and threw him into the pit, kodom!

Then there was a shout of distress by the people, "A! â! â! â!" and Ekwamekwa called out, "Catch him! catch him!" Mbuma-ty⊠ty⊠, lifting his feet, ran to his father-in-law's end of the town, and all the men came after him. His father-in-law protected him, and said to them, "You can do nothing with this stranger!"

At night, the Chief said to him, "Sir, you may go away tomorrow."

At daybreak, food was cooked. The Chief Njambu-ya-Mekuku, put his daughters into large chests. In one was a lame one; another, covered with skin disease; and another, with a crooked nose; and others, with other defects in other chests, each in her own chest. But, he put the wife into a poor chest all dirty outside with droppings of fowls, and human excrement, and ashes. In it also, he placed a servant and all kinds of fine clothing. Then said he to Mbuma-ty⊠ty⊠, "Choose which chest contains your wife."

The Gourd at once called him, and It said to him, "Lift me up!" It whispered to him, "The chest which is covered with dirt and filth, it is the one which contains your wife. Even if they say,

'Ha! ha! he has had all his trouble for nothing; he has left his wife,' do you nevertheless carry it, and go on with your journey."

He came to the spot where the chests were. The Chief said again, "Choose, from the chests, the one which contains your wife." Mbuma-ty⬛ty⬛ picked up the poor one. They shouted. But, he at once started on his journey, and on, until he came to the river, stepped into a canoe, paddled to the other side, landed, and went on, carrying the chest. Almost in an instant (by his magic Ngalo) he was at the place of the Great Tooth. It asked, "How is it there?" He replied, "Good!" The Gourd, in leaving, reported to Its mother, the Tooth, "A fine fellow, that person there!"

He went on with his journey, his feet treading firmly. Almost with one stride (by aid of his Ngalo), in the twinkling of eyes, he was near the spring at his own town.

Then he said, "Now let me open the chest here!" On his opening it, a maiden attended by her servant came stepping out, arrayed in the clothing which had been placed in the chest for her dress. One's eyes would ache at sight of her silks, and the fine form of her person. And you or any other one could say, "Yes! you are a bride! truly a bride!"

Two young women rose up in the town to go to the spring to dip up water. They were just about to come to the spring, when they saw their brother and his wife and her servant. They two went back together rapidly to the town, saying, "Well! if there isn't the woman whom Mbuma-ty⬛ty⬛ has married! They are two women and himself!"

The town emptied itself to go and meet them on the path. His father took powder and guns, with which to announce the arrival; and cannon were roaring. When the young woman came and stood there in the street, there was only shouting and shouting, in admiration.

Another brother, named Njâ, when he came to see her, was so impressed to get a wife like her, that, without waiting for the salutations to be made, he said to his mother, "My mother! make for me my mekima, too."

Mbuma-ty⊠ty⊠ entered into the house, he and his wife. At once hot water was set before them, and they went to bathe. When they had finished, they entered the public Reception-Room. Njâ, impatient to get away and, in impolite haste, said, "Now, for my journey!" His brother advised him, "First wait; let me tell you how the way is." He replied, "Not so!" And he started off on his journey.

The others sat down to tell, and to hear the news. They told Mbuma-ty⊠ty⊠ the affairs of the town; and he responded as to how he had come. When he had completely finished, he was welcomed, "Iy⊠! Oka! oka-O! But now, sit down and stay."

Now, when Njâ had gone, he met the two Millepedes fighting. He exclaimed, "By my father Njambu! what is this?" He stood there with laughter, "Ky⊠! ky⊠! ky⊠!" He clapped his hands, "Kwâ! kwâ! You! there! let me pass!" They asked, "Give us an ukima." He stood laughing, kwa! kwa! saying, "I will see this today! Food that is eaten by a human being! Is it so that they have teeth? As I see it, they, having no mouths, how can they eat?" But he opened his food-bag, took an ukima, and gave them a small piece. They rebuked him for his meanness, and laid a curse on him, "Aye! You will not reach the end." He responded, "I won't reach my end, eh? Humph! I'm going on my journey!" He left them; and they grabbed at the very little piece of ukima he had given them.

He cried out, "Journey!" and went on both by day and by night, traveling until he met the two Snakes fighting. He derided them, and took a club, and was about to strike them, when they cursed him, "You will not reach the end!" However, he gave them, at their request, an ukima, and passed on. As he turned to go, and was leaving them, they made signs behind him, repeating their curse, "He will not reach safely!" And they added, "He has no good sense; let us leave him."

He still cried out, "Journey!" and went on to that place of Ihonga-na-Ihonga whose size filled all the width of the way. He made a shout, raising it very loud, and repeated his exclamation, "By my father, Njambu! Thou who hast begotten me, thou hast not seen such as this!" Tooth asked, "Where are you going?" He, astonished, exclaimed, "Ah! It can talk! Alas! for me!" And he added a shout again, with laughter, "Kwati! kwati! kwati!" It spoke and said, "Please, split for me fire-wood." He replied, "What will fire-wood do for you?" He, however, split the wood hastily, ko! ko! ke! and left it in a pile. It said, "Leave me an ukima." He responded, "Yes; let me see what It will do with it now!" He opened his food-bag, and laid an ukima down disrespectfully, and said, "Eat! let me see!"

Tooth said to him, "Sleep here!" Said he, "If I sleep here, what is there for me to sit on?" It replied only, "Sleep here!" He said, "Yes!" Then he invoked his Ngalo, "A seat!" It appeared, and he sat down. In the evening, he invoked, "Ngalo, a house!" It appeared. "A bed!" It appeared. "A table!" It appeared. "Food!" It was set out. He ate, but did not offer any to Tooth, and fell into a deep sleep.

At daybreak, he was given water to wash his face, and food; and he ate it. Then the Tooth said to him, "Now, this is a Hova; go; the Hova will tell you what you should do." Said he sarcastically "Good! a good thing!" And he started on his journey. But, when he was gone, he despised the Gourd, and said to himself, "What can this water-jar do for me? I shall leave it here." And he laid it down at the foot of a Buda tree. There were many kuda (nuts of the Buda) lying on the ground. He prepared a seat, and sat down. He gathered the kuda nuts in one place. He took up a nut, broke it, threw its kernel into his mouth, and chewed it. He picked up another one, and was going to break it. Gourd warningly said, "I! I!" He replied, "Is it that you want me to give it to you?" Gourd answered only, "I-I!" And he said, "But, then, your 'I! I!' what is it for?" He broke many of the nuts, taking them up quickly; and finished eating all. And still his stomach felt empty, as if he had eaten nothing.

He then said, "The Journey!" He started, still carrying with him the Gourd, going on, on, until he came to the Bwibe tree (wild mango). That Bwibe was sweet. He collected the mibe fruits, and began to split them. He split many in a pile, and then said, "Now! let me suck!" He sucked them all, but he felt no sense of repletion, although the Gourd had warned him. He took the skins of the mibe fruit, and angrily thrust them inside the Gourd's mouth, saying, "Eat! You who have no teeth, what makes you say I must not eat? But, take you!"

He goes on with his journey. And he found water. He took his drinking-vessel, plunged it into the water, dipped, put it to his mouth, drank, and drained the vessel. He wanted more, plunged the vessel, and drank, draining the vessel. He took more again, disregarding the warnings of Gourd. The water said to him, "Here am I, I remain myself." (*i.e.* I will not satisfy you.) He gave up drinking, and started his journey again, journeying, journeying, crossed some small creeks, and passed clear on, until he came to the River. As he listened, he heard songs passing by. He said to himself. "Now! those who sing, where are they?"

The Gourd spoke to him, saying, "Call for the canoe!" He replied, "How shall I call for a canoe, while I see no people?" Gourd repeated to him, "Call!" Then he shouted out, "You, bring me the canoe!" Voices asked, "Who art thou?" He answered, "I! Njâ!" Some of the voices said, "Come! let us ferry him across." Others said, "No!" But the rest answered, "Come on!" Then they entered their canoe, laid hold of their paddles, and came singing,

"Kapi, madi, madi, sa!
Kapi, mada, mada, sa!"

And they came to the landing. He saw nothing but what seemed a log, and exclaimed, "How shall I embark in a log, while there is neither paddle, nor a person for a crew?" But Gourd directed him, "Embark!" So, he went in the log. They paddled, and brought him to the other side. He jumped ashore, and stood for a moment. Then he moved on with the journey, walking on to a certain town (that town of the Spirits). He saw nobody, but entered into the public Reception-House, and sat down.

Gourd spoke to him, saying, "Come, and escort me to the back-yard." He curtly answered, "Yes." He carried It, and stood It at the foot of a plantain stalk. Then he went back to the Reception-House and sat down.

A Bundle of Medicines came to salute him, and was about to sit on his lap. He jumped up saying, "What is this?" He sat down again. Another Bundle fell on his lap. He exclaimed, "Hump! what is that?" The Bundle being displeased, replied, "You will not come to the end." (*i.e.* you will not have a successful journey.)

The Gourd called him; and he went to the back-yard. The Gourd said to him, "Stand up!" And he stood up. Then the Gourd took a leaf, folded it as a funnel, and dropped a Medicine into his eyes; and he began to see everything clearly. He said, "This is the only thing which I can see that this Hova has done for me." He passed by, and entered the Reception-House again, and sat down. A person came saluting him, "Mbolo!" He responded, "Ai!" Another came, "Mbolo!" He replied, "Ai!"

They cooked food, and got it ready to bring to him.

During this while, he told his errand, and was given a wife.

Gourd called him. He went out to It: and It directed him, "When you are going to eat, you must take only one piece of plantain, and a piece of the flesh of the fowl. Then you dip it into the udika-gravy, and put it into your mouth; and you will chew it; and when you have swallowed it, then you leave the remainder of the food." He disregardfully said, "Yes! Yes!" And he laughed, "ky⊠! ky⊠! ky⊠! I do not know what this Hova means! And that 'remainder,' shall I give it to It?" And he entered the house again, and sat down.

The food was set out. Little children came; they said to each other, "Let us see how he will eat." He took up a piece of plantain, and put it in his mouth; he took a fowl's leg, put it in his mouth; and gnawed the flesh off of the bone. He took up another piece of plantain, dipped a spoon into the udika-gravy, and put it into his mouth; he took a piece of meat and a plantain, and swallowed them. The little children began to jeer at him, "He eats like a person who has never eaten before." He rose; but felt as if his stomach was empty.

He again seated himself, and he and his wife played games together. Soon he said, "My body feels exhausted with hunger"; food was again made and was set out; he ate. The result was the same. The evening meal was also prepared; he ate, and finished; and still was hungry.

In the evening, the Chief of the town called together the tribe and said to them, "Men! I see that this fellow has no sense; let him return to his place."

On another day, Njâ said to himself, "Let me try, as the Hova has advised me, about the food." They cooked; they set it on the table. He took a piece of plantain, and some flesh of the fowl; he placed them on a spoon, and dipped them into the udika, and put them into his mouth. He rose up, saying, "I have finished!" And his stomach felt replete. Then he thought to himself, "So! is it possible that this Hova knows the affairs of the Spirits?"

The next time when food was spread on the table, he did the same way; and his stomach was satisfied.

Another day broke, and his father-in-law said to him, "On the morrow will be your journey." When the next day dawned, the Chief brought out the chests containing his daughters, and said, "Now, then! choose the one that you will take with you."

The Gourd whispered to him, "Do not take the fine-looking one; you must take the one you see covered with filth." He responded, "Not I!" The one he chose was the fine one. He took it up, and carried it away. The town's-people began to cry out (in pretence), "Oh! he has taken from us that fine maiden of ours!" He was full of gladness that at last he was married. But, really, he was carrying a woman, crooked-nosed, and all of whose body was nothing but skin-disease, and pus oozing all over her.

He went on his journey, on, on, on, on, until the town of the Tooth. Said he, "Here's your Hova!" The Tooth requested, "Tell me the news from there." The Gourd whispered to Tooth, "Let this worthless fellow be! Let him go! He did not marry a real woman. So, he is not a person."

The man at once went on with his journey, continuously, until he came to the spring by his own town. Said he, "Let me bathe!" He put down the chest, and threw his body with a plunge, into the water. He bathed himself thoroughly, and emerged on the bank. Then he said to himself, "Now, then, let me open the chest!" The key clicked, and the chest opened. A sick woman stepped out! He demanded, "Who brought you here?" She replied, "You." Said he in astonishment, "I?" "Yes," answered she. He, in anger, said, "Go back! Do not come at all to the town!" He at once started to go to the town; and the woman slowly followed.

There were two children who were going to the spring. As they went, they met with her; and they cried out in fear, "Ay⊠! ay⊠! ay⊠! a Ghost! ay⊠!" And they went back together in haste to the town. The town's-people asked them, "What's the matter?" They said, "Come! there's a Ghost at the spring!" The woman continued slowly coming. Other children said, "Let us go! Does a Ghost come in the daytime? That is not so!"

As they came on the path, they met her. They asked her, "Who has married you?" She replied, "Isn't it Njâ?" The children excitedly cried out shrilly, "A! lâ! lâ!" They went back quickly to the town, saying, "Come ye! see the wife of Njâ!" The town emptied itself to go and see her. And they inquired of her, "Who is it who has married you?" She answered, "Is it not Njâ?" And the shrill cry of surprise rose again, "A! lâ! lâ! lâ!"

When they reached the town, Njâ rose in anger from his house, picked up his spear, stood facing them, and threatened with his spear, "This is it!"

He passed by them into the back-yard, and changed his body to that of a new kind of beast, with spots all over his skin. At once he stooped low on four legs; and thrust out his claws; and begun a fight with the people of the town, as a Leopard. Then he went, leaping off into the Forest.

From there, he kept the name "Njâ," and has continued his fight with Mankind. The hatred between leopards and mankind dates from that time. Some of the people of that country had said to Mbuma-Ty◻ty◻ that he would not be able to marry at the town of the Spirits, and had tried to hinder him. But he did go, and succeeded in marrying a daughter of Njambu-ya-Mekuku; while Njâ, attempting to do the same, and not waiting for advice from his brother, and treating with disrespect the Spirits on the way, failed.

A SNAKE'S SKIN LOOKS LIKE A SNAKE

Persons

Bokeli, Son of Njambe-Ya-Manga

Jâmbâ, Daughter of Njambe-Ya-Madiki

Ko (Wild Rat)

Mbindi (Wild Goat)

Etungi, A Town Idler

Kuba (Chicken)

NOTE

Bokeli was like a snake. When a snake changes and throws off his old skin, that slough, when it is left lying at any place, is almost as fearful to see, as the snake itself.

The list of the dowry goods for Jâmbâ is a good illustration of native exaggeration.

Njambe-of-the-Interior begot a daughter called Jâmbâ. And Njambe-of-the-Sea-Coast begot a son called Bokeli.

Many men arrived at the town of Njambe-of-the-Interior, asking Jâmbâ for marriage. There they were killed (Njambe's people were cannibals), not being able to fulfill the tests to which they were subjected. So, people said, "Jâmbâ will not be married!"

Finally Bokeli, the son of Njambe-of-the-Sea-Coast, said, "I am going to take Jâmbâ for marriage." He prepared for his journey; he went; and he arrived at the town. He at once entered into the public Reception-House, and sat down. There the people of the town exclaimed, "A fine-looking man!" And they saluted him, "Mbolo!" The young women at once went to tell Jâmbâ, saying, "What a fine-looking man has come to marry you!"

Previous to this, the mother of Jâmbâ, who was lame with sores, was lying in the house. If a prospective son-in-law laughed in her presence, she would say to her husband, "He is mocking at me!" Then that visitor would die. All the men who had come there to marry, were killed in that way.

Before this (as Bokeli understood the speech of all Beasts and of Birds) when he entered into the Reception-House, a Cock in the town spoke to him, and said, "If your hope for food rests on me, you will not eat! I will not be killed for you; neither shall you eat at all!" Also a loin of Wild-Goat meat, hanging in the kitchen, said, "For me, you will not eat!"

But Njambe (who had overheard the Cock, and who was thinking of food for his guest) ordered, "Today, catch ye Kuba!" But Cock ran off to the forest. Then the people said, "Take the leg of Mbindi!" The leg of Wild-Goat protested, "I?" And it rotted. They sought some other thing to cook for Bokeli; but, there was nothing. So, Njambe sent his sons hunting to kill wild beasts.

Then, the mother of Jâmbâ called for Bokeli, saying, "He must come; let me see him." So, he entered into her house, and he sat down. They began to converse. It was but a little while then that the mother said to her daughter, "Search for me on the drying frame (over the fire-place); you will find Ko there; take it for the guest, and cook it." The Wild-Rat spoke, saying, "If it is I, he will not possibly eat!"

At this, Bokeli broke into a laugh. The mother was displeased, and said, "You are laughing at me!" Bokeli replied, "No!" But, the woman flung into a rage, and threw herself down on the ground, ndi! She exclaimed, "Ah! Njambe! He laughed at me! Catch him! And let him go to die!"

They laid hold of him, and brought him out of the house. They were about to go a little further to the end of the town, when he suddenly pretended he was a corpse, and leaving his body, his spirit went back home, and assumed another body. They became quiet, all of them being startled. When they moved him, he was as cold as cold victuals. They said, "What shall we do here?" Some of them advised, "Let us take Jâmbâ and this corpse, and let us go together to his father, and explain, 'Bokeli is dead, but this woman is his wife.'" Others said, "What! lest his father will kill us!" Then they decided, "Not so! but, let us send as messenger some Etungi (useless person; no loss if he should be killed) to the father's town."

The Etungi went on that errand. When he arrived at Bokeli's town, he met Bokeli sitting at the village smithy, and, not recognizing him, was intending to pass him by. Thereupon, Bokeli called to him, "Brother-in-law! what are you doing? You have found me sitting here, but you seem about to entirely pass me by. Though all your family do not like me, come in to the Reception-House." The Etungi thought to himself, "Ah! I am dead! Is not this a brother of Bokeli?" Bokeli called to his mother, and told her, "Bring out that food of mine quickly that is there! My brother-in-law has come; he feels hungry!"

They set the food as soon as possible. And the Etungi ate.

Bokeli asked him, "Where are you going to?" The Etungi replied, "I'm on my way going to tell Njambe that his son Bokeli is dead." Bokeli said to him, "This is I." Then he gave the Etungi a shirt and a cloth and a hat, as proofs of his reality.

The Etungi returned to his town. And he reported to the

people in the town, "Bokeli is not dead; I met him at the bellows, working." They thought he was lying, and they said, "Let him be beaten!" But the Etungi replied, "True! see ye this shirt, and the cloth, and this hat!" He added, "He that doubts must first go and see."

Then went Kombe. When he arrived, he found Bokeli at the bellows. When Bokeli saw him coming, he arose at once, and went to his mother in the house; he seized a machete, and cut down a plantain bunch, yo! And he said to his mother, "Make haste to cook it!"

Kombe had by that time entered the Reception-House. Bokeli welcomed him, sa-a! and said, "Sit down!" Kombe sat down. Food had been cooked; and he ate. Kombe then says, "I'm going back!" Bokeli at once put down at his feet the dowry for Jâmbâ, cloths, shirts, hats, etc, etc. Kombe carried away the things. And having arrived at his town, he says, "It is true!"

Their father Njambe directed, "Come ye! over there with a present as a propitiation!" Then he gathered goats, fowls, ducks, plantains, dried meats, fishes, all sorts and kinds. He ordered, "Make ye a bier, and carry the corpse. I am going, even if I die!" (He still had a doubt about the real Bokeli.) They did so. They carried the presents, and they went, going on the journey.

When those in front had arrived at the half-way of the road, the father said to his children, "You must now remain here. I shall first go to the town. If you hear a sound of guns, you will know that I am killed; then ye must go back." The father Njambe took Jâmbâ to accompany him, and his wives with him.

When Bokeli saw them coming, at once the cannon were loaded, and were fired in a salute of welcome, and all the guns and musical instruments sounded, and people saying, "The bride is come!"

The children of Njambe who were left on the way, when they heard the sounds of the cannons and guns, said to themselves that their father was killed, and they scattered and hid themselves. But he hastily started and went back to the place where he had left them; and he found nobody there. He called them; and they came out of their hiding. He commanded, "Throw away this thing (the supposed corpse); take up the goods; come to the town of Bokeli."

Then they went to the town. They found Jâmbâ and her husband Bokeli sitting and playing. And they were treated with much kindness. Oxen and pigs were killed; they ate; they drank; and had great fun and very much enjoyment.

Njambe-of-the-Interior then said that he was ready to journey back to his town. But his friend Njambe-of-the-Sea-Coast said, "Not today, but tomorrow in the morning; then I will give you the dowry."

On the next day, they delivered the dowry; five millions of spear-heads (an iron currency); knives also, a million; one thousand hats; one thousand shirts; one hundred cloths; bags and trunks one hundred; bales of all kinds of white man's things; and native things in abundance; cattle also in abundance. Then they went away with them to their town.

And Bokeli and Jâmbâ remained in the seaside town with their marriage.

PART THIRD
FANG TRIBE

FOREWORD

In this Part, are tales told me by an old Batanga man, of the Banâkâ Tribe. He could not give me the time to come to my room, and tell me, sentence by sentence, as the other two narrators had done. But, having some education, he wrote the stories in his native language, and, at my leisure, I translated them. The translation is literal, except when the short phrases, clear to native thought, would have been an imperfect sentence to an English eye; or, where an allusion to well-known native customs, perfectly obvious to a native, would have been obscure to most readers. In such cases, I have sacrificed to clearness the concise native idiom. To a student of higher criticism, the sentences which are mine will reveal themselves. In my literal translations of the native, I have used very simple short words, mostly of Anglo-Saxon origin. In my own paraphrases, words of Latin origin have appeared.

Some tales of this Part are of Fang origin from the Bulu Tribe of the interior. My Batanga friend told me he heard them from Bulu people visiting at the Coast, and he wrote them as they were then current on the coast. After I had translated them from his Banâkâ vernacular, I found, and pointed out to him, that some of them had already been printed in Fang, as specimens of Bulu idioms, in a published Grammar of the Bulu-Fang Language ("Handbook of Bulu, by G. S. Bates"). This explanation is proper to be made, that while, unknown to me, Mr. Bates was collecting direct from his Bulu informants in the interior, my Batanga friend had collected for me, from his Bulu visitors; and the tales were in my possession, translated into English by myself, before I saw Mr. Bates' book, or even knew of its existence.

TALE 1
CANDOR

Persons
Ngiya (Gorilla)   Ingenda (A Small Monkey)

Gorilla, among all Beasts, was derided and jeered at by them. They called him "Broken-face."

So, he spoke to Ingenda of the Monkey Tribe, and ordered it, "Just examine for me this face of mine; whether it is really so, you tell me." The monkey was afraid to refuse, and afraid also to tell the truth. So it ascended a tree; and, as it went, it plucked the fruits. It said to Gorilla, "I must first eat before answering your question; I feel hungry." (As an excuse to give itself time to escape.)

So Ingenda went; and, by the time it had eaten two of the fruits, it was near the tree-top. Then it called to Gorilla "Look here! with your face turned upward." So the Gorilla looked, with its face upward. And Ingenda, being in a safe place, acknowledged, "It is really so, really so." Gorilla was angry; but was helpless to revenge itself on Ingenda for its candid statement; for, he had no way by which to catch him. And Ingenda went off, leaping as it went from tree-top to tree-top.

TALE 2
WHICH IS THE BETTER HUNTER, AN EAGLE OR A LEOPARD?

Persons
Mbela (Eagle)   Njᵄ (Leopard)

Eagle and Leopard had a discussion about obtaining prey.

Eagle said, "I am the one who can surpass you in preying." Leopard said, "Not so! Is it not I?"

Then Eagle said, "Wait; see whether you are the one to surpass me in preying." Thereupon he descended from above, seized a child of Leopard, and flew up with it to his nest.

Leopard exclaimed, "Alas! what shall I do?" And he went, and went, walking about, coming to one place, and going to another, wishing to fly in order to go to the rescue of his child. He could not fly, for want of wings; therefore it was the other one who flew up and away.

So it was that the eagle proved that he surpassed the leopard in seeking prey.

TALE 3
A LESSON IN EVOLUTION

Persons
Unyunge (The Shrew-Mouse)   Po (A Lemur)

NOTE

The development of the Shrew's long nose, and of the Lemur's big eyes.

Shrew and Lemur were neighbors in the town of Beasts. At that time, the Animals did not possess fire. Lemur said to Shrew, "Go! and take for us fire from the town of Mankind." Shrew consented, but said, "If I go, do not look, while I am gone, toward any other place except the path on which I go. Do not even wink. Watch for me."

So Shrew went, and came to a Town of Men; and found that the people had all emigrated from that town. Yet, he went on, and on, seeking for fire; and for a long time found none. But, as he continued moving forward from house to house, he at last found a very little fire on a hearth. He began blowing it; and kept on blowing, and blowing; for, the fire did not soon ignite into a flame. He continued so long at this that his mouth extended forward permanently, with the blowing.

Then he went back, and found Lemur faithfully watching with his eyes standing very wide open. Shrew asked him, "What has made your eyes so big?" In return, Lemur asked him, "What has so lengthened your mouth to a snout?"

PARROT STANDING ON ONE LEG

Persons

Njâku (Elephant)   Iwedo (Death)

Koho (Parrot)

NOTE

In former times, in the days of Witchcraft, it was the custom not to bury a corpse until the question was settled who or what had caused the death. This investigation sometimes occupied several days; during which time decomposition was hindered by the application of salt, and even by drying the remains in the smoke of a fire.

Elephant built his own town; and Parrot built also his.

Then the children of Parrot went a-hunting every day; and when they came back, the town had wild meat in abundance, hida! hida!

One day Elephant announced, "I must go on an excursion to the town of Chum Koho." He arrived there and found him, with that fashion of his, of standing with one leg bent up under his feathers hidden. His friend Elephant asked him, "Chum! what have you done to your leg?" He answered him (falsely), "My children have gone with it a-hunting." Elephant being astonished said, "On your oath?" He replied, "Truly!"

Then Elephant said, "I came to see you, only to see. I'm going back." The other said, "Yes; very good."

Elephant returned to his town, and said to his children, "Arrange the nets today; tomorrow for a hunt!"

The next day, the children made ready. And he, ashamed that a small Bird should do a greater act than himself said, "Take ye a saw, and cut off my leg." His children did not hesitate at his command, as they were accustomed to implicit obedience. So, they cut it off; and they carried with them, as he directed, the leg, on their hunt.

When they were gone, to their father Elephant came Death, saying, "I have arrived!" People of the town cried for help, "Come ye! Njâku is not well!" But, the children were beyond hearing, being still away at the hunt. During their absence, Elephant died. When they arrived, they found their father a corpse.

People wondered, saying, "What is this? Since we were born, we have not heard this, that hunting is carried on with the legs of one who remains behind in the town." When others, coming to the funeral, from other towns, asked the children, "Who was the person who counseled you such advice as that?" they said, "Himself it was who told us; he said to us 'Cut.' So we cut."

Then, on farther investigation, the people said, "The blame belongs to Koho," so, they called Parrot to account. But, Parrot said, "It is not mine. I did not tell him to cut off his leg." So, the charge was dismissed. And the burial proceeded.

TALE 5
A QUESTION OF RIGHT OF INHERITANCE

Persons

Utati-Mboka (A Sparrow)   A Man

Koho (Parrot)

NOTE

Sparrow based his claim on the grounds of companionship, and community of interests.

Parrot's claim is based on a very common line of argument in native disputes not only about property, but in all questions of liability.

Parrot and Sparrow argued about their right to inherit the property that a Man had left.

The Sparrow said, "The Man and I lived all our days in the same town. If he moved, I also moved. Our interests were similar. At whatever place he went to live, there also I stood in the street."

The Parrot spoke, and based his claim on the ground that he was the original cause of the Man's wealth. He said, "I was born in the tree-tops; then the Man came and took me, to live with him.

"When my tail began to grow, he and his people took my feathers; With which they made a handsome head-dress; Which they sold for very many goods; With which they bought a wife; And that woman bore daughters; Who, for much money, were sold into marriages; And their children also bore other children; Wherefore, for that reason, it is that I say that I caused for them all these women, and was the foundation of all this wealth."

This was what Parrot declared.

So, the people decided, "Koho is the source of those things." And he was allowed to inherit.

TALE 6
TORTOISE COVERS HIS IGNORANCE

Persons
Kudu (Tortoise)   Njⷧ (Leopard)
Ihⷧli (Gazelle)   A Vine

NOTE

It is customary for men to do some service for their fathers and mothers-in-law.

Tortoise arose and went to the town of his father-in-law Leopard. Leopard sent him on an errand, saying, "Go, and cut for me utamba-mwa-Ivâtâ." (The fiber of a vine is used for making nets.)

Then he went. But, while he still remembered the object, he forgot the name of the kind of Vine that was used for that purpose. And he was ashamed to confess his ignorance. So, he came back to call the people of the town, and said, "Come ye and help me! I have enclosed Ihⷧli in a thicket."

The people came, and at once they made a circle around the spot. But when they closed in, they saw no beasts there.

Then Tortoise called out, "Let someone of you cut for me, utamba-mwa-Ivâtâ." (As if that was the only thing needed to catch the animal which he had said was there.)

Thereupon, his brother-in-law cut for him a vine which he

brought to him, saying, "Here is an Ihenga vine which we use for making nets." Whereupon Tortoise exclaimed, "Is it possible that it was the Ihenga vine that I mistook?"

A QUESTION AS TO AGE

Persons

Asanze (A Shrike) And other Animals

Kudu (Tortoise) Njâbâ (Civet)

Uhingi (Genet)

Edubu (Snake)

NOTE

Differences in age as revealed by differences in taste for food.

Shrike was a blacksmith. So, all the Beasts went to the forge at his town. Each day, when they had finished at the anvil, they took all their tools and laid them on the ground (as pledges). Before they should go back to their towns, they would say to the Bird, "Show us which is the eldest, and then you give us the things, if you are able to decide our question."

He looked at and examined them; but he did not know, for they were all apparently of the same age; and they went away empty-handed, leaving their tools as a challenge. Every day it was that same way.

On another day, Tortoise being a friend of the Bird, started to go to work for him at the bellows. Also, he cooked three bundles of food; one of Civet with the entrails of a red Antelope; and one of Genet; and one of an Edubu-Snake. (Suited for different tastes and ages.) Then he blew at the bellows.

When the others were hungry at meal time, Tortoise took up the jomba-bundles; and he said, "Come ye! take up this jomba of Njâbâ with the entrails, and eat." (They were the old ones who chose to come and eat it.)

Again Tortoise said, "Come ye! take up the jomba of Uhingi." (They were the younger men who chose to pick it up and eat it.)

He then took up the jomba of the Snake. And he said, "Come ye! and take of the jomba of Edubu." (Those who took it were the youngest.)

After awhile they all finished their work at the bellows. They still left their tools lying on the ground, and came near to the Bird, and they said, as on other occasions, "Show us who is the eldest."

Then Tortoise at the request of the Bird, announced the decision, as if it was its own, "Ye who ate of the Njâbâ are the ones who are oldest; ye who ate of Uhingi are the ones who are younger men; and ye who ate of the Edubu are the ones who are the youngest."

So, they assented to the decision, and took away their belongings.

TALE 8

ABUNDANCE: A PLAY ON THE MEANING OF A WORD

Persons

A Hunter; Man   Bwinge (Abundance, or

Mbindi (Wild Goat)   "More")

A Dwarf, with Magic-Pow- Ngweya (Hog)

er   Ungumba (Riches)

NOTE

The Man's patience finally brought to him the Plenty which was promised him.

"Bwinge" might be the name of a person or of a thing; or, it could be the "abundance" for which the hunter hoped.

There was a certain Man who was very poor; he had no goods with which to buy a wife. He went one day into the forest to set snares. On the morrow, he went off to examine them; and found a Wild-Goat caught in the snares. He rejoiced and said, "I must eat Mbindi today!"

But the Wild-Goat said to that Man, "Let me alone, Bwinge is coming after awhile."

So, the Man, thinking that "Bwinge" was the name of some other and more desirable animal, at once let the Wild-Goat loose,

349

and went off to his town. On the next day, the Man went to examine the snare, to see whether Bwinge was there, and found Hog caught fast in the net. And he exclaimed, "I must eat Ngweya today!"

But the Hog said, "Let me go. Bwinge is coming." The man at once left the Hog, (still thinking that many more were coming); and it went away.

The Man wondered, and said to himself, "What Thing is it that is named 'Bwinge'?"

On another day, he went to set his snare. He found there a dwarf child of a Human Being; and, in anger, he said, "You are the one who has caused me to send away the beasts? Is it possible that you are he who is 'Bwinge'? I shall kill you." But the dwarf said, "No! don't kill me. I will call Ungumba for you." So, the Man said, "Call in a hurry!"

The Dwarf ordered, "Let guns come!" And they at once came. (This was done by the Dwarf's Magic-Power.) The Man again said, "Call, in a hurry!" The Dwarf called for women; and they came. The Man again said to him, "Call for Goats, in a hurry!" And they came, with abundance of other things.

Then the Man freed him, and said to him, "Go!"

The Man also went his way with his riches. And he became a great man. This was because of his patient waiting.

AN OATH, WITH A MENTAL RESERVATION

Persons

Ibembe (Dove)   Ngando (Crocodile)

Njɛ (Leopard)

NOTE

Covenants among natives are made under oath, by the two parties eating together of some fetish-mixture, called a "Medicine"; which, being connected with some Spirit, is supposed to be able to punish any infraction of the covenant.

Because Dove "abused" Leopard, that is, deceived him, the dove no longer builds its nest on the ground, through fear of leopards.

Dove was building in a tree-trunk by a river, because it preferred to walk on the ground. And Crocodile just then emerged from the river to the bank, and lay on his log where he usually rested.

They two said, "Let us eat a Medicine-charm."

So, Dove agreed, and swore, saying, "I say to you that, when anything at all shall happen openly, if I do not tell it to you, then may this Medicine find me out and kill me." Crocodile also uttered his oath, "When whatever thing shall come out from the river onto the ground, if I do not tell it to you, this Medicine must find me out and kill me!"

When they had finished their Covenant, Crocodile returned to his hollow in the ground by the river. Dove also arose, and went away, walking to his place. Then he and Leopard suddenly met, on the path.

Leopard asked, "Are you able to see Ngando for me? I want to eat it." Dove answered, "Ah! would that you and I were living in one place with an Agreement!" Leopard replied, "Come then! let us, I and you, eat a Medicine."

So Leopard began. He said as his oath: "Anything at all that shall come to my place where I dwell, if I be there, and it wants to get hold of you, if I tell it not to you, let this Medicine find and certainly kill me!" Dove also with his oath, said, "If I see Ngando, and I do not tell you, let this Medicine find me and certainly kill me!"

So, they made their promise; then they separated; and each one went to his own village.

Thus Dove and Leopard ate their kind of "Medicine," after Dove and Crocodile had already eaten theirs.

Then, one day, Crocodile came out from the river. Dove at once began to tell Leopard, saying, "He has emerged from the river and is about to settle on the log!" So, Leopard began slowly to come, and watching Crocodile, as he came. When he was near, in his advance, Dove spoke, telling Crocodile, and said, "Your watcher! Your watcher is coming! Do not approach here!"

Thereat, Crocodile slipped back into the water.

The next time that Dove and Leopard met, Leopard demanded, "What is this you have done to me? You swore to me this: 'If I see

Crocodile I will tell you; and you must come catch him.' Now, as soon as you saw me, you turned around, and told Crocodile, 'Fall into the River!' You have mocked me!"

And Leopard grew very angry.

TALE 10
THE TREACHERY OF TORTOISE

Persons
Mbâmâ (Boa Constrictor)   Njɛ (Leopard)
Kudu (Tortoise)

NOTE

Observe the cannibalism of the story.

Leopard married a wife. After awhile she was about to become a mother.

Boa also married a wife; and, after awhile, she also, was about to become a mother.

In a short time, like the drinking of a draught of water, the month passed, both for Leopard's wife and for Boa's wife also. Then Boa's wife said, "It is time for the birth!" So she gave birth to a child. And she lay down on her mother's bed. When they were about to cook food for her, she said, "I want to eat nothing but Njɛ!"

The next day, the wife of Leopard said, "It is time for the birth!" And she also gave birth to a child. Food was given to her. But she said, "I am wanting only Mbâmâ!"

When told of his wife's wish, Boa said, "What shall I do? Where shall I go? Where shall I find Mangwata?" (A nickname for

355

Leopard.) Also, Leopard said, in regard to his wife's wish, "Where shall I find Mbâmâ?" Then Leopard went walking, on and on, and looking. He met with Manima-ma-Evosolo (a nickname for Tortoise). Leopard asked him, "Can you catch me Mbâmâ?" Manima said, "What's that?" And he laughed, Ky⌷! Ky⌷! Ky⌷; and said, "That is as easy as play." Leopard said, "Chum, please do such a thing for me." And Tortoise said, "Very good!"

When they separated, and Tortoise was about to go a little further on ahead, at once he met with Boa. And Boa asked him, "Chum! Manima-ma-Evosolo! Where have you come from?" Tortoise answered, "I have come, going on an excursion." Boa asked to Tortoise, "But, could you catch me Nj⌷?" He replied, "That is a little thing." Then Boa begged him, "Please, since my wife has born a child, she has not eaten anything. She says she wants to eat only Nj⌷."

Tortoise returned back at once to his village. He called to the people of his village, saying, "Come ye! to make for me a pit." They at once went, and dug a pit. When they had finished it, Tortoise went to Leopard, and said to him, "Come on!"

Leopard at once started on the journey (thinking he was going to get Boa). When they came to the place of the pit, Leopard fell suddenly into it headlong, volomu! He called to Tortoise, saying, "Chum! Where is Mbâmâ?" (Leopard did not understand that he was being deceived.)

Tortoise did not reply, but started off clear to the village of Boa. He said to Boa, "Come on!" Boa did not doubt at all that he was going to get Leopard. He started, and went with Tortoise towards the pit. When he was passing near the spot, Boa fell headlong into the pit, volumu! And Leopard exclaimed, "Ah! now, what is this?"

Tortoise only said to them, "You yourselves can kill each other."

A CHAIN OF CIRCUMSTANCES

Persons

Etanda (Cockroach)   Uhingi (Genet)

Kudu (Tortoise)   NjⅩ (Leopard)

Kuba (Chicken)   A Man

NOTE

A Cause, from which came the enmity between Leopards, and other wild animals, and Mankind.

Observe the resemblance to "The House that Jack Built."

Tortoise was a blacksmith, and allowed other people to use his bellows. Cockroach had a spear that was known of by all people and things. One day, he went to the smithy at the village of Tortoise. When he started to work the bellows, as he looked out in the street, he saw Chicken coming; and he said to Tortoise, "I'm afraid of Kuba, that he will catch me. What shall I do?" So Tortoise told him, "Go! and hide yourself off there in the grass." At once he hid himself.

Then arrived Chicken, and he, observing a spear lying on the ground, asked Tortoise, "Is not this Etanda's Spear?" Tortoise assented, "Yes, do you want him?" And Chicken said, "Yes, where is he?" So Tortoise said, "He hid himself in the grass on the ground yonder; catch him." Then Chicken went and caught Cockroach, and swallowed him.

When Chicken was about to go away to return to his place, Tortoise said to him, "Come back! work for me this fine bellows!" As Chicken, willing to return a favor, was about to stand at it, he looked around and saw Genet coming in the street. Chicken said to Tortoise, "Alas! I'm afraid that Uhingi will see me, where shall I go?" So, Tortoise says, "Go! and hide!" Chicken did so. When Genet came, he, seeing the spear, asked, "Is it not so that this is Etanda's Spear?" Tortoise replied, "Yes." Genet asked him, "Where is Etanda?" He replied, "Chicken has swallowed him." Genet inquired, "And where is Chicken?" Tortoise showed him the place where Chicken was hidden. And Genet went and caught and ate Chicken.

When Genet was about to go, Tortoise called to him, "No! come! to work this fine bellows." Genet set to work; but, when he looked into the street, he hesitated; for, he saw Leopard coming. Genet said to Tortoise, "I must go, lest Njɛ should see me!" Then Tortoise said, "Go! and hide in the grass." So, Genet hid himself in the grass.

Leopard, having arrived and wondering about the Spear, asked Tortoise, "Is it not so that this is the Spear of Etanda?" Tortoise answered, "Yes." Then Leopard asked, "Where is Etanda?" Tortoise replied, "Kuba has swallowed him." "And, where is Kuba?" Tortoise answered, "Uhingi has eaten him." Then Leopard asked, "Where then is Uhingi?" Tortoise asked, "Do you want him? Go and catch him! He is hidden yonder there." Then Leopard caught and killed Genet.

Leopard was going away, but Tortoise told him, "Wait! come! to work this fine bellows." When Leopard was about to comply, he looked around the street, and he saw a Human Being coming with a gun carried on his shoulder. Leopard exclaimed, "Kudu-O! I do not want to see a Man, let me go!" Then Tortoise said to him, "Go! and hide." Leopard did so.

When the Man had come, and he saw the Spear of Cockroach, he inquired, "Is it not so that this is Cockroach's wonderful Spear?" Tortoise answered, "Yes."

And the Man asked, "Where then is Cockroach?" Tortoise answered, "Kuba has swallowed him."

Man asked, "And where is Chicken?" Tortoise answered, "Uhingi has eaten him."

Man asked, "And where is Genet?" Tortoise answered, "Njⵧ has killed him."

Man asked, "And where is Leopard?" Tortoise did not at once reply; and Man asked again, "Where is Leopard?" The Tortoise said, "Do you want him? Go! and catch him. He had hidden himself over there."

Then the Man went and shot Leopard,

Who had killed Genet,

Who had eaten Chicken,

Who had swallowed Cockroach,

Who owned the wonderful Spear,

At the smithy of Tortoise.

www.ingramcontent.com/pod-product-compliance
Lightning Source LLC
Chambersburg PA
CBHW070303030726
47505CB00004B/891